SUPERHERO JESUS: HAWAII

Thomas Bishop

CHAPTER ONE

Wednesday Morning

They peaked around the corner of the couch, sizing up their target. There were two of them, and they had a plan.

Matt Gold was on the floor in the giant living room. He knew the attack was coming, yet he didn't move. He waited. Even when he heard them coming, he remained still.

His attackers pounced. Matt struggled. One attacker had him around the neck, squeezing from behind. The other was standing on his lower back, jumping up and down.

Matt lay on his stomach and tried to reach around to defend himself. He grabbed for the first attacker's side, applying just enough pressure to send him shooting off in a fit of giggles.

The second attacker jumped again, aiming for the small of Matt's lower back, but Matt rolled over before impact, causing him to crash into Matt's waiting arms.

Matt sat up, trying to pin the rascal between his legs, but before he could gain the upper hand, the first

1

attacker landed on Matt's back, reaching around his neck again, hanging on for dear life.

Matt used one hand to reach around and grab a handful of shirt, pulling the attacker over his shoulder and on top of the other one. He pinned them in front of him, shifting to his knees for leverage.

"Okay," Matt said, looking them in the eyes. "Which one of you is Jace?"

"He is. He is," said the attacker on the right.

"No, no. He is!" said the one on the left.

They were both struggling to squirm free, giggling with energy.

Matt leaned in for a closer look. "How do I tell these monkeys apart?" he asked his sister.

Sarah Gold sat on the couch flipping through channels and watching the battle. She knew Matt didn't need help telling them apart, but she played along as usual. "Jace is the monkey on the right."

Matt's eyes widened, looking at Jace. "So ... you lied to me?" he said, squeezing his hand around Jace's small rib cage. Matt turned to Jace's brother, Alex: "And so did you!" He had both boys pinned, effectively tickling them as they kicked and fought, pretending they weren't loving every minute of playing with their uncle.

"Hey, check it out," Sarah said, nodding to the television.

Matt let the twins go and looked at the fifty-two-inch flat screen mounted above the fireplace. The boys bounced to their feet and escaped, running out of the room and down the hallway to safety.

"That's the best yet," Sarah said.

Matt held his hands in the air. "Seriously? C'mon!"

It was a local news channel, and there was a photo of Matt over the news anchor's shoulder. It was a picture of him on a beach. He was holding a beer bong in the air and wasn't wearing a shirt. Sarah turned up the volume.

Coming up after the break, we've got new photos of local hero and Los Angeles Police Officer Matt Gold. You may know him as Superhero Jesus, but we're going to show you him in a whole new light. Stay tuned.

Matt rubbed both palms into his eyes and let out a sigh. "And the nightmare continues."

"This ought to be good."

Sarah loved the attention for her brother, but Matt wanted to crawl into a hole and hide.

Matt sat next to his sister on her enormous sectional couch. He'd been hiding out at her house in Santa Monica since video footage of him went viral, a video that was the culmination of sixteen months of undercover work. It was Matt's first assignment, and now, thanks to his popularity, likely his last.

His assignment was to investigate a small steroid ring working out of CrossFit studios in the Los Angeles area, but that small steroid ring turned into one of the largest heroin busts in the state's history. And it ended with amateur footage of Matt swinging from a burning hotel. A video that changed Matt's life.

Matt heard the twins running back down the hallway. He looked back, but they weren't there. He strained to look over the couch, seeing them crawling on the floor around the side. "I think a surprise attack is coming," he whispered to his sister.

He waited, but they didn't strike.

"We should be recording this," Sarah said. "I can't wait to see what photos they dug up on you."

So far, the media had been kind to Matt, but slowly the stories became more personal and less about the viral video of his heroics.

Jace and Alex sprang from the side of the couch, each jumping on one of Matt's outstretched legs. They wrapped their arms and legs around him, laughing.

Matt stood up, reaching down and prying Alex off. He hoisted him over his shoulder and grabbed Jace with his other arm, holding him on his hip. "That's it. I think it's time to call the zoo. Send you two to the monkey cages where you belong."

The twins screamed in mock fear and excitement.

Sarah turned up the television. The news was back.

We're learning more about local hero Matt Gold. We have photos from his college days at the University of Hawaii.

In addition to the photograph they showed before the commercial break, there were several more that made Matt shake his head and grimace. One was Matt dressed up as a hula girl for Halloween. He had a long, dark wig and a coconut bikini top. Another was Matt wearing an aloha shirt and Puka shell necklace with an experimental feathered hairstyle.

"Damn that Facebook," Matt said. "This is embarrassing."

Several of the photos included Matt's good friend, Daniel Palakiko. Sarah looked at her brother, knowing the photos must hurt. "Danny looks good there," she said.

"Yeah," Matt agreed.

The twins began to shake Matt's legs, trying to bring him back to their game.

"Boys, leave your uncle alone."

They didn't listen.

Matt bent down, putting his hands on their heads and keeping his eyes on the television. The boys laughed and strengthened their grips.

Jace and Alex didn't know the story. They didn't know that Daniel Palakiko was a Honolulu Police Officer. They didn't know that he was Matt's best friend from college, and they didn't know that he was murdered two days ago.

The news story ended, and Matt snapped away from the television. "I'm going to shower. We'll leave in about an hour?" he said to his sister.

"Sure."

He looked down at the boys. "I sure hope your dad is home by then, or we'll have to lock you monkeys in the closet."

He walked out of the living room, carrying Jace and Alex on his legs, both boys giggling.

In less than four hours, Matt would be on a flight to Honolulu. He'd be escaping the craziness the viral video brought, but he'd be heading to the funeral of his best friend.

Hopefully, he'd also find the rest he needed so badly.

****

Detective Solosolo Fauatea was at his desk looking over the file of the deceased Honolulu police officer Daniel Palakiko. Solo, as he was known by just about everyone, was born in Samoa and moved with his family to Honolulu almost four decades ago. At fifty-six, Solo was just a year away from retirement. Thirty years—that was his goal.

Solo didn't know Officer Daniel Palakiko well. They'd crossed paths once or twice on the job, but Solo made little effort to befriend young street cops, and Danny was no exception. Since beginning the investigation, however, Solo felt like he'd gotten to know Danny better than anyone, as there was no shortage of people willing to sing his praises.

Danny was a positive influence in Waimanalo. In a community suffering with addiction, increasing poverty, and petty crime, Danny was heavily involved in trying to turn things around. He worked the streets diligently and was known by every addict, dealer, thug, homeless person, wife-beater, and petty criminal in town. But the business owners, the teachers, the moms, dads, and kids, they knew him too. Even some of the tourists got to meet Officer Palakiko, although they often met under unfortunate conditions, mostly from car break-ins and DUIs.

The lack of physical evidence stressed Solo. Danny was shot down in his home during what seemed to be a burglary gone wrong. A few items were noticeably missing: Danny's laptop, wallet, and police badge. Odds were the burglars were meth heads, looking for cash or items to sell for drug money. Solo had seen it hundreds of times, usually without a dead cop involved.

There were, however, a few points that struck Solo as unusual. First, the neighbor who heard glass break called the police. The glass was from the back door and presumably the point of entry. Why didn't the neighbor hear the gunshots? Second, from the position of Danny's body, it appeared he was coming from the bedroom toward the living room. If he was responding to the sound from the broken window, why didn't he grab his service revolver from the nightstand? This led to the third point that really got to Solo: The spare bedroom Danny used as an office was ransacked, but his bedroom appeared to be untouched. His gun was in the nightstand, all the drawers were intact, and the closet door closed. Bedrooms are almost never left untouched. They're the most common place to find money, jewelry, and other valuables, but whoever killed Danny spent more time going through the filing cabinet.

Solo had three logical conclusions as he looked over the evidence. One: meth heads can be illogical. Hardcore users are often so tweaked out of their minds that they don't act rationally. They grabbed what they could and took off. Percentage wise, this was the likely conclusion. Two: this was a burglary gone wrong. The burglars weren't expecting anyone to be home, and Danny's murder was not part of their plan. Three: Danny's murder was a hit. Whoever broke into his house tried to make it look like a burglary, but they were there to kill Danny. They were also there to find something, possibly a file.

Solo tried not to listen to his gut; it told him to put money on theory number three.

CHAPTER TWO

Wednesday 10:00 p.m.

Matt heard his name over the PA system: "Mr. Matthew Gold, flying Hawaiian Airline's direct to Honolulu, please report to the counter at gate twenty-three. Matthew Gold, please report to the counter at gate twenty-three."

Matt was sitting across from his gate in the most secluded spot he could find, trying his best to hide from the crowd. He had his hat pulled low and face buried in his Kindle, yet he could see the two women working at gate twenty-three looking directly at him.

He'd already had looks and fingers pointed his way, but if there was anyone in the airport who hadn't recognized him yet, they were sure to spot him now.

Matt had been all over the news. It was a local Los Angels news station that first coined the nickname "Superhero Jesus." That was before they knew his real name. All they had seen was the amateur video of Matt's heroics and an overly excited cameraman who must have said, "It's Jesus, oh my God, it's Jesus" about fifty times. CNN was the first to take the story international, and also the first to suggest that the cameraman might have been high. A media storm followed.

It didn't take long for the full story to come out: Matt was working undercover for the LAPD. He cannot fly. The white robe from the video was from the Hyatt. Yes, he did save a lot of lives. No, he couldn't turn water into wine.

Far from holy, Matt had to admit he resembled Jesus, at least a little. With his shoulder-length, dirty blonde hair and rugged five-o'clock shadow, he'd been called Jesus on numerous occasions. This was, however, the first time he'd been called Superhero Jesus. Combine that with the fact that he'd been called it on international news, and Matt was starting to develop a complex. He'd already heard it several times today; everyone from his taxi driver to airport security had a comment. And now he approached a young Hawaiian Airlines employee, smiling like she was about to meet a movie star.

"Mr. Gold, can I have your ID and boarding pass? We've upgraded you to first class."

Matt could feel people watching, but he managed to focus on the girl at the counter. "Sure," he said as he watched her look over his driver's license. "I guess it's my lucky day."

"I'd say it's more than luck, Mr. Gold," she said. "We're overbooked in Economy, so someone gets bumped. We think you deserve it." She was blushing.

Matt glanced at the two attendants preparing for the boarding process. They had the same silly smiles as the counter attendant.

"Thank you. That's very kind."

"We saw you on the news," she giggled. "That was amaaaazing."

Matt gave her an awkward nod, one he couldn't seem to get right no matter how many times he did it.

Before he could retreat to his hiding spot, one of the flight attendants said, "We're ready to begin boarding, Mr. Gold. I can take that."

Matt handed her the boarding pass. He cut right in front of the people who had lined up early, giving them a weak smile and avoiding eye contact. If he had thought about it, he never would have cut, but it happened too fast. She asked for his pass, and he gave it. Now he felt like an asshole.

He led the passengers down the jetway and was greeted by two flight attendants and two pilots as he boarded, all wearing the same silly smiles.

For the next twenty-five minutes, Matt watched the other passengers board, each one looking directly at him. Some said hello, others smiled. An attractive Korean girl held up the line to take a picture with him, which would have been more acceptable if she'd have asked permission. All she said as she took the picture was, "Say … Kimchi!"

Matt felt trapped, and he didn't like the attention. He found himself thankful to the few passengers who walked on by without looking his way.

The winner of the who-sits-next-to-Jesus contest was an older man from Texas.

"Jesus Christ!" he said as he took his seat. "It's not every day I get to sit next to a celebrity. Walt's the name." The Texan reached out to shake Matt's hand.

"You can call me Matt."

The Texan was big in a Texan kind of way, and Matt noticed he was the only passenger on the plane wearing a suit. It was gray, and his bolo tie was silver and topaz.

It matched his belt buckle and tan cowboy boots. Nothing screamed "mainlander" in Hawaii more than a suit, but the Texan's cowboy suit was rugged, like a rancher.

"So, heading to Hawaii on business or R&R?" asked the Texan.

"Well... a little of both," Matt said. All Matt wanted to do was put on his headphones and close his eyes. The flight to Honolulu took around five hours, and Matt was tired of being under the spotlight. However, manners prevailed.

"You?" Matt asked.

"Just some business in Honolulu. Nothing exciting." The Texan waved his hand to stress that Matt didn't want to hear more about it. "Me and the ol' lady seen you on the news. That was some real cowboy shit you pulled. Boy, I ain't never seen nothing like that outside a movie. Better than the last Die Hard, that's for sure."

Matt smiled weakly.

Walt continued: "I can understand why the media calls you Superhero Jesus, although there are folks in my neck of the woods that take issue with it. You know, the bible thumpers. Unless you're religious, I guess."

Matt didn't comment.

"Hell, it doesn't matter to me." Walt let that sit for a second before leaning in and saying: "Seriously, though, that was some mighty cool shit."

Matt had heard this kind of remark many times since the media storm, but this was the first time he was trapped next to his interrogator. It was no problem to throw a bone or two at the reporters who ambushed him going to his car, but he couldn't stand the thought of a five-hour conversation, no doubt one that included eves-droppers as well.

"Well, the media tends to sensationalize things," Matt started. "Truth is, I did what any cop would've done in that situation."

"Any cop? Well, I don't know about all that. You were undercover, right?"

"Heck, forget about cops. Walt, I bet you'd have done the same thing if you were there. People talk about fight or flight, but it all matters what kind of situation you're in. It wasn't just my neck. I had to think of those other people." Matt said.

Walt raised his eyebrows and considered objecting to this. The man known around the world as Superhero Jesus was telling him he'd have done the same thing. The Texan liked this idea, but he didn't believe it. Everyone likes to believe they could be a hero, but Walt couldn't picture himself doing what Matt did. He couldn't imagine himself in the video.

Matt continued: "I'm no superhero, Walt. I'm just a guy who was doing his job. All this attention … I'd like to forget. I'd like it to all go away."

"I can understand that," Walt said.

"And let's be honest, what I did was more foolish and reckless than brave. I don't think the media should be celebrating it."

Matt could feel that the Texan wanted to object, but he didn't give him a chance. His plan was to move the conversation past what happened in LA.

"I hope I'm never in a situation like that again. It's a bit traumatizing, you know? Now I'm on my way to Hawaii. You'd think to relax, but I'm actually on my way to a funeral."

"I'm sorry to hear that," the Texan said.

Matt continued before the Texan could say more: "A close friend recently passed. He was a police officer." Matt closed his eyes hard and put his hand to his head. He let out a big yawn. "Walt, it's been nice talking to you, but I'm starting to feel the sleeping pill kick in. It's been tough to sleep recently, so I thought I'd catch up during the flight. You understand, right?"

"Aw, heck, I understand. Can't imagine going through this myself. You get some rest. I'll make sure no one wakes you." Here was the southern gentleman Matt hoped for. He hated using his friend's death as a ploy, but it had the desired effect.

There was no sleeping pill. Matt made that part up, but as soon as he said it, he kicked himself for not scoring some Ambien before the flight. It wasn't his style to take pills, but he did need the rest. Sleep had not come easy lately, and things weren't about to get easier for Matt.

As Matt pretended to sleep, he thought of his dead friend. They met in college where they both played volleyball for the University of Hawaii. Matt was the star of the team, a six-foot-four-inch center with a thunderous spike and full scholarship. Danny Palakiko was a five-ten walk-on from Waimanalo, attending UH on a Native Hawaiian scholarship. Unlikely friends from the start. *Stupid fucking haole*, thought Danny when they'd first met. Growing up in Waimanalo taught Danny that white people are not just haoles, but stupid fucking haoles. It had a nice ring to it.

Matt was the one to reach out to Danny. He invited him to hang out at the beach with some friends. Danny didn't hesitate to accept, and he'd later admit to Matt that he was only interested in meeting white girls, who he assumed would be there. For some reason, as Danny had explained to Matt later, white girls weren't stupid fucking haoles. Especially white girls in bikinis.

But from that day at the beach, Danny saw Matt in a whole new light. He noticed how Matt treated everyone the same. How he didn't prejudge people or treat anyone differently. He was considerate and respectful, not arrogant and entitled.

It wasn't what Danny expected. Matt wasn't a stupid fucking haole after all.

They became close. So close that they became roommates their sophomore year, and Matt started to get invited to family barbecues. He never seemed to notice that he was one of the few white guys there, if not the only.

Matt was also the one that kept Danny in school. Although he'd always been a good student, Danny knew the odds were against him graduating. He planned to make it as far as possible and then join the military. For a kid from Waimanalo, Danny considered those options as pretty bright. This was in stark contrast to Matt, who never had an ounce of doubt about graduation.

Matt had been a positive influence in Danny's life, but now Danny was dead. Matt couldn't help but feel somewhat responsible.

Danny's funeral would be big. Family ties ran deep in local communities, and nearly every law-enforcement official on the island would attend. Even the governor would be there.

He was worried about how he'd deal with Danny's family, especially Danny's mom, who had welcomed him into the family. She always told Matt that if he were going to act like Danny's brother, she'd act like his mom.

It was going to be tough.

The Texan thought about what Matt did and about what he said. He thought about what he'd have done in that situation, and if it's true that when other's lives are in danger there is no fight or flight, but only fight. Walt wondered if he could he have flown like Matt? Could he have saved all those people? No, he reckoned he couldn't have. But it sure was a nice thought.

CHAPTER THREE

Thursday 6:00 a.m.

Kinu had been joining dawn patrol since he moved to Oahu in 1994. He moved into his auntie's small house in the Palolo Valley when she became sick, and when she passed away, she left the house to Kinu. It was a small, one-story Hawaiian-style home and a bit rough around the edges, but it was more than Kinu needed.

Dawn patrol was Kinu's favorite part of the day. Most surfers at dawn were locals getting in a morning surf session before work. Being summer, the best waves were on the east side, which suited Kinu just fine; the drive from Palolo to Waikiki took less than ten minutes, and at dawn, the waves weren't overly crowded with tourists banging into each other.

Kinu's mornings were usually the same. He'd wake up to the sounds of the neighborhood rooster just before the sun came up. After sliding on his board shorts, he'd hop in his old Nissan pick-up and head for the parking lot of the Waikiki Zoo, longboard in tow.

The Waikiki Zoo's parking lot was right across from the beach, and within twenty minutes of waking up,

Kinu was in the water and paddling out to the breaks. By the time he hit the water, the morning grogginess was gone, and Kinu's long, lean arms were powering him out to his morning session. A lifetime of surfing and working manual labor gave him the wide shoulders and ripped body so typical of the dawn patrol regulars, and Kinu was a dead ringer for surfing legend Duke Kahanamoku. He'd even stood next to the statue of the famous surfer in Waikiki for a photo once. A tourist remarked that it'd make a great Facebook profile picture, unaware that Kinu didn't have a computer, let alone a Facebook account.

Today started like most days. After catching a few waves, Kinu paddled out past the surf breaks for his morning shit. It was like clockwork. He often joked that his favorite part of the day was the peace he found while clutching his surfboard as he dropped a deuce in the clear waters of Waikiki. He thought the view was spectacular, even after all these years. Tourists pay to ride out on catamarans for the view, but Kinu got it for free. He was so used to shitting in the ocean, he couldn't remember the last time he sat on a toilet. Anytime he heard someone complain of being backed up, he'd say, "Brah, dawn patrol … no betta' time."

On ordinary days, Kinu would continue surfing after his shit. He'd head back to the break and ride a few more waves before finally riding one all the way into the beach. He'd wash off at one of the beach showers, rinse his board, and head back to his truck. Recently he'd been working on a construction job, rebuilding a house on the beach in Kahala, one of the richest neighborhoods in all of Hawaii. The Japanese billionaire who bought the house in the 1980's let it fall into disrepair and recently decided to bulldoze it and rebuild from scratch. Kinu's local connections got him the job, but for unknown reasons, the work had come to a sudden stop, which Kinu didn't mind.

Money wasn't top priority to Kinu. His house and truck were paid for and he had no family to support, so when work dried up, he welcomed the chance to spend more time on the water. Today he decided to paddle down to Diamond Head for his post-shit waves.

He didn't make it. Just in front of the Waikiki Aquarium, about four hundred yards from his surf spot, he saw a silver briefcase floating in the water. As he pulled it out of the water and onto his board, he noticed a handcuff attached to the handle, sawed off in the middle.

Kinu sat on his board with the briefcase in front of him for a long time. It was strange to find something floating in the ocean. Even stranger that it was a locked briefcase, and extremely strange that it had a handcuff attached to it. A little voice inside Kinu's head told him to paddle away. *Leave it! Paddle away, brah.* But that voice was the little voice. The big voice was louder. It was the voice that appealed to Kinu's curiosity. The voice that said, *Maybe it's cash. Maybe it's diamonds. Maybe it's ... who knows? Take it! Take it you big dummy!*

Kinu did what anyone else would've done. With the briefcase on his board, he turned and paddled back towards his truck.

****

Matt woke up as the flight attendants were preparing for the final descent into Honolulu, which only left about twenty minutes of chat time with the Texan. The conversation was light, and Matt felt great as the

Hawaiian Airlines' flight finally touched down on the runway.

Matt was the first passenger off the plane. He was happy to be back in Honolulu; it'd been too long, and from the first few steps off the plane, Matt could smell the island. It was so distinct, and so many good memories came rushing back: the beaches, jogging at Kapiolani Park, hiking Makapu'u, surfing, scuba diving, shrimp trucks on the North Shore ... too many great Hawaiian memories. Even inside the terminal, he thought he could feel the trade winds blowing. There was nothing like landing in paradise, even if it was for a funeral.

Matt made his way to the baggage claim and his mood soured fast. He had a welcoming party. A group of at least twenty were waiting, some holding a lei, others holding signs. "Aloha Superhero Jesus," was the first one he noticed. A granny in a purple muumuu practically threw it in his face. Matt was nearly choking in leis in a matter of seconds. It reminded him of his graduation at the University of Hawaii.

There were news cameras. Unknown to Matt, a video of him making his way to the Hawaiian Airlines counter in the LA airport was uploaded to YouTube. The clip showed Matt smiling with two female counter agents and then boarding a Hawaiian Airlines flight to Honolulu. The clip also showed Matt posing for a photo with a sexy, young Korean girl in his first class seat. It was titled "Superhero Jesus Goes to Hawaii: First Class." A university student with over ten million YouTube subscribers uploaded it just before takeoff. The video had been viewed over a million times before the flight even landed.

19

Matt accepted the situation graciously, but he declined interviews. The news channels would still run with the story, but it didn't get more than a few seconds on each station: *"And finally today, take a look at who arrived in Honolulu this afternoon... That's Superhero Jesus, who flew in first class for a little R&R ..."* Shots of Matt covered in leis and smiling at the welcoming crowd were seen all over the state.

Matt didn't like the attention. He managed to keep his smile intact, but his focus was on the baggage claim. As soon as his bag popped up, he was out of there.

He grabbed his bag and made a beeline for the shuttle bus. He regretted checking luggage, and now he was regretting not having a friend pick him up from the airport.

Before he left LA, Matt sent out emails letting friends on the island know he'd be in town, but he made a point to tell them he didn't need a ride from the airport. He'd need a car, and renting one from the airport made the most sense. Luckily, the shuttle pulled up right as Matt made it to the curb, and the driver never even looked him in the eye.

****

Detective Solosolo Fauatea looked over the crime scene at Kahanamoku Beach. Located on the west end of Waikiki, Kahanamoku is located immediately in front of the Hilton Hawaiian Village and just before the Ala Wai Harbor. The beach curls out towards the sea, creating a small peninsula and a serene spot for tourists to snap pictures of Waikiki and Diamond Head. When the currents are right, it's also an excellent location to catch floating debris, like lost beach balls and boogie boards. Today the peninsula caught itself a twenty-one foot

Boston Whaler. A lucky tourist was up for pictures of the sunrise and ended up with the first shots of the bloody boat.

Solo looked it up and down. He knew the make and model well. It was a twenty-one foot Montauk, popular with fishermen, skiers, and anyone looking for a simple boat to get out on the water. It's hard to get more basic than a Montauk. Solo remembered a case six months ago involving a similar boat. A group of friends was skiing in the Hawaii Kai marina when the driver decided to go bowling through a club of standup paddleboarders. He was watching his girlfriend ski and never saw the group in front of him. He left one dead and two injured, one of which was his girlfriend. She ramped off a board and ended up with a broken arm and concussion. She was lucky. He was drunk.

"Fill me in, Chun," Solo said to the first officer on the scene.

"Yes, sir. The boat was about twenty yards out. A tourist called it in. He said he grabbed the anchor from the bow and walked it to the beach. Claims he didn't touch anything else."

"Haven't found a body yet, huh?" Solo asked.

"Not yet. We've got men canvassing the area, and the Coast Guard is on the way, but it's unlikely they'll find anything in the water unless it's nearby. Once the current moves past here, it usually pushes everything out to sea."

Solo gave the officer a look out of the corner of his eye and wiped the sweat from his balding head.

The center console was smeared with blood, as were the seats in the rear. The severed hand was on the deck just in front of the center console. There was a streak of blood behind it; it looked like it'd been kicked there.

"Anyone around here lose a hand?" Solo asked.

"Not that we know of yet, Detective. We're checking the hospitals. Doesn't look like the owner of the hand bled out here. There'd be more blood."

Solo mumbled agreement as he continued to size up the scene. It was a good observation for such a young street cop. Officer Chun was a rookie, but Solo had known his dad. Detective Raymond Chun was gunned down five years ago by a whacked-out meth head. He'd spent over thirty years on the force. A damn fool for not retiring, Solo thought. And here was his son, following in dad's footsteps.

Officer Chun continued: "CSI Ikawa is on her way, and we've got the area roped off all the way back to the Hilton. The harbor side, too. Any orders, sir?"

"Nope," Solo said as he began to walk back to his car, still not giving the young officer any compliments. Solo had more important things to do. He was hungry.

****

Kinu felt terribly suspicious as he walked to his truck. He tried to sandwich the briefcase between his board and his side, but there was no way to hide it completely. Aware that most people don't surf with their briefcase, he knew it could draw attention his way. He managed to hide the handcuff by pressing it between the case and his body, but it was painful to have the cuff jabbing into his ribs.

Kinu tried to open the case before he got out of the water, but it was obvious he wasn't going to be able to break the locks without a tool. He had some tools in his truck, so he tried to open the case using a hammer and screwdriver, but he couldn't even put a dent in it.

The briefcase would have to wait. He could take a crowbar to it once he got home, but for now, he had more pressing needs. Kinu worked up a mighty appetite on the water. He could hear the Spam and egg scramble at Zippy's calling his name.

Kinu threw the case on the passenger's seat. He strapped down his board, finished drying off, and put on a shirt he grabbed from the floorboard. He felt energized. He was content with his life, as uneventful as it was, but this briefcase felt like a buried treasure. At first, Kinu mostly hoped it would be full of money, but now he had a better scenario playing out in his head. Money would be nice, but Kinu didn't need it. Instead, he had images of finding something important: documents, a rare piece of art, priceless family heirlooms. His imagination only went so far, but what he could imagine was the praise he'd get if the contents turned out to be important. He'd be a hero. Maybe there'd be a ceremony: Kinu, the local surfer who saved the day. Kinu never had half the recognition that he imagined in his head. That's the ultimate reward for people who do the right thing: recognition.

Kinu felt charged. His mood was positive, and he was feeling finer than he'd felt in a long time. He put his truck in reverse and backed right into reality. He crashed into the front side of a passing HPD patrol car.

Breakfast would have to wait.

CHAPTER FOUR

Thursday 9:00 a.m.

The man with one hand couldn't stop picking at his face; he had the itch.

It'd been twelve hours since his last fix, and he needed to smoke. The events that had unfolded since his last high were unusual, even for his fucked-up life. He lost his hand, but he considered that a small price to pay for his new opportunity.

He sat on the dirty mattress, back against the wall, waiting for the man with the neck tattoo. It was a typical junkie apartment: frameless mattress, soiled clothes, trash in the corners. The walls had turned yellow from a combination of dirt and smoke, but they weren't shit-stained, and his power was still on. He hadn't fallen as far as many meth heads, but he wasn't too far away from sleeping in the park.

He looked at the stump at the end of his arm, bloody with grains of sand stuck in the gauze. It wasn't supposed to go down like that. The plan was for him to take the package, make the drop, and then wait for his payday.

There was nothing about losing a hand. Nothing about the package being handcuffed to him.

But soon ... soon he'd have enough money to buy all the ice he could handle. All he had to do was wait a little longer. The longer he waited, the more it felt worth it. He'd survive. Things he learned in his pre-junkie days assured him of that. He'd need more gauze and a proper cleaning, but that could wait for now.

He kept thinking about a hit. And money. He was going to buy enough meth to last at least a month, and he'd have plenty of money left over. No longer would he have to steal from friends and family. No more petty shit. No more degradation ... or less of it, he believed.

Where is that giant fucker with the neck tattoo?

The man with one hand never thought he'd turn into a junkie, of course. Like most of his addict friends, he came from a middle-class family. High school was average. He played football and dated cheerleaders. He got good grades. He was popular. Some booze and weed on the weekends, but he never even saw a stronger drug until he got to college.

His college roommate was an Asian-American kid who dealt drugs, mostly weed and mushrooms, but his personal drug of choice was cocaine. A few lines of coke here and there with the roomie never fazed the man with one hand. It was manageable. He always had control, but as too many addicts can attest, it's that false sense of control that ultimately leads to downfall.

The first time he tried meth, he couldn't sleep for two days. He didn't eat and found it hard to pass the time. He plucked at his guitar until his fingers chapped. He never wanted to do it again. But the seed was planted. The rush he felt burned through his memory, and although he didn't need it again right away, it was only a matter of time until he was at a party where he came across it. And then another party. And then another. And another. Soon he was looking for it, and then he was lost.

Meth controlled his life, but he still clung to hope. Not hope for a bright future, or for a family, or that he'd get clean, but hope that he could earn enough to support the habit. And what better way to do that than to deal? His new job was the most profitable of his criminal career, but he couldn't go on losing hands. No, that wasn't supposed to happen. He deserved major brownie points for his sacrifice. Maybe even a bonus. Right now, more than anything, he needed to get high.

The man with the neck tattoo finally arrived; he walked right in and left the door open behind him.

"Finally. Fuck, I'm bleeding out over here. Where've you been? I need to ... Hey!" The man with one hand stopped talking when he saw the gun. It was the first time he'd ever seen a silencer.

****

Detective Solosolo was finishing up his breakfast when he got a call.

"Detective, we got the tests back on the bullets used to kill Officer Palakiko. Turns out the murderer used a silencer. Thought you'd like to know."

"A silencer, huh? Thanks, Skippy," Solo said. "Any match to the bullet?"

"It's Fran, sir."

"What's that?"

"My name, sir. My name is Fran. Joe Fran."

Solo knew CSI Fran and thought Skippy was a fair nickname. "Don't be an asshole. How about that bullet?"

"Um, no match to the bullet, sir."

"You got anything else for me?"

"Yes, sir. I mean ... no, sir. That's all."

"Thanks, Skippy." Solo hung up and rubbed his temples. That rules out junkies. In all his time on the force, he'd never seen a junkie with a silencer. Things weren't adding up the way he'd hoped, and he was starting to feel stress from the case. The whole police force wanted answers to Danny's murder, and it was no secret that it might be more than a random break-in gone wrong.

Solo thought about the evidence. The murderer probably staged the broken window. He could have picked a lock, or it's possible that Danny didn't keep the back door locked. He should have known better, but it was still a possibility. Danny was shot three times in the chest. Twice from a level angle, and once from an angle that suggests Danny was already down. The third shot was likely unnecessary, just an insurance bullet. Aside from the trashed office, nothing noticeable was out of place, and forensics failed to turn up much.

He picked up the newspaper on the table and focused in on a small article on the front page: Superhero Jesus Visits Hawaii. The article went a little further than last night's newscasts. Matt Gold was in Honolulu for his close friend Daniel Palakiko's funeral.

Great, that's just what the case needs: more attention.

Solo had seen Matt's antics on CNN. His first thought: *Get a haircut, hippie.* Solo felt there was a way law enforcement officials should look, and Matt didn't fit the bill. He was too pretty with his hair tucked behind his ears and five-o'clock shadow. He reminded Solo of a younger Lorenzo Llamas, like the kind of guy who women think are sexy and rugged, but then they sure seem to spend a lot of time on their hair.

Solo's second thought: *People from LA suck.*

Solo's primary concern was the extra attention Matt might bring to the case, and the possibility of Matt trying to get involved. The last thing he needed was a hotshot media-whore from LA stepping on his toes. Solo preferred to be under the radar, which was already hard enough, and would be impossible with someone who was all over the news getting involved.

Solo was thinking about a refill on his coffee when his lieutenant called.

"Solo, where are you?"

"Zippy's." Solo didn't even consider lying— everyone's got to eat.

"That call you took this morning, the one with the hand, I think we've got a match. There's a junkie with three bullets in the chest and one missing hand. There's a witness. Get over there and check it out."

"What's the address?" Solo asked as he waved over a waitress. He went ahead and got that refill. After all, the body wasn't going anywhere.

****

Shauna Ikawa was the CSI working on the Montauk. The Montauk was stolen from the Ala Wai Harbor, and the owner was unaware of the crime until informed by the police. This wasn't too uncommon. There were a lot of rich people in Hawaii who owned boats, yet they rarely got the chance to take them out. They were too busy golfing and shopping. Shauna verified the boat was last cleaned two days ago, so whatever clues she could find would likely be from the crime.

Shauna also knew that the boat couldn't have drifted from the Ala Wai Harbor to Kahanamoku Beach. The current would've pushed it west, out towards Magic Island and on past Pearl Harbor. It also wasn't possible that the boat came from the south. The likely conclusion was that the driver beached the boat somewhere along the Waikiki strip and departed on foot, leaving the boat behind. Ditching a boat in Waikiki would result in witnesses, but so far nobody had come forward. She knew anyone out late in Waikiki would likely be drunk tourists, and a boat pulling up on the beach probably wouldn't look too suspicious.

Her initial assessment of the scene didn't turn up much. Whoever took the boat left it as clean as they found it, aside from the blood and hand of course. There were no bottles, cans, or trash that could turn up clues. The hand, which was obviously the biggest clue, was bagged and taken back to the lab. The boat was taken back to a dry dock for further processing.

When Shauna got back to the lab, her first action was to process the hand. It was filthy, covered with scars and dirt under the nails. Shauna ran the prints and came back with a Joshua Allen.

Moving on to the boat, Shauna was careful to work systematically to preserve any clues left behind. The two workers who cleaned the boat days ago were brought in for fingerprinting and DNA samples. Shauna expected to find a few of their prints, as well as some from the severed hand. She also hoped to get lucky and find a few more.

She enjoyed processing the boat. Boats are easier to work than cars. With every surface of the boat wiped down only days ago, there were likely to be some fresh prints somewhere. Clean prints are never as easy to get as they are on television, but Shauna was able to pull a few. After excluding the two cleaners and Joshua Allen, Shauna found new prints from the rub rails, the gunwale, and a rear cleat.

She didn't have enough to start drawing up comprehensive theories, and she knew better than most cops that she needed to wait for the evidence, but she couldn't stop her mind from working on possibilities. She thought the mystery prints belonged to the driver of the boat, probably a man. She wanted to believe the severed hand to be from an innocent victim, maybe caused by an accident, and she hoped for a call from a local hospital confirming the news. That would make her job much easier. But Shauna knew that the longer she didn't get that call, the more likely it was that the man would turn up dead. Odds were he was already shark bait. Smart money would be on a body dump in the ocean.

Just before running the prints from the boat, Shauna got a call from Detective Solosolo Fauatea.

"CSI Ikawa, I think I have a body to go with your hand. Just found a junkie with three holes in his chest and a freshly severed left hand. Want to come have a look?"

"Joshua Allen, huh? You've got the body, and I can confirm I've got the hand."

"Joshua Allen … Three bullet holes, two first names, and one hand. You get anything from the boat?"

"I'm working on it. I'll get someone to run the prints I pulled. We'll test the blood too."

"You've already pulled prints? That's why I tell everyone you're the best. Quick, efficient, and lovely." In stark contrast to how he treated young male officers, Solo was a big softy to the women in the department.

"Come on, we both know you don't say that."

"Hey, I might. I'm a sweet guy. I like to dish out praise where praise is due. I like to keep it positive."

"Yeah, that's your reputation—Mr. Sunshine."

"I've been watching Tony Robbins videos on my off time."

"Lord Jesus, I've heard it all."

Solo laughed. "Okay, well I guess you'd better come for a look. You can enjoy my charisma in person. There's a witness, so I'll be around for a while. You know the Lilikai Garden Apartments?"

"Yeah, classy place. I think that's where they filmed most of *Dog the Bounty Hunter*. Give me thirty minutes."

CHAPTER FIVE

Thursday 10:30 a.m.

The woman with two black eyes and a busted nose sat on a stool in front of the tiki bar and was pissed; her boss should have been angry as well, but he was cool as usual, sipping an espresso and inspecting his manicure. He sat under an umbrella next to the pool. The woman had been upset since coming back to the rented Kahala beach house the night before.

He took another sip and asked: "So you're sure the briefcase won't be found? How do you know it won't get washed up on the beach?"

"For fuck's sake, would you forget about the briefcase, Alvi? Look at me. I mean, seriously, stop going on about the god-damn-fucking case."

"Take it easy, now. You still look as beautiful as usual," the boss said with a grin. He was dressed head to toe in Tommy Bahama. He wore a silk aloha shirt, white linen pants, tan boat shoes, and a palm fedora.

"I need to go to the hospital. I don't trust that chink bitch you call a doctor. Where did you find her? She probably gives better blow jobs than medical care. If my nose is permanently crooked, I'm going to hold you as responsible as that big motherfucker who punched me."

Alvaro Garcia Menendez joined her at the tiki bar. "Come on, now. I'm sure her medical skills are more than adequate. Besides, there's really no way to test which one she's better at. I mean, they're two very different skills …"

"Stop, Alvi! Just stop right there," she cut him off. "How do you expect me to trust a doctor with a boob job? Get me someone else or I'm going to the hospital. I need to get my nose set or something. She just looked at it and said it was broken. One of your goons could've done the same."

"We'll see how you feel. Alright? If you're not feeling better tomorrow, we'll find another doctor, okay? You know you can't go to the hospital." He moved to the stool next to her. "Now, about the briefcase."

"I threw it in the ocean, just past Diamond Head, on the Waikiki side. If it didn't sink, it got carried out to sea. Nobody's going to find it."

"You said that already, but are you sure about that? Seems like if it sinks, a snorkeler or scuba diver might come across it eventually. And last time I checked, the waves seem to push things towards the beach. You think there's any chance it turns up?"

"Nobody snorkels out there, and do you ever see trash on beaches here? That's right, you don't, and do you know why? Because the currents take everything out, that's why. It'll be pushed out to sea. Probably turn up in China or Peru or somewhere like that."

"Hmm," the boss said as he sipped his espresso, "forgive me for being skeptical, but I'm not entirely convinced. And you're sure you threw the case with the samples?"

"I think so. I'd have thrown both if I could've. And that big fucker. I would've like to have thrown his ass overboard, and then ran over him a few times with the boat, grinding his body up with the propellers, and then watching the sharks come and eat..."

"Whoa, all right. Damn, slow down. I get the point."

"Fuck that. Look at my face. Totally unnecessary. I tell you, I'm gonna get that asshole."

He looked at her face. It was still attractive, despite the broken nose and two black eyes. "We'll figure out who he is, and then we'll go from there. Nothing to worry about."

She rolled her eyes and let out a sigh. "What about the Wu Tang? Think we have to worry about him?"

"That'd be Woo Lee. I think you need to get your racial slurs straight. The doctor is Japanese, not a chink, which is a derogatory term for Chinese people. I believe the Wu Tangs are an African-American hip-hop group, and Woo Lee is Korean." He sat back and adjusted his fedora, leaning his back to the tiki bar and looking out past the pool to the beach.

"And what's the derogatory term for you? You look like Panama Jack and Speedy Gonzales' love child. Why do you dress like that? You look like an asshole."

He let out a big laugh. Despite his laid-back attitude, nobody else would dare talk to him that way. He enjoyed it.

"Without that tan, you'd look like Don Knotts on steroids," she added. "Gayer than Cristiano Ronaldo in a speedo."

He was rolling. "I'm glad you can keep your sense of humor in a time like this. And does it really look like I'm on steroids? I have been working out …"

"Sense of humor? Who's joking?" she said with a straight face. "And the Wu Tangs?" she asked again.

"Woo Lee?" He waved to dismiss the name. "Don't worry about him. He's my problem."

****

"What the fuck is this?" asked Rachel. She looked at the kid who handed it to her.

The kid seemed indifferent. He'd heard the same question at least twenty times in the last couple of hours. He knew how the conversation went. "That's the new packaging." He was sitting on a picnic table in Kapiolani Park, right across the street from Waikiki Beach. He had his shirt off and was trying to flex his abs.

Rachel looked at the package and back at the kid. "What the fuck is this?" she repeated. "This is sugar. Sweet Maui Brown. I put this in my latte."

"Yeah, I know," said the kid, as he looked her up and down. He'd sold to Rachel before. Usually, she paid and left. No questions. Not as much small talk as he'd of liked. She was at least five years older than him, probably early twenties, and he noticed he puffed his chest out a bit when she came, just for her. He guessed she lived in Waikiki. Probably waited tables.

"This is Sweet Maui Brown, the same shit I see at the coffee shops. What the fuck is this?" the girl repeated once more.

The kid pulled down his Oakley's. "It's meth. Ice. Crank. Tutu. The Yammer Bammer. The Barney Dope. Chunky Love. Hawaiian Salt. Poop …"

She cocked her head. "Are you fucking with me?"

"Nope, and if you've got any sugar packets in your purse, you might want to be careful." He gave her a wink.

She cocked her head the other way. "You think I'm so dumb I won't know the difference?"

"Not that," the kid said. "I mean, I don't think you'll smoke sugar, but I can see someone dumping it in their coffee. You know, just by accident. Packets look the same, yeah?" He figured this was the most they'd ever spoken to each other.

"You've got a point there," Rachel admitted.

Rachel kept inspecting the packet. "It does look and feel exactly like sugar. How long do you think until the cops have this on their radar?"

The kid hadn't even thought about it, but he played it cool. "It'll take a while, but even after they figure it out, there's no way they'll be able to search every sugar packet on the island."

Rachel was impressed. "How much for this?"

"Same as usual."

She looked at him for a second and then at the Sweet Maui Brown. She felt the packet through her fingers, trying to measure the quantity by touch. "Same price, huh? Here ..." She took all the money out of her wallet, "... give me two more."

She wondered if anyone had ever thought of this before.

****

CSI Shauna Ikawa arrived at the Lilikai Garden Apartments and found Detective Solosolo Fauatea sitting on a lounge chair next to the pool. He was talking with an auntie in a fluffy white robe with bright red lipstick. He appeared to be enjoying himself quite a bit.

"Detective Solo," Shauna said to get his attention.

"Aloha, Shauna," Solo said with a big smile on his face. "I'm just interviewing Ms. Dubois. She saw a big haole with a tattoo on his neck leaving the apartment. She was down here walking her dog, Peaches."

Shauna looked her up and down. She was attractive for an older lady, but there was something a little off about her. Who wears a robe, pink slippers, and what appears to be no shirt this late in the day? Shauna thought there was a real possibility of a boob popping out any second. Solo was grinning ear to ear.

"Well ... I'll leave the interviewing up to you. I'm going to head up to the apartment," Shauna said. She shook her head as she walked away.

"Third floor. There's an officer at the door. I'll finish up with Ms. Dubois and be up shortly." Solo nodded up to where the first officer on the scene was leaning over the railing.

Shauna went up to the room. She heard a laugh from Ms. Dubois, but couldn't imagine what Solo could have said to earn it. She knew Solo well enough to know he's just having fun. He's the family-man type. Although overweight, he's handsome, burley, and can be charming from time to time. Still, she was impressed to see his powers taking hold of Ms. Dubois, regardless of the fact that she might be totally lolo.

When Shauna reached the apartment, the officer filled her in on the necessary details. He was first on the scene, and most of his information was what Shauna could see for herself. The body was on the dirty mattress. Despite the filth, there didn't appear to be any signs of a struggle. Shauna knew she'd have to process everything, including all the trash and what she could only image would be a disgusting bathroom.

Shauna's eyes kept going from the bullet holes in his chest to the bloody gauze on his wrist. It was going to take some time to process everything, but the search for answers is what kept Shauna motivated.

"Quite a way to start the day, hey?" Solo said as he made his way to the front door. "Lots of action in Honolulu, and it's not even lunchtime yet."

"I have a feeling I'll be skipping lunch today. How'd it go with Ms. Dubois? Anything … you know, slip out?"

"The lovely Ms. Dubois, Dotty to her friends, saw a big man with a tattoo on his neck leaving the apartment. Said he walked right on by her …" Solo noticed the expression on Shauna's face and picked up on her comment. "Oh, slip out? No no, nothing. She … she managed to keep her, um, well, the robe did its job," he said with a smirk.

"Oh, don't act all innocent. You were eating it up out there. Did she even comment on your wedding ring?"

"I don't know what you're talking about. Someone has to question the witnesses. I'm just here to serve and protect."

"Right, and if you see a little nipple while serving and protecting …"

"Then I guess it's just part of the job," Solo said. "Anyway … Dotty—Ms. Dubois—said that she noticed the man when he walked out of the apartment. She thought it was strange that he didn't shut the door behind him, and after he had left, she went up and peeked in. That's when she saw the body. Didn't hear gunshots, though. Said she didn't hear anything before she saw him leave."

Although calm and collected when he delivered this news to Shauna, Solo got chills when he first heard it himself. If a silencer was used, how long would it take for everyone in Hawaii to draw the connection to Officer Danny Palakiko's murder.

"Silencer?" Shauna said under her breath. They both looked back at the body. "Coincidence?"

"Awe, fuck," Solo said, rubbing his temples.

****

Kinu couldn't believe his luck. After backing right into the patrol car, he thought he'd be taken "downtown," as they say in the movies. As he sat at Zippy's eating his loco moco, he shook his head and wondered how he'd gotten off so easily.

As soon as he realized he hit something, he immediately pushed the briefcase to the floorboard. Shocked to see that it was a cop car, he got out of his truck to face the officer. Although it felt like he hit the patrol car with some force, he was surprised to see very little damage. The officer got out with a big smile on his face. Although big and lean, Kinu felt tiny as he saw the officer get out of the car. Well over six feet tall and probably pushing three-hundred pounds, the officer made Kinu feel small. His partner stayed in the car, but Kinu could tell he was also the built like a linebacker. Very typical in Hawaii.

Kinu gave a concerned smile and turned on the local charm. Lots of "braddahs" and "sirs" were mixed in with his apologies, and the officer could tell that Kinu was just a local surf bum. With some pity, the officer let Kinu go without even giving him a warning. Just said that the car was already scratched up in that area. No worries.

Kinu started to get carried away with the apologies, which the officer rightfully took as nervousness. Anyone who backs into a cop car would act the same way. Little did he know that Kinu was in a near panic as all he could think about was the briefcase on the floorboard. Even though he did nothing wrong, the fact that the case had handcuffs attached to it made Kinu feel as if he were doing something illegal. He would have broken down, but the officer saved him. Just told him to be more careful. That's it. No ticket. Didn't even search Kinu's truck. Nothing.

Kinu couldn't believe the day he was having.

****

Matt Gold checked into the Outrigger Hotel in Waikiki to little fanfare. He was relieved the front desk treated him just like any other guest, and as far as he could tell, he made it all the way to his room without too many people doing a double take.

The Outrigger Hotel is located on Kahanamoku Beach, less than fifty yards from where earlier in the day Detective Solosolo Fauatea investigated a twenty-one-foot Montauk with a severed hand in it. But Matt didn't know about that yet. He just knew that the Outrigger was on one end of Waikiki, opposite the Diamond Head side and next to Fort De Russy Park. He booked it because it was affordable and convenient. It was also in a prime location. Not in the heart of the Waikiki strip, but close enough to everything. Easy to get out, yet minutes from most of Honolulu.

Most of Danny's family lived across the island on the Waimanalo side, but since Matt had always lived in Honolulu, Waikiki was the logical place to stay. He did have offers to stay with Danny's family, but after recent events, and the grief that he was sure the family was going through, he knew a hotel in Waikiki was the best bet.

Still, he had to face what he was here for. He stood by the window and looked out at Diamond Head. He took a minute to enjoy the view, and then he made the call to Danny's mom.

CHAPTER SIX

Thursday 10:45 a.m.

Alvaro Garcia Menendez sat next to his pool at his rented Kahala mansion and thought about his next move. Shit hit the fan last night. He lifted up his fedora and ran his fingers through his hair as he wondered if he had enough manpower. Two of his men were outside with him, and two more were inside. All armed. It was hard to know how pissed Woo Lee would be, or if he had anything to do with what happened last night, but Alvaro knew one thing: If Woo Lee wanted him dead, he wouldn't stand a chance.

The deal last night should have been simple enough. Woo Lee's people were bringing the money, and Heather was taking the samples. How it got so messed up ... he couldn't quite figure out. Why Heather was punched in the face and thrown overboard, he also couldn't figure out. He knew it'd take time to figure out the Hawaii crime scene, but he never expected to be challenged so soon.

"All right, time to go," he said as he hopped up and motioned to his men.

In typical Hawaiian style, the back windows of the house completely opened up to the outside, creating a seamless transition from the pool area into the living room. Great for paradise living; bad for protection. His other two men were sitting in the kitchen playing with their smartphones.

"You guys know the drill. When Heather wakes up, don't let her leave."

"Sure thing, Alvi."

"You got it, boss."

Alvaro took a look in the mirror and adjusted his fedora. He rubbed down his eyebrows and checked his teeth.

"All right, let's hit it," he said to the other two as he put on his sunglasses.

****

Alvaro met with Woo Lee in Chinatown. Although Woo Lee was Korean, he owned one of the most stereotypical Chinese restaurants in the area. He sat in the corner by himself, the rest of the restaurant empty. Alvaro couldn't hold back his expression of disgust as he noticed the tackiness of the red and gold decor. Chinese lanterns were hanging everywhere. There was even a large aquarium with some ugly fish. Not the pet kind of fish, but the eating kind. Woo Lee sat there in a white t-shirt, khaki shorts, and rubber sandals. Not exactly a pillar of fear.

"Woo Lee, how are you?" Alvaro said as he took a seat. Woo Lee was around twenty years older than Alvaro, probably in his mid-sixties. Rumor had it that he was a merciless gangster back in the day. He ran with the Korean gangs working out of Seoul and Hong Kong, and Alvaro heard that Woo Lee never backed down and always got his way. There are stories of him taking on three or four guys at a time. Stories of him using all kinds of weapons on guys: bats, crowbars, pipes, and pliers … Stories Woo Lee told Alvaro himself, and stories Alvaro found hard to believe. Unfortunately, the men who worked for Woo Lee, they were not softies. Alvaro also heard stories about them. Not the kind of guys you want to mess with, but he didn't see any of them here.

"Alvi, good to see you. Have a seat. Do you like my restaurant?"

"Thanks for meeting me. Wow, this is your place, huh? It's … um … nice."

Woo Lee leaned in and put his elbows on the table. "So, Alvi, how are your kneecaps?" Woo Lee gave an exaggerated look under the table.

"Um, fine I guess. That's kind of an… um, strange question."

"How about your rittle fingers? Your elbrows?"

"Yeah, uh, good. I'm all good, thanks." Alvaro adjusted himself in the chair and looked around. There were no signs of other customers or workers, and the restaurant felt eerily quiet. He looked at Woo Lee's t-shirt: *Matsumoto's Shave Ice.*

Woo Lee kept it up: "How about your achirrrries tendon? That good too? Alvi, you know I care about your health. You work so hardly. You must take care of health."

"Hardly? No, Woo Lee, I've been working very hard. Very, very hard. That's the problem. All this work, and then last night …"

"Yes, you work so hardly. Hardly! It's adverb. You run quickly. You walk slowly. You work hardly! My Engrish teacher teach me."

"No, Woo Lee, see, 'hardly' means not a lot. Like, I hardly ever come to a tacky Chinese restaurant in Chinatown. 'Hard' means ... well, it means with a lot of effort, like how I've been working. I've been working hard."

"Hard." Woo Lee demonstrated by knocking his knuckles on the table. "But hardly, it's adverb!" He looked at Alvaro with a grin and shook his head. "Alvi ... you live in America long time, but your Engrish ... not perfect. You need learn adverb."

Alvaro conceded. "Ok, fine, I work so hardly. Now, about last night ..."

"Yes, Alvi, you work so hardly, but last night ... Big fucked last night, yes?"

"Well ..." Alvaro shrugged. "You know what happened then, right? We brought the samples. So ... what happened with the money?"

"The money?" Woo Lee's eyes lit up. "Alvi, I gave your money. My man gave it."

Alvaro shook his head. "Um ... no, no money. One of your guys punched my girl in the face, dragged her around the boat by her hair, and then threw her overboard. He broke her nose."

Woo Lee had a look of genuine shock on his face.

"You didn't know about this? About ..."

"Alvi, I know I have no sample. Nothing. And money gone." Woo Lee cocked his head and squinted at Alvaro. "So, what do you know?"

Alvaro leaned in. "I know a big asshole with a neck tattoo tried to take the samples and not pay. I know that my girl was able to throw the case with the samples in the ocean. That's when he roughed her up." As soon as Alvaro said it, even he heard the tone of concern in his voice. The idea of a floating briefcase full of their crystal meth was a scary thought, but the idea of some giant psychopath was even more concerning.

Woo Lee shrugged. "Alvi, I don't know about this. You believe your girl?"

"Yeah, sure do. She didn't break her own nose. So who was the big fucker with the neck tattoo? Do you know him?"

"Alvi, let me worry about that big fucker with neck tattoo. If he didn't get you your money, I'll take care of it. He fuck with both of us." Woo Lee smiled at Alvaro and leaned back in his chair.

This news was bittersweet for Alvaro. He let out a sigh: "Hard to know who to trust around here." Before coming to Hawaii, all Alvaro heard about was how everyone knew everyone on the island, and this was especially true for the criminal element. If Woo Lee didn't know the big fucker, that was bad news. On the other hand, if there was a problem, Woo Lee was the man to fix it.

"So, your girl. You say she got punched in face?"

"Yeah. Broken nose. Two black eyes. One angry temper. How's your man?" Alvaro asked. "The one who lost a hand."

Woo Lee looked surprised again. "Don't know. Lost a hand? Guess I find out soon." Woo Lee's expression of concern turned to a smile. "You tell me about you. How's business? I mean, how's our business?"

"We're on track. Everything is still a go," Alvaro said as confidently as he could. "Big shipment is arriving soon."

"That's good news."

"Listen. Woo Lee, we haven't known each other long, but you know I've got a boss. He trusts you, I trust him, and he trusts me. After last night, I have to admit, I don't know ..."

"Alvi, Alvi, Alvi, prease. Rook at me. Okay. You trust me. Your boss, yes, we have deal. He called me. I know him. Mexican boss is powerful boss. Me? I don't want trouble. I want to live aroha, braddah. I want to pray with sexy wahine and eat fish and poi. We run business and then pau hana. Live aroha, yes?"

Alvaro had more trouble with Woo Lee's broken pidgin than his broken English. He threw him a bone: "Shoots, let's live aloha."

Alvaro smiled. Woo Lee laughed. "Ho, Alvi, you do have aroha spirit."

"Yeah," Alvaro said still smiling. "But I've also got some concerns, and now I've got some money issues."

Woo Lee's laugh faded out. He just sat with a grin and nodded his head.

Alvaro looked around and still didn't see any sign of another person; it made him uncomfortable. Then he looked at his Rolex. "Whelp, lunch crowd is bound to be banging down the doors soon. I should probably be doing the ol' skedaddle."

Woo Lee looked confused for a moment but quickly got the gist when Alvaro stood up to leave. "Haha, yes, the ol' skreedittle. Okay, yes. Talk to you soon, Alvi. Don't worry. I take good care of you. We good, braddah?"

"I hope so, Woo Lee. I really do."

****

Kinu sat on the tailgate of his truck and looked at the briefcase. He was very disappointed at what he saw.

The briefcase was full of Sweet Maui Brown sugar packets. He picked one up for a closer look. The packets were dry and in perfect condition, and they were utterly worthless to Kinu. Why in the world would someone have these things in a fancy briefcase with a handcuff attached to it—Kinu didn't have a clue.

He closed the case and left it in the bed of his truck along with the crowbar he used to open it. *Oh well*, Kinu thought. *Nothing exciting ever happens to me anyway.*

CHAPTER SEVEN
Thursday 11:30 a.m.

After a quick nap and shower, Matt was ready to visit the Palakikos. Danny's mom said she'd be around all day; she told Matt to come by whenever he could—she'd be waiting. Danny's youngest brother, Duke, would also be around in the afternoon, so it'd be great if Matt could see him as well.

The fastest way to Waimanalo was to cut across the island on the Pali Highway. This would take Matt over the mountain towards Kailua, which was only about ten minutes from Waimanalo. Matt, however, decided on the more scenic route that headed around the eastern tip of the island.

Getting out of Waikiki was always slow-going, and Matt was happy to take his time. He drove down Kalakaua Avenue past all the hotels on the strip, past Kapiolani Park and the zoo, past Diamond Head and into Kahala. He made a few wrong turns, eventually ending up on Waialae Avenue. From Waialae, he finally found an on-ramp to the H1 highway.

From the H1, it was hard to get lost. The highway led into Hawaii Kai, where it turned into the Kalanianaole Highway, a much slower road with stoplights that gradually turned into two-lane traffic. The Kalanianaole Highway runs through Hawaii Kai, heads up past Hanauma Bay and several scenic points, and then right into Waimanalo. After meeting Danny's mom, Matt planned to continue to the North Shore. What better way to spend the day than an island tour? Perfect therapy.

Matt stopped at a Starbucks in Hawaii Kai for a coffee. As he stood in line, he was almost certain that nobody gave him a second look. Maybe it was his genius disguise: a University of Hawaii ball cap and aviator sunglasses. Or maybe nobody cared. Either way, it was nice to fit into a crowd.

Matt could already feel the therapeutic effects of driving on the island. Stopping for a coffee wasn't exactly stalling; it was more like adjusting. He enjoyed being back on the islands for so many reasons. When he moved away to Los Angeles, Matt assumed he'd return to Hawaii someday to live, but life in LA happened, and his plan to return kept getting delayed.

After getting a coffee, Matt drove past Hanauma Bay and along the rocks and cliffs of the eastern point of the island. He drove past the lookout point where tourist buses stopped for photos of Molokai and Maui. Past the blow hole. Past Sandy Beach. And eventually up past Makapu'u Point, where Matt could see down to the Waimanalo and Kailua coast, one of the most beautiful views on the island.

The road led right into Waimanalo, and as Matt turned on to Danny's mom's street, he found himself excited to be there. Danny's family was down-to-earth, welcoming, and always showed him a lot of aloha. Exactly what Matt needed after being in LA for so long—unless they weren't coping well. That'd be tough.

Danny's little brother busted out of the front door as soon as Matt pulled into the driveway. "Ho, Uncle Matt, good to see you, braddah! Been too long." Duke hadn't seen Matt in years, and they'd both changed: Matt was about forty pounds of muscle heavier, and Duke had gone through puberty. Duke gave Matt a hug.

"Yeah, it has been too long," Matt said, returning the embrace. "What's up with the eye, champ?" Duke's eye was purple and swollen. He also had a swollen lip and Matt noticed some scratches on his arm.

"Just kicking ass and takin' names. You know me." Duke threw some shadow punches at Matt and did a little foot shuffle. "Nah, just kidding. I got rolled in the park after playing ball the other day. Meh, it happens."

Danny's mom came out of the house before Matt could ask any follow-up questions. Within two minutes, she'd hugged him so hard that he thought she was going to crack a rib, asked why he wasn't married yet, and presented her case why Danny's death was more than just a robbery gone wrong. She led him around to a table in the backyard. Matt hardly said a word.

She talked. Matt listened to her theories.

He got the impression that she expected him to do something about it.

****

Detective Solosolo Fauatea sat in Lieutenant James Nishi's office and listened to him explain what he wanted Solo to do. He didn't expect Solo to go along with it willingly, but the orders came from the top, and

Lieutenant Nishi didn't get where he was today by not following orders from his superiors. He was used to dealing with Solo, so he knew he'd have to go through the routine. "So, what do you say, Solo? Think you can handle it?"

Solo let out a deep sigh and put both hands up to rub his temples. He let his hands move down to rub his neck as he let out another sigh.

"Why do you do this to me, Jimmy? Can't you just let me do my job?"

"Sorry, Solo, but you know it comes from the top. What can I do?" Lieutenant Nishi shrugged. He adjusted himself in his chair, leaning back as far as the springs would allow. Lieutenant Nishi was even bigger than Solo, and the chair squeaked with his weight.

"Hey, easy there Jimmy. I'm not sure that chair's built for a man of your … um … stature."

"You're one to talk." Lieutenant Nishi nodded to Solo's gut. He smiled and shook his head. "Now listen, we all appreciate your goodwill to the Los Angeles Police Department, and your continued efforts to find the murderer of Officer Palakiko. You are a model public servant, and we are all in your debt. On behalf of the city of Honolulu, the entire department, and the mayor, I'd …"

"Save the bullshit, Jimmy." Solo looked again at the newspaper that Lieutenant Nishi tossed at him when he first came in. "Superhero Jesus Visits Hawaii." It was a different article than the one Solo read over breakfast, but the information was mostly the same.

"Do you know if he wants to be part of this?" Solo asked. "The papers seem to think he's here on vacation."

"No clue, but it's just a matter of time before they connecting the dots between him and Danny. We need to get ahead of it before the papers do."

"Yeah, I think you already mentioned that."

"Give him a call today. See what he thinks. If he doesn't want to help out, great! If he does ... well, maybe you'll get your picture in the paper." Lieutenant James Nishi gave Solo another smile.

"Sure thing, Jimmy. Tell the governor I'm on it. Solving murders and babysitting pretty boy celebrities at the same time. No problem."

Solo left Lieutenant Nishi's office and went straight to his car. He didn't want to spend more time in the office than necessary. He headed over to Aloha Mart to grab a Spam Musubi and bag of chips. He needed to call Danny's mom and see what she thought about inviting Matt to help him with the investigation. He also wanted to tell her about CSI Ikawa's discovery: the bullets used to kill Danny matched the bullets pulled from a one-handed junkie found dead this morning in Honolulu. And they have a lead: a big guy with a tattoo on his neck. He didn't have to share this information, but he wanted to.

Solo finished his chips, wiped his hands on his pants, and got out his phone. She answered on the second ring.

"Ms. Palakiko, this is Detective Fauatea." Before he could get to the point of his call, she told him that she was sitting in her yard talking to Matt Gold. "Have you heard of him?" she asked.

"Yeah ... I've heard of him," Solo said.

He invited himself over.

****

53

Kinu came out of the Aloha Petro Mart with a cup of coffee. He put a half a tank of gas in his truck and grabbed two packets of Sweet Maui Brown from the case in the bed of his truck. He didn't drink coffee often, but there was something about the Sweet Maui Brown. For Kinu, it was fancy. And it was something he found in a fancy briefcase. Yes, it was a disappointment, but Kinu wanted to taste his small treasure, regardless of how ordinary it was. Sugar was something he'd never buy, and almost never use when free, but he found it, so why not?

He poured the packets into his coffee and stirred it the best he could using the wrappers. He knew that a lot of the sugar would settle at the bottom, which he could mix later by swirling the coffee around in his cup. Kinu looked forward to those last drinks, which he knew would be the sweetest.

He sipped the coffee as he turned onto Beretania Street. He was heading to a barbecue at Magic Island. One of his surf buddies invited him. Every weekend Kinu would end up at a picnic or two, and now that he was temporarily out of work, he could meet up with friends anytime. He was looking forward to this one all week—mainly because of a certain wahine friend that Kinu knew would be there.

Kim Carson was from the mainland. California, if Kinu could remember correctly. She had long blond hair, was tall, and had the kind of body Kinu liked. She wasn't skinny, but she wasn't fat, and she had the curves in the right places. Kinu wouldn't usually go for a haole girl, but Kim had lived in Hawaii since she was a child. She had a plumeria tattoo on her ankle, turtle stickers on her Nissan Pathfinder, gold bracelets on her wrist, and she belonged to an outrigger paddling club—all the signs of a long-term Hawaiian resident. She had heaps of aloha, something Kinu found attractive in a white woman.

She was also divorced. From a local Hawaiian. Kinu liked that, too.

He continued to drink his coffee as he turned onto Piikoi Street. He started to notice how great he was feeling. The coffee was starting to kick in.

Kim Carson seemed interested in Kinu. They'd met at a couple of barbecues. She always seemed happy to see him. She liked to talk, and Kinu liked to listen. He didn't know it, but that's what Kim liked about him. After the first time they met, Kim Carson told her friend: "That Kinu ... When you talk to him, he makes you feel like you're the only person there. Like everything you're saying is the most important thing in his world. I've never met anyone who's made me feel like that." Her friend hadn't noticed. She considered Kinu another uneducated local surf bum, but what she had noticed was Kinu's body. He was ripped for a man in his forties.

Kinu didn't know that he made that kind of impression on Kim. Kinu, always the nice guy, thought Kim saw him as just an ear to talk to. Just a friend. He thought she was out of his league. Beautiful, educated, and she had a good job as a nurse at Queen's Medical Hospital. He figured she only dated doctors or lawyers or rich guys with BMWs.

But then he heard she asked about him. She's the one who invited him to the barbecue. Not directly, of course, but through a mutual friend.

Maybe he had a chance.

Kinu turned left onto Ala Moana Boulevard. He entered Ala Moana Beach Park from the opposite end as Magic Island. The road followed the beach about a half mile down to where Kinu would park. He always came into the park at the opposite side of where he was going. The traffic was bad at times, and it would often take a while to get from one end to the other, but Kinu liked the drive. He liked the view of the beach.

Entering on the west side, Kinu got a nice view of Magic Island, which was actually a peninsula that shot out at the east side of the park. Behind Magic Island, he could see the Ala Wai Boat Harbor, Waikiki, and views all the way to Diamond Head. A great spot for a barbecue.

Kinu gave the last bit of his coffee a swirl and gulped it down. He felt confident. He was looking forward to talking to Kim, but the traffic was driving him crazy. He couldn't wait to get to the barbecue. Today was his day with Kim Carson. The day he'd do the talking. The day he'd pull out his charm. He could feel it.

He could also feel his legs tingling.

His heart was beating faster.

The traffic was driving him crazy. All these tourists who didn't know how to park their rental cars. Too many locals who were taking their sweet-ass time. Magic Island seemed so far away, and Kinu felt an unfamiliar wave of anxiety overtake him.

Kinu began to honk at cars in front of him. His peaceful drive into the park was now too much for him to handle. He thought about pulling over, but he could see the Magic Island parking lot. Just a little farther.

He felt a rush to his head. Something was happening to him, and it was freaking him out. Maybe it was a caffeine rush. Or maybe something with his blood sugar levels, whatever that could mean. Or … a stroke? Maybe he was having a heart attack?

Kinu had no idea, but he felt like he was losing control of his legs. The tingling sensation was moving to the rest of his body, and his heart was about to jump out of his chest.

He was scared. But he'd also never felt better. There was a euphoric wave sweeping through his body, mixing with an urgent sense of panic.

He drove to the back of the parking lot, trying to get a spot as close to the barbecue as possible. He could barely steer his truck into a parking space.

Kinu's friends spotted his truck, and Kim said she'd see if he needed help carrying anything. She was looking forward to seeing him as much as he was to seeing her.

As Kim walked to the truck, she was surprised that Kinu wasn't getting out. She could see his head through the rear window. He didn't seem to be moving. She wondered if Kinu even had a phone that he could be looking at? What could he be doing?

Kim called his name as she approached the truck, but Kinu's head still didn't move.

"Kinu?" she said again in a soft voice.

She looked through the window and noticed why Kinu hadn't responded. He had vomit running down his chin and all over his shirt. His eyes were rolled back in his head.

Kim looked back at the barbecue and shouted as loud as she could: "Call 911! Somebody call 911!"

CHAPTER EIGHT

Thursday 1:00 p.m.

The woman with a broken nose and two black eyes was Heather Brown. A military brat, Heather moved around the world a lot as a child. She spent time in Germany, Japan, Guam and Hawaii, and during her senior year in high school, her family moved to San Diego where her father decided to spend the final years of his career as a drill sergeant at the San Diego Marine Corps base.

In Heather's opinion, this was a suitable job for her father. Like most career military men, Heather's father was a stickler for discipline. He ran a tight ship around the Brown household, and Heather's mom was always happy to play the good military wife.

Heather didn't hate her parents. In fact, she always considered herself lucky. She got to travel around the world and make all kinds of friends. She also learned how to stick up for herself.

When Heather was in fifth grade, her father was transferred to a base in Chiba, Japan, where Heather met Jovina Jackson. Jovina was from Alabama and was the biggest girl in class. When the teacher went out of the classroom on the first day, Jovina decided to have a little fun with the new girl. She turned around in her desk and said loud enough for the entire class to hear: "Hey, white girl, welcome to Japan. Konnichiwa you little white bitch."

Heather smiled.

Jovina didn't like that. "Yeah, I called you a little bitch. That's what you are, a little white bitch. What? You think you're tough? You sit there with that ugly-ass smile on your face thinking you're tough—I'm gonna show you who's tough after class. You'd better run your little white-girl butt all the way home." She turned back around, thinking she proved her status to the new girl.

Jovina was only bluffing, but Heather learned from her father to stand up to bullies. She stood up and took three quick steps at Jovina, jamming her pencil directly into Jovina's forearm. Jovina cried in front of the entire class, and Heather was never bullied again in Chiba, Japan.

Heather learned two lessons that day. First, don't take shit from anyone. Second, make everyone afraid of you.

As Heather moved from school to school, she learned a third, even more valuable lesson: She didn't have to stand up directly to confrontation. She could lose a battle and still win the war.

This third lesson molded Heather as she aged. In seventh grade, her family moved again, and she had a new classroom of students to meet. Natalie Pruney waited for Heather after school. She pushed her down, kicked her, punched her, got her in a headlock, and just all around pummeled her. Heather chalked it up to being the new girl. She didn't fight back. She didn't run away. She didn't say anything. She just took the beating.

59

She knew she couldn't beat Natalie in a fight, so she'd have to win another day.

"Fucking-A right," Natalie said as she gave one more kick before walking away, leaving Heather lying on the ground.

That night she went home, cleaned herself up, and she thought. She thought all night about what happened. She thought about how she knew Natalie was a bit fucked in the head, and probably came from a messed up family, but Heather couldn't forgive her for that. She had to get revenge, and she thought about the appropriate response.

The next day Heather acted like nothing happened. She came to class and sat down just like any other day.

During science class, as the students were working on problems by themselves and the teacher was sitting at her desk, Heather closed her book, stood up, and walked over to Natalie.

"Hey, Natalie."

As Natalie turned to look up, her face was met square on by Heather's hardback science book, swung with all the torque Heather could muster. Natalie went down fast. She was on the floor holding her nose. Blood was everywhere. She was crying and covering her face, not understanding what just hit her. Not knowing what just broke the bridge of her nose.

Heather leaned over her and slowly, very slowly, began to spit on her. It was a slow spit, the kind where the saliva hangs from the mouth, like a rope. Natalie was looking at her hands, seeing the blood. She had tears in her eyes and didn't see the spit slowly working its way from Heather's mouth.

Heather was aiming it, trying to stretch it out until the perfect moment to let it loose. It landed on Natalie's eye right as she looked up. It hit at the same time the teacher finally pulled Heather away. "Fucking-A right," said Heather.

The class looked on in shock.

Heather's acts of revenge evolved as she got older. In college, Heather stopped with the violence and instead went for public embarrassment. A girl who failed to do her part of a group project was Heather's first target. The girl was responsible for the conclusion and final editing. Instead, she turned it into the professor directly and told him that Heather was the one who didn't finish her part. Heather only found out after she got her grade.

Heather didn't complain. She knew what circles the girl ran in, and her plan was simple.

Step one: sleep with the girl's boyfriend. That was simple. She knew he was in a fraternity. She happened to bump into him at a party, feed him some shots, and then suggest that they go to his room. She flew under the radar at parties as she almost never went to any, but she knew she was hot enough for any drunken fraternity guy to bang.

Step two: wait for him to pass out and then take a picture of him naked. She only had to wait about five minutes. She took out her cell phone and took a picture of him with his shriveled little penis poking up. She made sure she got his face.

Step three: search his phone and computer for naked pictures of his girlfriend. She figured this was a long shot, but it only took her about two seconds to find the photos. They looked like photos he took while his girlfriend was passed out. She sent them to herself as she thought about the irony.

Step four: she printed thousands of the naked pictures and then dropped them around campus. Some around the dorms. Some in lecture halls. Some around the fraternity and sorority houses. Anywhere and everywhere.

Both the girlfriend and boyfriend withdrew from school within the next week. Heather didn't bother finding out what happened to them.

Now, as Heather Brown looked at her broken nose in the mirror, she thought about that big fucker with the neck tattoo. She thought about his square jaw and enormous shoulders, and how he yanked her up by the hair and threw her out of the boat like she was nothing. She thought about his senseless actions. How she was sure he had no brains, and how he had no clue the fire he lit inside her.

She looked in the mirror and gently touched her nose. She felt the pain and could still see dried blood in her nostrils.

She'd never wanted revenge so badly in her life.

****

On the other side of Honolulu sitting in a shitty old Ford Taurus, the man with the neck tattoo wasn't thinking about Heather Brown. He was thinking about money. His money, and how he could make more. He never wanted to see Heather Brown again, and when he did think about her, he wondered if he should have just killed her.

The night on the boat was already a distant memory to him. He knew using handcuffs to secure the briefcases was dumb. He knew there was no need for it, yet it still happened. He let it happen, and he prepared for it.

He also knew they didn't need a boat. But, yes, he agreed that two people meeting for an exchange with briefcases handcuffed to their wrists would be better off traveling by boat. That would be more discreet. But ... why do we need to use handcuffs, he had questioned again.

He knew it was because of the money. He didn't know how much money would be there, but to use handcuffs ... it had to be a lot. He bought a hacksaw at Walmart and some gauze. He also brought a camping ax just in case. He was prepared.

The plan was for one of Woo Lee's men to pick up Heather at a private dock in Kahala. The dock was accessible from the beach, and the house it belonged to was for sale, so there'd be no one to complain.

He was to take Josh and drop him off at the dock. Josh would walk to a spot down the beach to meet one of Alvaro's men. He'd then take Heather back to meet Woo Lee, and then take Heather back to the dock and pick up Josh.

It was a stupid plan. Too many steps. Too complicated. The man with the neck tattoo suggested he take the briefcase and make the switch himself. Simple. Efficient. But his suggestion was politely refused. This was too much of a game for some.

When he pulled up to the dock, he made Josh sit near the bow and told him to shut up and act scared. Josh didn't have to pretend.

He turned a gun on Heather and gave her a simple choice: get in the boat or get shot in the head.

She got into the boat, her briefcase handcuffed to her wrist.

She tried to ask questions as the man with the neck tattoo drove the boat back to Waikiki. He didn't answer.

He stopped the boat in front of Waikiki. The beach and hotels seemed so close. Maybe too far to swim, but close. Too close to dump a body, Heather hoped.

The man with the neck tattoo grabbed a bag near his feet and approached Heather. He grabbed her by the hair and pulled her down hard on the floor of the boat. He quickly yanked her back up and threw her forward, causing her to drop headfirst near the bow. She felt him on top of her. He had his knee on her shoulder and leg across the back of her neck. She felt him stretch out her arm. He pulled the handcuff to stretch out her wrist, and she heard the saw grinding into the metal handcuffs.

His leg was crushing her neck, and she struggled to breathe. It seemed like hours until Heather felt the tension leave her arm and the leg move off her neck. He yanked her back up by the hair and threw her back into her seat.

She wanted to say something, but she knew she was in no position. She needed to get off the boat.

The man with the neck tattoo turned to Josh. "Your turn." He didn't give Josh time to reply. He grabbed him by the arm and neck and slammed him to the deck, positioning him the same way as Heather. His giant leg crushing Josh's neck in the same way.

The man with the neck tattoo began to saw at Josh's handcuffs, but he stopped, took a deep breath, and reached for his bag. "Fuck it. We need to speed this up."

Josh felt the man with the neck tattoo shift his weight, and he was able to turn his head toward the hand with the briefcase attached to it. He expected to see the saw.

Then he heard a whack.

And then the pain came.

Josh was able to see his severed hand only inches from his face. He saw the stub of his wrist and blood. Lots of blood. He screamed. Too shocked and in too much disbelief to say anything, he just screamed.

The man with the neck tattoo got off Josh and reached for the bag. He threw it at Heather. "There's gauze in there. Wrap him up."

Josh's screams slowly turned into sobs.

After a few seconds of shock, Heather took the gauze and did her best. Josh made no move to get up. He was on his back, his head turned away and eyes closed, sobbing and shaking.

The man with the neck tattoo started the engines and turned back to Kahala.

"What the fuck is wrong with you?" Heather yelled over the engines, still working the gauze.

She got no response.

"This is fucked up," Heather said. "Why cut his hand off? I could've sawed the cuffs off. Shit, he could've done it himself." She was feeling the anger build. She shouldn't be in this situation. This plan. This ... psycho. This boat in the ocean. Some big asshole she didn't even know. Fucking Alvaro for putting her getting her into this. She saw her briefcase still on the deck next to Josh's severed hand. "Well, you're not getting this," she yelled as she chucked the briefcase into the ocean.

Easing up on the throttle, the man with the neck tattoo lunged down at Heather, connecting his right fist directly between her eyes. She felt the bridge of her nose break and her body crash to the deck. He lifted her with one arm by her hair. She hung briefly before she felt his other hand on her hip, throwing her overboard.

The man with the neck tattoo regained control of the boat and turned back to Waikiki. He watched Josh sob on the deck. She was right, and he knew it—there was no reason to chop off his hand. Either of them could've sawed off the handcuffs. He only brought the ax as a last resort, but he was too impatient. Always too impatient.

He looked down at the briefcase of money and reminded himself what Josh was: a hired junkie. That's all. What difference did it make if he didn't have two hands? Harder to smoke crack, that's all. Fuck him, and fuck the chick he threw off the boat. He had his money—a nice little bonus he wasn't expecting.

He knew his days in Hawaii were numbered. He didn't see any harm in doing what he had to do to make and extra buck.

****

Detective Solosolo Fauatea pulled into the Palakikos' driveway and parked behind Matt Gold's rental car. He walked to the backyard where Ms. Palakiko told him they'd be sitting and saw her and Matt talking. She got up and greeted him with a hug.

"Detective Fauatea, I'm so happy you came over," she said as she squeezed him.

He gave her a kiss on the cheek. "It's good to see you. Please, call me Solo."

Solo needed to do a balancing act. He needed to treat Ms. Palakiko with his soft, concerning side while also showing Matt that they weren't going to be buddies. He wanted Matt to decline his offer.

"Detective Solo, this is Matt Gold. Have you heard of him? He's been all over the news. He was a good friend of Danny's. They graduated from UH together."

"Yes, I've heard," Solo said, wondering if Ms. Palakiko remembered having the same conversation on the phone a short time ago.

Matt stood to shake his hand. "Detective."

Solo noticed that the pretty boy's hat and sunglasses were on the table.

"I was just telling Matt about the case," Ms. Palakiko said to Solo. "I think I've got him up to date on what I know. Are there any new developments?" Ms. Palakiko could have been a cop in another lifetime.

"Yes, actually, there's been a lead," said Solo. He was glad she got right to the point. Solo knew she'd want to talk story later, but new information trumped the island's social protocol.

"We matched the bullets from Danny's murder to a murder in town. The murderer used a silencer in both cases."

"Oh, a silencer? What does that mean? Who was the victim?"

"He was a junkie. Had track marks all over. We found him on a dirty mattress in an otherwise empty apartment."

She let the information sink in. "Just a junkie? Do you think ...?"

"He had a record for dealing, but so far we haven't found much. Just found his body this morning. There was a witness."

Ms. Palakiko perked up with this news.

"Another resident in the apartment complex saw a man leaving the victim's room. She's a bit of a ... well, she's unique, but … her story sounds solid," Solo said. He held back a smile as he thought of his morning with Ms. Dotty Dubois and her revealing robe.

Matt just listened, trying to make sense of the details.

"He's a big haole. Taller than me according to the witness, and she said he's full of muscles. He also has a distinct feature: a neck tattoo. We're working on it."

Ms. Palakiko and Matt were both silent. They were trying to connect the dots, thinking of possible connections and motives. Her mind was working almost as fast as Matt's.

"Oh, and he was missing a hand. The victim, that is. I almost forgot." Solo waved his hand as if it were a minor detail. "Found it in the bottom of a Montauk in Waikiki this morning."

"A hand? Why in the world …?"

Matt didn't say a word. He watched Ms. Palakiko process the information. She'd been going through details of the murder all morning, and now she was thrown a curveball.

Solo didn't give time for questions. He turned to Matt: "Officer Gold, the Honolulu Police Department wonders if you'd like to assist in the case. Due to your high profile, we figure there'll be a media spectacle. I mean, not that you're a spectacle, but … there will be a lot of media speculation is what I'm trying to say. Speculation as to why you're here and your involvement. So maybe something official would, you know, put a cap on the attention."

Matt sat up in his chair, obviously surprised by the offer.

Solo continued: "Of course, I'd understand if you're not interested. I mean, if I were you … Shoots, no way would I jump into this. You know, media and all."

"Oh, Matt, please. You need to do this. Danny would want you to. I know it. Please, help the detective." Ms. Palakiko was more encouraging than Solo was expecting.

"Detective Fauatea, I really appreciate the offer to help. I came here for Danny's funeral. I wanted to pay my respects to his family, and I wanted to say goodbye to my friend. I'm not sure if you caught my story on the news, but I've been going through some stress recently. I've been having a hard time with it. What you said earlier, about the media spectacle, I couldn't agree more."

Solo nodded. He liked the way this was going.

"But," Matt continued, "I didn't come here thinking I'd get involved in any way. Even driving over here today, I didn't even consider that I might be able to help. I really don't want to—"

"Matt," Mrs. Palakiko put her hand on his, "please."

Shit, thought Solo.

Matt looked Danny's mom in the eye. She gave him a smile, and her eyes pleaded with him to accept. He knew he wouldn't make a difference. He was no real superhero, but … but how could he say no? "Sure. Detective, whatever I can do, I'm willing to help out."

Solo wanted to talk him out of it, but he could see he'd be wasting his time. He saw the expression on Mrs. Palakiko's face. Nobody was going to say no to her. The deal was done.

"I guess I'll pick you up tomorrow We'll see what we can find out," Solo said, pulling his notepad and pen from his pocket. "Where are you staying?"

****

Alvaro smoothed out his eyebrows as he talked to his boss on the phone. They used the latest in bad-guy technology to make sure their phones weren't tapped, but they still tried their best to speak in code.

"Listen, Alvi," his boss said. "The cruise starts on Monday. It's all-inclusive and, um, don't forget to tip your waiters. If ... um ... you ... you need to make sure you've checked your reservation, and ... or ... there's another cruise later. It's a bigger boat. Much bigger. Like ...four times the size."

Alvaro's boss was calling from Mexico. He started as a small time drug dealer who worked hard to turn his operation into a moderately successful operation. They focused on running drugs across the U.S.-Mexican border, but due to stiff competition and lack of muscle, he decided to find new markets.

He thought talking in code would be easy, but he was already running into trouble. "The cruise ... um, I'm interested in a later one. Maybe something to Maui, or um ... Honolulu."

The first place on the list to expand was Hawaii. Alvaro came to him with the idea. At first, the boss was skeptical. He suspected that Alvaro just wanted to get out of the shit-hole Mexican town they were working out of and move to paradise, but Alvaro was persistent, and it did seem like a decent plan.

Alvaro continued: "So it's basically the same plan—I mean—same cruise we talked about before?" The code-talking was getting on his nerves, and he wasn't sure he was still following the conversation.

"Yeah, um, everything on the ... cruise sounds good. How about our Asian friend?"

"He's on board." Alvaro wanted to tell his boss about the broken nose and missing samples, but he didn't know how to put that in cruise-ship talk. He'd let it wait.

"Good good," his boss said.

Alvaro got off the phone and walked to the tiki bar. He was in the backyard of the house he was renting in Kahala. He was comfortable here. He had his men stock the bar with top-shelf liquor, beer, and lots of mixers. He could just as easily whip up a martini as a lava flow, complete with paper umbrella.

"Something to drink?" he asked Heather Brown, who was on a lounge chair next to the pool. She was looking as natural as could be expected from someone with a broken nose and two black eyes. "Maybe a mai tai?" he said as he pulled out the shaker and bottle of rum.

"What kind of beer you got?" Heather didn't even look up from her iPad.

"Beer? Come on, beer is so boring. How about a pina colada? Or a margarita?"

"I'll have a beer. Corona is fine. Or a Longboard. Whatever." She still didn't look at him.

Alvaro made himself a mai tai and brought Heather a Hinano. "From Tahiti," he said. He stocked the bar with the Tahitian beer because he liked the Polynesian girl on the label, and because he thought beer from Tahiti was cool. Heather didn't care.

"So, what did the boss have to say?" Heather had never met Alvaro's boss. She worked for Alvaro, and the big boss never seemed to leave Mexico. To Heather, he was just the man on the other side—the supply side.

Alvaro was going to ask her to put the iPad away, but he let it go. "He just babbled some bullshit about cruises. He's too scared to talk on the phone. It was worthless."

He sat next to her in a lounge chair and took off his fedora.

She put the iPad down. "Are you going to help me find the bastard or what?"

"Whoa, hey, slow down. Can we enjoy our drink for a second? Don't you love this time of day? The sun's starting to go down, the trade winds are blowing, and look at those puffy white clouds ..."

"Yeah, it's beautiful. Now, are you going to help me find the fucker who broke my nose, or are you going to sip your cocktail and admire the fucking palm trees?"

With a smile and a shrug he said, "I guess I can try to multitask, but I have to warn you, multitasking doesn't really work, you know? I mean, right now I'm focusing on this cocktail and the 'fucking palm trees,' but if you want me to help you, I'm not sure I can give my full attention."

She reached over, grabbed his mai tai, and finished it off in one drink. "There. One less thing to focus on."

"Hey, come on, seriously? I just made that!" He was happy to see Heather drink. She'd be easier to handle with a few drinks in her. The alcohol should mix well with the poolside paradise.

"Oh, I'm sorry. I thought you were just using it as an accessory ... to match that fruity-ass shirt of yours. I'll tell you what Jimmy Buffet, you tell me what you're going to do to help me get even with that asshole, and I'll go over and make you another drink. What do you think about that?"

"Gladly," said Alvaro. "While you were sleeping earlier, I was working." He flashed her a smile and looked at his empty glass.

"All right, put your veneers away and keep talking," she said. She moved the iPad off her lap and got up to go to the bar. "You guys want something?" she asked Alvaro's two men at the table.

They looked at each other before replying almost in unison: "No, thank you, ma'am." They could never tell when Heather was being nice or when she was about to be a bitch. They played it safe.

Alvaro continued: "So while you were sleeping, I was meeting with Woo Lee. If anyone on the island can get to the bottom of this, it's Woo Lee."

"You mean, if there's anyone that *you* know on the island who can help, it's Woo Lee. How many other connections you got? And surely Mr. Neck Tattoo works for him."

"Whoa, hey, easy," Alvaro said. "I've got all kinds of connections." He didn't like Heather calling him out in front of his muscle. "I can't deny that Woo Lee is the biggest, but I've got others." He half expected her to ask him for names.

"Anyway, what's that Chinese bastard have to say? And don't you think he knows full well what happened? I think it's about time we stop trusting him."

"Well, that Korean gentleman said he's on it. I'm sure he's as concerned as we are."

"We? I think I'm a tad more concerned than either of you two assholes," she said as she pointed to her face. "How'd Mr. Miyagi take it? You know, what happened last night? He seem pissed or what?"

Alvaro had thought about that a lot since he left the meeting. "You know, hard to say. He didn't seem too upset. You should have seen the old guy. He was wearing a t-shirt and rubber sandals. He looked like he was about to go fishing or something. He did say that he was working on it. I don't know ... seemed confident to me. You know, like he's not worried about it. But he was surprised when I mentioned that his man lost a hand, and he acted surprised that the guy with the neck tattoo was there. I'm not sure what he knows."

"And you? Any theories?" She handed him a fresh mai tai.

"Hey, who's my hero? This looks great. You even put a new umbrella in it."

"It must be the fucking palm trees. Making me soft," she said. "So, Panama Jack, got any insight for me? What do you think?"

"Honestly, I'm not sure who the neck tattoo guy could be. Maybe some local thug taking advantage of a situation," Alvaro said as he sipped his drink.

"Right. A local thug, huh?" Heather sat next to the pool and put her feet in. She braced another Hinano between her legs and fumbled with the bottle opener. "A local thug quite possibly, but he had an ax for Christ's sake! Who just happens to bring an ax? And who would know we were going to be there? You have to have an idea, right? I mean, this is Hawaii, not fucking Utah, or wherever it is that people just walk around with axes."

"Heather, babe, relax. The last thing we need is for you to go off picking a fight with the wrong people. Let's wait for Woo Lee to get back to us. I'm sure he'll get to the bottom of this mystery man. Don't forget, his man lost a hand. I'm sure he won't let that slide."

"His man was a shitbag junkie. You think he gives a fuck about that asshole?"

Alvaro didn't say it, but he knew she had a point.

CHAPTER NINE

Thursday 6:30 p.m.

CSI Shauna Ikawa was finishing her shift when she got the text message: *Shorebird. 7:30. Reservation is under Mitchell. See you there.*

She didn't want to go, but she decided to force herself. She had to hurry. She needed to run by her studio apartment in Makiki to change and freshen up. After a day of dealing with blood, body parts, and a dead junkie, she needed to get some of the filth off of her. And she couldn't show up at the Shorebird without putting on something nice.

She thought about calling Solo to tell him the bad news: After processing most of the evidence, she didn't have many clues to go on. But if there was one thing she knew about Solo, it was that he could wait until morning, and if he were worried about it, he wouldn't hesitate to call her. She just hoped he wouldn't call during dinner.

Shauna arrived at the Shorebird about ten minutes late. The hostess took her to her table where she saw Dr. David Mitchell waiting for her. He was pale, overweight, and looked nothing like his photo. She thought he had hair plugs.

"Shauna, you're late," he said. "But that's fine. I went ahead and ordered a Jack and Coke. Wasn't sure how long you'd be."

Not the best first impression, but maybe he's just nervous, Shauna thought. She always was on first dates.

"Sorry I'm late," she said as she sat down.

"One second," Dr. Mitchell said to the hostess. "Shauna, would you like something to drink?"

"Um, I'm still thinking about it," she said to the hostess. Shauna waited tables during college. She wasn't about to place a drink order with a hostess.

Dr. Mitchell liked what he saw. Shauna looked even better in real life than her profile photos. She was wearing tight jeans and a skimpy, yet classy blouse. He noticed that her arms looked toned. There wasn't any of that tricep fat his ex-wife had so much of. "You look pretty fit. Really toned arms. You surf or something?"

"Yeah, I surf most mornings and sometimes evenings after work. How about you? You ever get out on the waves?" She already knew the answer.

"Me? No. Right, can you picture me on a surfboard? No, I don't get in the sun much. I spend too much time at my practice."

It looked as if fifteen minutes in the sun would turn him into a lobster.

Shauna knew this date was going nowhere. It was her fifth online dating experience, and she vowed it would be her last. Dr. David Mitchell surely thought his money could get him laid, which it probably often did, but Shauna wasn't interested in money. He was rude, arrogant, and just not her type. All this she figured out in the first two minutes—no CSI training needed.

At the end of dinner, she wouldn't even let him pay for her meal. She insisted. That should have been a big enough hint, but Dr. Mitchell still suggested they hop in his BMW and go back to his place for a drink.

It didn't happen.

Shauna went home and deleted her online dating profile. She hoped that she wouldn't break down and put it back up again, but it was hard to meet guys in Honolulu unless she wanted to date a coworker, which she wasn't about to do.

****

Kinu lay unconscious in a hospital bed. He had one arm handcuffed to the bed, and an IV hooked up to the other.

Kim Carson was in the lobby talking to a doctor and police officer. She found it hard to believe that Kinu would overdose, but she didn't know him that well. She knew he could be a user.

The police officer told her it was standard procedure to handcuff Kinu to the bed. "We have to wait until the drug is out of his system. There's no telling what he might do if he wakes up," the officer told her. "Most people in his situation would try to leave. Or worse."

Kim had heard about this before. Although she worked in the maternity ward, she heard many nurses share their stories of drug overdoses.

The doctor added, "It's for everyone's safety. Actually, he's very lucky he vomited. He came in with a rapid heart rate and a dangerously high body temperature. If he wouldn't have got some of the drug out of him, he could've had a heart attack or stroke, which, thankfully, is the only way to overdose on methamphetamines."

Kim had asked about that. She figured it was easy to overdose on meth, just like heroin or crack. Even after all her years in the nursing field, she didn't fully understand the differences in most hardcore illegal drugs.

"Once he wakes up and the doctor gives me the okay, I'll take the cuffs off," the officer said.

"Then we'll see if he's in a state to take a visitor," the doctor added.

Kim thanked them both and headed over to where some of the friends from the barbecue were waiting. As soon as the ambulance left with Kinu, the barbecue was packed up and most of the people went straight to the hospital.

"Kinu will be fine," she announced. "He overdosed on methamphetamines. The doctor thinks he drank it somehow."

"Ho, no ways," one of Kinu's friends said. "Kinu never take no ice. Braddah clean."

"Yeah, maybe a little of the pakalolo sometimes, but meth? No ways," another said.

Kim wasn't surprised by the insistence that he was clean. His reputation was solid as far as she knew. But still ... a lot of users hide it well from their friends and family. She'd heard too many stories.

"Besides, who drinks meth? Neva' heard of dat," added the first friend.

"That's what the doctor thinks," Kim said. "Maybe Kinu will tell us what happened when he wakes up."

"When can we see him?"

"The doctor said they'll keep him sedated until tomorrow morning. That junk is still in his system. He might be able to receive visitors then," Kim answered. "Until then, there's not much we can do. Might as well call it a night."

With that, the group said their goodbyes. Hugs and kisses were given and a few plans were made to come back tomorrow. Kim was touched. She was well aware of the ohana spirit, and it made her feel good to see such support for Kinu.

As they drove home, Kinu's white 1988 Mazda pick-up truck was making its way to Island Towing Express over in Waimanalo. The tow company cruised the parking lots of all the state parks that forbid overnight parking, and when they saw Kinu's truck in the Magic Island parking lot after hours, they went in for the kill. Easy money.

Once the truck was back in the lot, the tow truck driver checked the doors. Locked. He shined his flashlight through the window. Not much.

Even though the company charged over two hundred dollars to release a towed car, the drivers always tried to make a little more by searching glove compartments and consoles for money. It was late, and the driver didn't think it was worth picking the lock of a shitty old truck. Besides a briefcase on the floorboard, there wasn't much inside.

CHAPTER TEN

Friday 8:25 a.m.

Solo told Matt he'd pick him up at eight o'clock sharp in the hotel lobby. Twenty-five minutes after eight, Solo pulled up to the Outrigger Hotel and saw Matt standing out front waiting with two cups of coffee.

"Good morning, Detective Fauatea," Matt said, giving Solo one of the coffees and pronouncing his name perfectly. He said nothing about the time.

"You hungry?" Solo asked.

"I had a protein bar, but I could always eat."

"Good," Solo said.

They headed out of Waikiki in silence. Solo figured Matt would be full of questions. Matt figured Solo was a grumpy old detective who didn't really want to be playing host to Superhero Jesus.

They were both right.

"Zippy's okay with you?" Solo asked as he pulled into the Zippy's parking lot on King Street.

"Yeah, I love Zippy's," Matt answered.

Solo was a little surprised. He imagined Matt as the alfalfa sprout and green smoothie kind of guy. He was even more surprised when Matt ordered the Zippy's chili omelet with a side of Portuguese sausage. He didn't even look at the menu.

When the food came, Matt loaded his omelet with hot sauce. Solo put a layer of salt on his loco moco.

"I used to come here all the time," Matt said after taking the first bite. "We'd throw our boards in Danny's truck, go down to Waikiki for dawn patrol, and then we'd skip class and come here for breakfast. Actually, we'd usually hit the other Zippy's on King. The one down by Magoo's. What's the park over there ... Moilili?"

"Yeah, behind the supermarket? That's Moilili," Solo said.

"We used to play softball there."

"With Chuck?" Solo asked.

"Yeah," Matt was surprised Solo knew Chuck. "Yeah, we played in the Thursday co-ed league. I mean, we mostly drank beer and hung out, but there was a softball game in there somewhere."

"Chuck's been running those leagues for years. I used to play on a team or two back in the day."

"Who knows, maybe we played against each other. Do you remember a bunch of punk kids who drank too much and lost badly?" Matt asked. "That'd have been us."

"Seems like there was always one or two teams like that. Nobody wanted to be the team to lose to them. Too embarrassing. Some of the guys I played with took that league very seriously. They looked forward to it all week. They'd even practice."

"Yeah, we weren't exactly going to the batting cages. We'd load up the cooler, make sure we had our gloves, and we'd just have fun. Nobody cared about winning or losing. You know ... Danny was probably the worst player on the team. He always wanted to play shortstop, but at least two or three balls would go through his legs every game. Nobody cared."

"So, you and Danny, you guys were close?" Solo asked.

"Yeah, really close," Matt said. "With his family, too. It's still hard to believe he's gone. It's surreal."

"Surreal, huh?"

Solo could tell where the conversation was going. He knew he'd need to tell Matt his theories and all the details of the case, but he decided not to do it in the restaurant. They finished their meals with little small talk.

"I'm going to use the bathroom. Why don't you pay the bill and I'll buy you something fancy for lunch?"

"Fancier than Zippy's?" Matt asked.

"Hard to believe, huh?"

****

The kid's mom woke him up. "Timmy! Timmy, time to get up," she yelled. "Breakfast is ready!"

The kid rolled over to look at the clock. "For the love of God, mom. It's the crack of freaking dawn. How many kids wake up with the roosters during summer vacation?"

She stood in his doorway. "It's after eight, sleepyhead. I cooked breakfast."

"Are you wearing an apron?"

"Wakey wakey eggs and bakey. Wakey wakey eggs and bakey," she sang.

"For the love of Christ." Timmy threw his pillow towards the door, but his mom was already off, singing the line over and over.

He stumbled over to his blackout curtains and threw them wide open. The sun nearly blinded him. It was already up over Diamond Head, and he could see Waikiki coming to life down below. Another beautiful day in paradise.

The kid moved to Hawaii the year before from Newark. His mom divorced her second husband, took him for half he was worth, and decided to retire to Honolulu.

"Timmy, come on. It's getting cold," she yelled.

"It's 'Tim,'" he said, making his way to the table. She used to be the only one to call him that, but in Hawaii, it seems people are always putting a "y" on names: Timmy, Jimmy, Tommy, Mikey ... Tim didn't like it.

"Good morning, my little Grumpy McGrumperson. How'd you sleep?"

Tim's hair was sticking up and he rubbed his eyes. "Ahhh, need more sleep. Grumpy need more sleep. No like mom. Mom gay."

"Don't talk to me that way," she said, giving him a little smack on the head as she put his plate in front of him. "You want coffee or juice? I have fresh guava juice I bought at the farmer's market."

"Both."

"Coming right up, Mr. McGrumperson. You want hot sauce for your eggs?"

"Yes."

"At your service," his mom said. "And what are your plans today? How are you going to spend this lovely day in paradise?"

It was the same conversation they had every morning of summer vacation. "I'll probably play ball over at Kapiolani. Maybe head over to Jared's later." This was his standard reply.

"Well, would you like to hear what your mother is planning?" asked his mom.

"Not really," said Tim.

"Well, I'm going to tell you anyway, grumpy-butt. Your young, adventurous mother is going to hike to Manoa Falls. What do you think of that?"

"Whoa, settle down Indiana Jones, that's like a twenty-minute hike. You going to wear your heels?"

"You could join us, you know? We're going to the Waioli Tea Room after for lunch. It's going to be a good time. Sometimes there are chickens under your table, and all the aunties working there wear muumuus."

The kid held two fingers in his mouth and pulled the imaginary trigger. His imaginary brains sprayed on the wall behind him.

"Fine, drama queen. Whatever. You're the one missing out. Go play with Jared. Or for all I care, you can go play with yourself."

Timmy laughed.

"Oh, grow up. You know what I mean."

Timmy ate while his mom cleaned the kitchen and sang. They'd been through lots of ups and downs together, and he liked seeing her this happy. Living in Hawaii had completely changed her, and Timmy loved to see it.

After breakfast, he headed to a three-story apartment building on Date Street. It was a short walk from his apartment in Waikiki, but there was a noticeable change in the neighborhood. The apartments were mostly three or four stories, and many were old and a bit worn down.

He knocked, but there was no answer. He knocked harder, and finally the door opened.

"Hey, Frances," the kid said.

"Timmy, come on in."

Frances was old. The kid guessed at least in his seventies. He reminded Timmy of his grandpa, but older. And more local. And homosexual, which didn't matter to Timmy.

"How'd it go yesterday? You know, with the Sweet Maui Brown?" Frances asked.

"Smooth as butter," Timmy said. "Only one guy opened the packet to look, which was surprising. I thought more people would want to see what they were buying. And a lot of people bought extra," Timmy said.

"Well, that's good. Not sure when we'll get more; we're back to the regular stuff today. You got the money?"

Tim tossed the money on the counter. "What's the deal? Why we going back?"

"Don't ask me. I get what I get." He took the money and went to the back bedroom. He came back and tossed a bag at Timmy. "See you tomorrow, right?" he asked.

"Yeah. Nothing else to do."

Timmy put the bag in his backpack and headed for the park.

****

The man with the neck tattoo was up early. He sat in his car across the street from a rented Kahala beach house.

The house had a gate around it and was a one-story beauty. Easily worth a couple million. He could see the front of the house through the gate, but not much besides that. He assumed the back of the house had a pool, or at least a big barbecue area. Maybe a hot tub as well, and it seemed to have beach access. Not bad if you can afford it.

When a black SUV pulled out of the gate, the man with the neck tattoo followed. The SUV went down Kilaeua Avenue, turned right on Alohea, and then cut over to Kapahulu. The man figured that the SUV was heading for the H1, but it turned into Leonard's Bakery, home of the famous malasada, also known as a Portuguese donut.

The SUV pulled up and parked in front. The man backed into a space across from the side exit. When he saw the driver get out and go inside, he grabbed his crowbar and walked over to the SUV.

The driver, one of Alvaro's men, ordered a dozen malasadas.

"What kind of coating do you want?" said the kid behind the counter.

"Um ... I don't know. What do you have?" asked the driver.

"Original, cinnamon, and li hing."

The driver had no idea what li hing was. "Um, I guess I'll just have the original," he said.

"Hey, is that your car?" the kid said as he looked out the front.

The driver turned to see a large man with a neck tattoo winding up with a crowbar.

"Holy shit!" said the driver.

"Holy shit!" said the kid.

They both watched as the crowbar bounced off the passenger's side's rear window. The man swung again.

Again, the crowbar bounced off the window. It was damaged, split out like a spider web, but the bulletproof glass wasn't going down to a measly crowbar, even with a giant swinging it.

He lifted the crowbar over his head and brought it down hard on the side view mirror, snapping it clean off.

"Holy shit, that's fucked up," the kid working the counter said. "You think I should call the cops?"

Other customers and employees stood motionless. They watched as the man with the neck tattoo took a couple more swings at the SUV.

The driver thought about pulling his gun, which was tucked discreetly under his oversized aloha shirt, but instead, he just stood there, watching the man. He was big. Looked mean. He'd be a handful in a fight, but then again, the driver was no creampuff marshmallow himself.

The man with the neck tattoo calmly walked back to his car. He put the crowbar in the back seat and then got in. Slowly, he pulled out of the parking lot. He even used his blinker.

"I think he put his seatbelt on," said the kid. "That was crazy. Do you know that guy?"

"Not really," the driver said.

Everyone looked at the driver. He turned back to the kid and asked, "So, how much for these donuts?"

****

Just as Solo and Matt were pulling into Danny's driveway, the site of his murder, Solo got a call from CSI Shauna Ikawa. She told him what she had: "There was a hit on some fingerprints pulled from the Montauk. They came back to a thirty-two-year-old named Heather Brown. There was also blood on the gunwale that didn't

87

match the blood from deck—could be hers. She was in the system from her military records. She wasn't active duty, but her father was. I was able to get her file sent over from Pearl."

"Well, that's good news," Solo said. "Anything else?"

"Not much, but I've got a little. So far I've found out that she had quite a few incidents while growing up. Her military school records show lots of run-ins with her classmates. Seems like she was a bit of a fighter, but she was never charged with anything. No criminal activity. She spent time in Hawaii as a high school student, but then she moved to the mainland her senior year. She hadn't been back to the islands until two weeks ago. She came in on a one-way flight from San Diego. No local address. Her last address on record is in Burbank."

"It's a start," Solo said. "What kind of work is she in?"

"Not sure. She graduated from UCLA, and she filed taxes for three years after. She worked for Maston Shipping, but there are no tax records for her for the past few years."

"Married? Kids?" Solo asked.

"Never married. No kids. Parents live in San Diego. No siblings. That's about it."

"You check her Facebook page?"

"Yeah, nothing. There are a lot of Heather Browns on Facebook, but not the Heather Brown we're looking for. The military sent over a copy of her old military ID, and I've got a copy of her California driver's license. I'll text them to you."

"Mahalo." Solo hung up and turned to Matt: "I've got a few more details that I should probably fill you in on." He got out of the car. Matt followed as they walked around back. The police tape was down, and Danny's house looked like any other house on the street.

"That was one of our CSIs on the phone. We have a lead that seems related to our case."

Solo led Matt through the back gate. It was Matt's first time to Danny's, but he'd seen pictures. Danny invited Matt to come out for his birthday, but Matt was too deep undercover at the time. The case was over, and now Matt thought about the part of his life he gave up and the things he missed out on.

Solo continued: "When I met you at Ms. Palakiko's last night, I might have left a few things out, and there are a few details we haven't worked out yet. Something that's too much of a coincidence not to be related to the case, but I didn't want to tell Ms. Palakiko. I don't want to keep her in the dark, but I'm trying to keep her on a need-to-know basis. You know what I mean?"

"I know what you mean," Matt nodded.

"Yesterday morning we found a severed hand in the bottom of a small boat just off the beach in front of your hotel. A little later in the morning, we found a junkie with some bullet holes in his chest. He was missing a hand. There were some prints on the boat, which we've matched to a Heather Brown. That's what I just found out."

"Does that name mean anything?" Matt asked.

"Not yet, but it's a lead. We haven't worked out a motive. Maybe she can shine some light on things. The bullets from the dead junkie match the bullets used to kill Danny. It's possible we're dealing with some junkies and bad luck, but that doesn't sit right."

"Yeah, definitely not something you see every day." Matt thought for a second. "So ... what's your theory?"

Solo led Matt to the back door. "Look over here. We know the killer came through the back. The window was broke, but the way we found the glass, we think that might have been staged." Solo opened the back door. "I think the murderer either picked the lock or the door was open. I think he came in this way and surprised Danny. Maybe broke the window on his way out. Look back here."

Solo led Matt through the living room. Danny's blood was still visible on the carpet. "Look in here; now look in the bedroom."

Matt took a quick glance at both the office and bedroom. He tried not to look at the blood, and he tried not to think of Danny. "Looks like whoever was here didn't even go into the bedroom," Matt said.

"Exactly. That alone makes me want to rule out a robbery. We've got a witness who saw a man leaving the junkie's apartment. He's a big white guy with a neck tattoo. I'd say he's prime suspect numero uno. And we've got a match from the prints on the boat—a Heather Brown. Now all we need to do is find one of them."

"Easy ..." Matt looked at Solo, "so how do we do that?"

****

Kinu woke up in a haze. It took him a second to realize where he was. The last thing he could remember was having a panic attack as he pulled into Ala Moana Beach Park.

He moved his legs and looked at his body for signs of injury. Seemed fine, except for being handcuffed to the bed.

"Hello … ?" he said. He could barely talk. His throat was dry, and he was dizzy. His head was pounding.

Kinu waited until a nurse came in. "What happened? Why am I here?" he asked.

"Good morning, Mr. Anapu'ui. How are you feeling?"

"Been bettah," Kinu said.

"You had a methamphetamine overdose. Do you remember?"

"I hadda what? Overdose?"

"We'll let the doctor explain." She handed him a glass of water, which Kinu drank in one drink.

Just as the nurse was leaving, Kim Carson came into the room. "Kinu, you're awake," she said with a smile.

Shit, Kinu thought. He instantly became self-conscious. "Kim, what the …? How are you? What are you …?"

She cut him off: "How are you feeling? Do you need anything?"

"No … I'm …" He didn't know how to answer. "I'm okay, I think. Not too sure what happened."

"Kinu, you had an overdose. Do you remember?"

"No." He shook his head. "Not really."

"You ingested a large dose of methamphetamines. Large enough that the doctor had to pump your stomach and give you medicine to calm your heart rate. He was worried. He said you could've gone into cardiac arrest."

"Whoa, what? Ingest? You mean I ate meth?"

"Drank, probably."

It started to come back to Kinu. "I stopped and got a coffee on my way to the barbecue. I remember feeling kind of funny driving into Ala Moana. Maybe it was the

91

coffee? Maybe there was something in it. You know, like laced or something."

It was what Kim hoped to hear, and she believed him instantly. "Yes, that's possible. We need to tell the police about this. If the coffee was laced, this might have happened to other people. Did it taste funny?"

Kinu thought about it for a second. "You know, I don't know. Don't drink much coffee."

****

Heather Brown was pissed. "So that big motherfucker just randomly decides to take a crowbar to your SUV? In broad fucking daylight?" she screamed at Alvaro.

Alvaro sat on a stool at the tiki bar in the backyard of the rented beach mansion. His four men sat around the table."Easy, babe," he said. Trying to calm her down was starting to feel like a full-time job.

"Easy? Oh, 'take it easy, babe.' I'm getting tired of hearing that. We need to take this fucker out. We should be taking crowbars to his shit, not the other way around." Heather was behind the bar with a bottle of Hinano in one hand and her sunglasses in the other. "What's he doing following your car? You're not concerned that maybe he's looking for you? Maybe that crowbar was meant for your pretty fucking head, huh?"

Without looking up from his smartphone, the driver said, "I'd have shot him."

Heather shot him a look. "Great! Guido would've shot him. Simple."

"Guido? I'm Irish," he lied. "And you can call me Iceman." He gave her a wink.

Alvaro couldn't help but smile, and his three other guys tried to hide their grins.

"Listen, fucktards, can we focus here? Alvi, you need to find out who this guy is. We don't need this trouble. What if he shows up tonight? You think of that?"

"How's he going to know about tonight? Besides, there's one of him and six of us. If he shows up tonight, we'll take care of him. Easy."

"How'd he know about last night? Hell, how'd he know shit-for-brains over there was going to buy donuts this morning? I feel like we're going to be having this same conversation again tonight. He just keeps showing up, and you just keep fixing your hair."

"They're called malasadas," Iceman said.

"What?" Heather snapped.

"They're Portuguese donuts. And why you gotta always be calling us names?"

Heather ignored him and sat next to Alvaro. "Alvi, listen, it's a real possibility that he shows up tonight. We need to kill this asshole as soon as possible. Call your Chinese boyfriend if you have to, but figure out who he is and who he works for. Don't let this one guy fuck everything up. We don't need this."

CHAPTER ELEVEN

Friday 10:00 a.m.

"Hey, are you the kid selling meth in sugar packets?"

Timmy was sitting on a picnic table at Kapiolani Park. "I don't know what you're talking about." In Timmy's short time as a drug dealer, it was the first time he'd been scared.

"Come on, it's gotta be you. I'm friends with Rachel. You know, brown hair, small tits, nice ass ... Rachel. She described you perfectly. Said she buys from a white kid in the park with too much gel in his hair and who's always trying to flex his abs. Dude, come on, that's gotta be you."

"Sorry, man. I don't know any Rachel." *What a dick*, the kid thought. He wished he had his shirt on. This guy had tattoos covering his arms and was probably about ten years older. He wasn't tall, but he was thick, and he looked a little off. He had a hollow look in his face and dark rings around his eyes. He smelled bad.

"Come on, man. It's cool. I just wanna buy." The guy flashed a smile of rotten teeth and a small wad of cash.

"Sorry, not me," said Timmy, trying to stay cool.

The smile vanished. "Listen, I know it's you." He took a step closer. "I want some of those sugar packets. Some Sweet Maui Brown. Come on, you going to hook me up, or are we going to have a problem?" The guy was dangerously close. He went from friendly dick to violent asshole in two seconds.

"Man, it ain't me. I don't know what you're talking about." He couldn't believe Rachel told this guy about him. Timmy couldn't picture her hanging out with this scumbag. He was getting nervous.

"Bullshit. Come on, asshole. Sell me some shit. I've got money. When the fuck did drug dealers get picky?"

He took another step closer, and Timmy did a back-roll off of the picnic table and started running.

"Hey … what the fuck? Come on, man. Where you going? I've got money, man. Come back."

Timmy didn't stop running until he was well out of sight. He had some bags in his pocket, but the rest of the meth was in his backpack stashed back in the park. He'd have to go back and get it, so he doubled back when he was confident he wasn't being followed.

Once the coast was clear, he went back and sat on the picnic table. What the hell, might as well go back to business.

The advantage of this spot was that he could see people coming in all directions. He was fast, so as long as he saw someone coming, he felt confident that he could outrun just about anyone. Today was the first time he ran, and although he was a bit scared at the time, he didn't expect the guy to be back.

Timmy debated whether he should've just sold to the guy. The guy had a point—Timmy was a drug dealer. Why should he care who he sells to?

He started selling drugs shortly after moving to Honolulu. He found a bag of ecstasy in the locker room at school, and after trying some with his only friend Jared, he got the idea to sell to his classmates. Actually, it was Jared who got the ball rolling. He told a guy that Tim had some. That guy told another guy, and that then that guy's friend asked Tim if he could buy some from him.

The next thing Timmy knew, he was somewhat popular. He had senior girls asking him to hook them up, cool kids texting him, and most people in school knew his name. The only problem: Timmy wasn't really a drug dealer.

Fortunately for him, weed was easy to come by in large quantities, and since he already had the reputation as a dealer, his business stayed brisk.

At the beginning of summer vacation, Timmy got hooked up with Frances, his new supplier, who talked him into selling meth in the park, and here he was three weeks later. High school customers evolved into customers of all ages, many of whom looked like anyone off the street.

The park was full of homeless ice-heads, but he didn't deal with any of them. Most of them slept under trees during the day, and the kid never stayed in the park after dark. Today was the first time he didn't want to sell to someone, and it was something he never even considered before.

He assumed there were different classes of meth users. He wanted to deal to the middle class; white people were his bread and butter, followed by a mix of locals. All it took was his supplier to point a few regulars his way, and slowly the word got out. He had no idea where all the homeless junkies got their drugs, but he wanted no part of that. He didn't even like using the park bathrooms on the chance that a homeless person would be in there.

He'd only been sitting for about five minutes when he spotted another guy heading his way. Like the other guy, he was big.

Timmy thought about taking off, but he decided he was a drug dealer, and drug dealers sold drugs, so he stayed put.

"Hey ... how'z it? You a ... you wouldn't happen to be holding, would you?" the guy asked. "Do you know Rachel? Bartends at Lulu's. Cute girl. She said you could hook me up."

This guy seemed all right. A little bit of manners goes a long way. This was the kind of customer Timmy was looking for. "What are you looking for?" he asked.

"I hear the Sweet Maui Brown is good."

"I meant how much? I don't have the fancy packaging today, just regular bags."

"Oh, okay, um ... I guess that'll work."

The guy paid, said thanks, and took off. Tim felt a little of his confidence come back, but he needed to have a talk with Rachel. He wanted to find out about the first asshole. And he wondered how many people she was sending his way. He didn't know much about dealing drugs, but he knew enough to know a little discretion is important.

He saw more new faces that morning. Some said they knew Rachel; others knew someone else he sold to the day before. Most asked for Sweet Maui Brown, and then they all bought what he had. He told them he didn't know what he'd be getting tomorrow. They didn't complain, but a lot of them said they'd be back.

By eleven o'clock he was out. Unheard of. The earliest he ran out before was around three. He'd have to ask for more tomorrow.

****

Alvaro met Woo Lee at Ala Moana Beach Park next to the lawn bowling court. Woo Lee was sitting on a picnic table throwing bread to the birds when Alvaro walked up.

"Alvi, so good to see you so soon."

Alvaro looked around but couldn't see any of Woo Lee's guys. *No way he was here alone*, Alvaro thought. His guys must be in a car watching, but he couldn't spot them.

"Woo Lee, how are you?" Alvaro shook his hand and took a seat next to him on the table. "What's in the bag," he said.

"My rawn bowring balls." He motioned to the lawn. "Do you pray? I have match today."

Alvaro shook his head. "No, I didn't even know this was a game." Sitting next to Woo Lee on the picnic table, Alvaro couldn't help notice Woo Lee's rubber sandals. They looked like they came from Walmart, and his toenails looked like they hadn't been cut in years.

"You want to pray? There's one sexy wahine praying today. You can pray with my balls."

"Really? A sexy woman is playing?" Alvaro looked at the people around the lawn bowling court. He didn't see anyone who looked under 60. "I think I'll pass this time, thanks. And thanks for the offer to play with your balls."

"Okay, maybe next time," said Woo Lee. He threw some bread over the pigeons, causing a minor scuffle as they relocated to the new feeding ground.

"So ... I know we talked about it yesterday, but I had another run in with our neck tattoo friend. He took a crowbar to my car this morning. You got anything for me yet?"

"Oh, Alvi, I'm sorry to hear that. You not hurt?"

"No, I wasn't even in the car. I sent my guy for malasadas. The guy hit the car there."

"Did he go to Leonard's? Those are so yummy. So ono," Woo Lee said smiling. "You making me hungry."

"Yeah, of course. Where else?" Alvaro said. He noticed that "ono" was the second Pidgin word Woo Lee used. He was really going native. Alvaro continued: "But you can see my concern. He seems to be coming at me, and I don't even know who he is. It's mo' bettah' I get the jump on him," Alvaro said in his best local pidgin voice.

Woo Lee seemed please. "Working on it, Alvi, but it takes time. I'm on it. Don't worry, braddah." He gave Alvaro a slap on the back.

Alvaro was worried, but he couldn't help but laugh. Here was this old Korean gangster wearing rubber slippers and a tacky aloha shirt trying to speak Hawaiian Pidgin.

He looked around again but couldn't imagine where Woo Lee's men were. It seemed that he was alone. Two of Alvaro's men sat less than thirty yards away and were armed. But Woo Lee's men ... nowhere to be seen.

"Anyways, Alvi, I need to warm up. Game starts soon." Woo Lee hopped off the picnic table and grabbed his balls. "I'll be in touch."

Alvaro got back in his car. He saw the damage from the crowbar, which now served as a reminder: He needed to keep an eye out, especially for an angry asshole with a neck tattoo.

"Hey, take a ride around the parking lot. See if you can see anyone that looks like they might work for Woo Lee," Alvaro said.

"Sure thing, boss," said Iceman.

They cruised up and down Ala Moana Beach Park, but there was no sign of Woo Lee's men.

"You think he's alone, boss?" said Alvaro's man in the front passenger's seat.

"Sure seems like it, but did you see what the old kook was wearing? Hell, his men could be dressed like him. Not a bad disguise on this island. Look like they're all going to a Don Ho concert" Alvaro said.

"I think Don Ho's dead, boss," the driver said.

"Okay, fine, then that Brother Iz guy. You know what I mean."

"I think it's 'Braddah Iz,' boss. And he's dead too."

"Jesus, Iceman, you've been doing your Hawaiian music homework, huh?"

Iceman smiled. "Yep. Loves me some Israel Kamakawiwo'ole."

They did one more pass by the lawn bowling court. Alvaro could see Woo Lee laughing with an older Hawaii lady. She was wearing a purple muumuu and seemed to be enjoying his company.

"Weird," Alvaro said. "Okay, let's pick up Heather. We need to be at the docks by noon."

****

The man with the neck tattoo drove by an apartment on Date Street. On his first pass, he didn't notice anything unusual. The building was a three-story walk-up, and it looked like it might be low-income housing, but that was normal for Honolulu. There was only one apartment on the ground level, with space under the other apartments used for parking. The second and third floor had four or five apartments each. The entire block looked nearly identical, with only slight variances in size and color.

The man with neck tattoo knew this was the right apartment. He followed a black SUV here on two occasions and watched a man make a drop.

On his second pass, after making sure the SUV was nowhere in sight, he parked a little ways up from the building. He grabbed his gun from the glove compartment and tucked it into his black slacks. His oversized aloha shirt covered it well, but the handle was visible if someone was looking for it.

He knocked. No answer. He knocked harder, and finally an old man answered the door. The man with the neck tattoo pushed the door open and shoved the old man on the floor.

"What kind of drug dealer opens his door for strangers?" The man drew his gun and looked around the apartment. "You alone?"

"Just you and me, buddy," said the old man as he started to get up.

The man with the neck tattoo kicked him over and moved towards the back rooms. After making sure they were alone, he came out and saw the old man trying to get up again. This time he grabbed him by the back of the shirt and shoved him on the sofa.

"Thank you," said the old man. "This is just where I was heading."

The apartment was incredibly tidy. The living room opened to the kitchen, where the man with the neck tattoo sat at one of the kitchen stools. There was a coffee table and a plastic lawn chair in the living room, and nothing much in the kitchen except a coffee maker. There was a small television next to a loaded bookshelf.

"I like what you've done with the place," the man with the neck tattoo said. "Very minimalistic."

"That's very kind of you to say, sir. Can I get you something to drink? Coffee? Guava juice?"

The man with the neck tattoo got up and went to the refrigerator. "I do love guava juice," he said. "You want one, old man?"

"It'd be rude to say no, wouldn't it?"

The man with the neck tattoo took two cans of guava juice from the refrigerator. He wound up and threw one as hard as he could at the old man. The can bounced off the old man's shoulder.

"Ah! Oh … I … I should've caught that. My bad," he said as he grabbed his shoulder. The can of juice fell on the floor and rolled back towards the kitchen. "Maybe I'll just drink that later," said the old man.

"Franny—that's your name, right?"

"Frances." Said the old man, still rubbing his shoulder. "Or Franny. Whatever."

"Franny, I heard a little rumor. That rumor said that you're selling some sugar, and I just so happen to be interested in some sugar." He leaned back and put his arms behind his head. Frances noticed that the man's arms were bigger than most men's legs. "Sweet. Maui. Brown."

"Well, I'm not sure where or how you heard that rumor, but I have to disappoint you. I think I had what you're looking for, but I don't have any right now."

"That is disappointing," said the man with the neck tattoo. He got up and moved to the plastic chair. The old man wasn't sure the chair would hold him. "When do you plan on getting some more?" he said as he placed his gun on the coffee table.

"I don't know," said the old man. "Ain't up to me."

"That's not the answer I was hoping for." The man with the neck tattoo took a glance around the apartment. "You know Franny, I'm not totally sure I believe you. How about you tell me where your stash is, and I'll have myself a look?"

Frances knew he was going to give up his stash. There was no way to talk his way out of this. His best bet was to try to get out of the situation without getting killed. "It's in the trunk in the bedroom on the right. There's a false bottom."

The man with the neck tattoo nodded in approval. "You know, Franny... When you make things easy for me, that makes me happy." He got up and started to walk to the bedroom. "You just sit tight. I'll be back in a second."

He left the gun right there on the coffee table. Right in front of the old man. Frances picked it up.

"Excuse me, sir." he said as he started to walk towards the bedroom.

"Sit tight, Franny. I'll just be a sec."

Frances was at the door: "You left your gun on the table."

"Did I?" The man was taking out the blanket in the trunk. He didn't even turn around. "Franny, I told you to sit tight." He took out the false bottom. "Jackpot," he said. "On second thought, where do you keep your plastic bags? I'm going to need something to carry this. Make yourself useful." He turned and looked at Frances.

Frances was holding the gun in his right hand and pointing it at the floor. The man was relaxed. Frances checked that the safety was off when he picked it up, but he didn't check the clip for bullets. He'd never used a gun before, and he didn't really want a dead body to deal with. *Not worth it*, he thought. "I've got some bags in the kitchen. Hold on."

"Hey!" the man nodded at the gun. "Leave it, Franny."

Frances tossed the gun on the bed and started to head to the kitchen.

"Grab two bags, Franny. I know you've got some cash around here. I'm going to need that, too."

Frances grabbed the bags and went back into the bedroom. He gave one to the man and kept the other one. He flipped down the quilt on the bed and began putting bound stacks of money into the other bag. "Might as well save us some time," he said.

"Franny, it's been a pleasure robbing you. How much cash would you say is there?"

"About thirty grand." The amount of money Frances kept in the apartment fluctuated daily. Fortunately, thirty thousand wasn't too large of an amount.

"And how much are these drugs worth?"

"About the same. Probably a little less."

Here's what's going to happen, Franny. I'm keeping all this shit, but as soon as you get some more of that sugar, I'm going to need you to call me." He grabbed Frances by the shoulder and squeezed hard.

"Ahhh … Ouch, ouch, ouch …" He dropped to one knee.

"Think you can do that?"

"Yeah, yeah, yeah … Okay, okay."

The man yanked Frances up to his feet and let go. "Good. Now, if you don't call, well … I'll kill you. I'll probably torture you a bit, and then … maybe strangle you. Maybe shoot you. I don't know. But I do know I'll kill you. That's kind of what I do, you know—it's my thing."

"I believe you," Frances said as he rubbed his shoulder, "but …"

"But what?"

"If I give you my drugs, someone else is going to kill me. That's kinda how it works. So … you see my problem?"

"Franny, if you call me, I'll bring cash. Honestly." He held up the bag of money, and then he pulled out a card with his number on it and put it in Frances' front shirt pocket. "Besides, I wouldn't worry about those people if I were you. I'm not."

Frances agreed, but he knew this was bad news. He couldn't be doing business with this asshole.

"Franny, I'm going to go. It's been a pleasure. Sorry about the shoulder, and thanks for the guava juice." The man with a neck tattoo put out his hand.

Frances shook it.

CHAPTER TWELVE

Friday 11:45 a.m.

Detective Solosolo Fauatea and Matt Gold pulled into the Honolulu CSI unit's parking lot a little before lunch.

"This is probably going to be a little more ... rustic ... than LA," Solo said.

"I've never even been to a CSI lab in LA," Matt said, "but I've seen quite a few on television. I'm expecting something like that."

"Yeah, right. A lab like that'd take up about eighty percent of the HPD's budget."

They went inside where Solo had to sign Matt in. The officer working the front desk recognized Matt from the news. He was a huge Hawaiian. Bigger than Solo and as tall as Matt.

"Hey, ho, Superhero Jesus." He shook Matt's hand. "Nice to meet you, braddah. Hey, Solo, you gonna get yo picture in da paper hangin' with this guy. You got the paparazzi following you around?"

"Nah, but I haven't paraded him up and down Waikiki beach yet. Maybe after lunch."

"I think the attention is dying down," Matt said. "I hope so, at least." Matt meant it. He was tired of moments like this one.

"Ho, braddah, you gotta use dat. A pretty boy like you—you could be knocking down the ladies left and right, eh? Fo reals, you got wahines coming out your 'okole, eh?"

Solo cut in, "Matt's from LA. You know, Los Angeles," he said as he gave a wink to the officer. "You know what I mean …? Maybe he's not into the wahines."

The officer knew what Solo meant: "Ohhh, hey that's cool. Shoots, whatevers, man."

"Not into the wahines?" Matt said. The implication wasn't initially clear to Matt, but he finally caught on. "Hey, no, Solo … no, I'm not gay."

The officer put his hands in the air: "Hey, to each his own, brah."

"Come on, Solo, don't be telling people …"

Solo let out a laugh, "Okay, Jesus, settle down. I'm just having some fun."

Solo led Matt down to where CSI Shauna Ikawa was still processing items from the dead junkie's apartment. Although Solo knew just about everyone who worked in the CSI building, he tried to avoid as many as he could. He usually talked story with the older ones, and he liked to stop and give the younger guys a hard time. Not today. He didn't want to introduce Superhero Jesus to the whole police force.

"Shauna, aloha," Solo said as he entered her lab.

"Hey, Solo, I've been expecting you," she said as she dropped an old Jack in the Box bag. She smiled at Matt.

"This is Matt Gold. Celebrity police officer by day, underwear model by night," Solo said as he peeked around at the contents on the table.

Matt smiled at Shauna and shook his head. "Nice to meet you."

"You too." She took off her glove to shake his hand. "Don't mind Solo. He's a big softy on the inside."

"Yeah, I'm a big fucking teddy bear." He noticed how Shauna tucked her hair behind her ear as she smiled.

"He is. Don't worry, Matt. You've got to break down Solo's tough exterior. Keep at him. He'll come around."

"Yeah, good luck with that," Solo said as he poked through some of the trash from the apartment.

"What's this about being a celebrity police officer?" Shauna asked.

"Wait …" Solo looked up from the trash. "You don't know our friend Superhero Jesus here? Don't you watch the news? Read the papers? Have that social media thing that all you kids are talking about these days?"

Matt was uncomfortable.

"No clue, Solo," said Shauna. "Fill me in." She looked at Matt as if she were trying to place him. He didn't look familiar. She'd have remembered.

"No kidding? You haven't heard of him?" This news made Solo happy for some reason. "He's here from LA. He's going to be helping out on Danny's case. You might want to get his autograph."

Matt just shook his head. "Trust me, Shauna, it's no big deal. Boring story. Really."

"Well, maybe you can tell me about it? Let me decide." She tucked her hair behind her ear again.

Solo moved behind Matt and tried to mouth to Shauna: "He's gay … gay … likes men." Then he said out loud: "I'm sure we'll have time to talk story later, but we need to see what you've got. It's almost lunchtime. Find anything promising in all this?"

Matt was thankful for Solo moving on.

Shauna shook her head and smiled at Solo. "Nah, nothing here, just trash. We didn't get much from the boat either, but I dug up some more information on the victim." Shauna grabbed some files. "You know, Solo ... I'm getting kind of hungry myself. It *is* about lunch time, isn't it? Maybe we could go over everything ..."

"Shit. Walked right into this one, didn't I?" Shauna smiled and waited for what she knew was coming.

In a flat tone, Solo said, "Say, Shauna, how about joining us for lunch?"

She smiled at Matt. "I'll grab my bag."

****

Alvaro Garcia Menendez and Heather Brown rode with two of Alvaro's men in the SUV with the crowbar-damaged window. Alvaro's other two men lagged behind in a rented U-Haul. They turned onto Sand Island Boulevard.

Sand Island was the entry point for Honolulu Harbor and where most of the island's cargo was brought in. It was also a large industrial area and the home of Maston Shipping. They passed several nondescript warehouses and a few bars and restaurants, many of which had been in business for decades.

"Park around back," Alvaro said to his driver. They pulled into the parking lot of an old building. The front was decorated in traditional Hawaiian style, and there was a large sign on the wall that said, "Welcome to Johnny's." The entrance had a tiki awning and torches on the sides.

"What is this, a strip club?" Heather asked.

"What? You don't know Johnny's?" Alvaro looked at her with genuine shock. "No way! You don't know Johnny's? Come on. Iceman, tell her what Johnny's is."

"No clue, boss. Looks like a strip club."

"Oh, mios dios! It's Johnny's! The last old-style tiki bar on the island. How can you not know about this place?"

"Do we look like the tiki bar crowd, Alvi?" Heather asked.

Alvaro looked back and forth at Heather and Iceman. "Yeah, good point. But I tell you, you're missing out. Best cocktails on the islands. And ukulele players that'd make Don Ho proud."

"Looks tacky, but I can see why you'd like it," Heather said. She looked at his aloha shirt and rolled her eyes.

"What?" Alvaro looked at his shirt. "You don't like it? This is vintage. Three hundred dollars!"

"You're an idiot. Looks like it came from the ABC store."

Alvaro looked like he had his feelings hurt. "Whatever. You don't know. I go into Johnny's in this shirt, I'm going to get respect. You'll see."

Heather didn't say anything; she just gave him a look and shook her head.

"So it's not a strip club?" Iceman asked. He sounded disappointed.

The U-Haul pulled in before Heather had time for a smart-ass comment. "My ride's here." She started to get out of the SUV.

"Tootles," Alvaro said. He waved his fingers at her and smiled. "Good luck with Maverick and Goose."

Iceman smiled.

She rolled her eyes as she went to get into the U-Haul. "Slide over," she said to the guy in the passenger's seat, who she assumed would now be referred to as Goose. "Pull out and make a right." She was running the show.

The U-Haul pulled into a Maston Shipping storage area. There were shipping containers stacked on a lot the size of a football field, some stacks reaching as high as six containers. The security guard waved her right on through the gate.

The area was mostly for empty containers. Depending on the season, sometimes more containers went back to the mainland, and sometimes the extra containers were kept in Honolulu until business picked up the other way. By the looks of things, Heather could tell that a lot more was coming into the islands than going out.

They pulled the U-Haul around the side of the storage yard and parked behind a medium-sized warehouse. Waiting for them was a man named Chester Pile.

Chester was leaning against a forklift wearing aviator glasses and an aloha shirt. He was easily over six feet tall and weighed around one hundred and fifty pounds. The way the trade winds caught his shirt, he looked like he could fly away any second.

"You see that? That's a real man, boys," Heather said as they pulled the U-Haul next to the forklift. They couldn't tell if she was trying to be funny.

"Right," said the driver. "We'll be sure not to give him any trouble. Wouldn't stand a chance against that beast."

Chester was smiling as Heather got out of the U-Haul, but then he saw her face. "Jesus, what the fuck happened? You get into a fight?" He took off his aviator's.

"Settle down, Nancy. I'm fine. Nothing to get your panties in a bunch about."

"What the fuck happened?" Chet repeated. "Tell me that didn't happen because of … you know … Like, was it an accident or something?"

"Yeah, some big asshole accidentally punched me in the face. He didn't even say sorry."

"What the fuck? Hold on, man … Nobody said anything about violence and shit. This is supposed to be a peaceful operation, right?"

"Relax, hippie. Nobody's going to chop you up. We'll take these boxes off your hands, and you can go pay off your alimony, or whatever it is you need to pay off."

Heather met Chester when they worked together for Maston Shipping in LA. She knew him as a bit of a creep. He'd been married three times, had a kid with each wife, another kid with another woman, and he was always dodging bill collectors. He was also a bit of a drunk, and she guessed he had a coke problem.

"Is this everything?" Heather asked. She noticed he looked nervous. He kept running his hand through his hair and looking the guys up and down.

"Yeah," Chester answered. "So, you got something for me, right?"

One of Alvaro's men opened the back of the U-Haul and took out a silver briefcase. Heather recognized it. It was the same style case as the one that was handcuffed to her hand less than two days before. Chester looked anxious.

"Nothing stupid, Chet," Heather said. "If you fuck this up by drawing attention to yourself, I'll kill you. Comprende?"

He took the briefcase from Alvaro's man and didn't even open it. "I'm paying off some debts and burying the rest in the back yard," Chester said. "Honest to God." He crossed his heart and held up two fingers. "Scout's honor."

Alvaro's men began loading the boxes into the U-Haul.

Chet knew Heather believed him. She had quite the reputation when they worked together back in LA. Everyone knew Heather was "one tough bitch," as they used to say about her. He had his doubts about helping Heather smuggle drugs to Hawaii, but he had the connections to make it work. And he needed the money. Now, as he noticed a gun sticking out of one of Alvaro's men's waistbands, he realized the consequences of fucking this up. He felt his heart skip a beat or two. He was suddenly more worried about the guys Heather was working with than her.

"I've got to go," he said to Heather. "You guys can handle this, right?"

"Chet … I'll be in touch," Heather said. She'd told Chester that it'd be a one-time deal, and she'd told Alvaro he was fully in. She knew how it'd work out. They needed a regular shipment, and Chester was going to be their guy. He was stuck.

"Um, okay," was all he could say. He didn't want to think about what she meant, but he knew he needed to get the hell out of there.

Heather watched Chester's skinny ass hurry to his shiny new truck. He fumbled with a cigarette before pulling away. She noticed the NASCAR sticker on his back window. She was surprised when he threw his hand out the window and gave a shaka for goodbye. "Yeah, hang loose, Chet," Heather said under her breath. "See ya soon, braddah."

She couldn't help but smile as she turned back to see Alvaro's men loading the boxes in the U-Haul. This was easier than buying a futon off of Craigslist.

Once they had the boxes in the back of the U-haul, they pulled out of Maston Shipping's parking lot and dropped Heather off at the tiki bar.

Alvaro's two men then drove less than three blocks to a storage shed that Alvaro rented under a false name. They unloaded most of the boxes there, and then they drove to another storage shed near Kahala Shopping Mall, which was less than a mile from Alvaro's rented beach house. After unloading most of the other boxes, they went to drop off the U-Haul and moved the remaining boxes to their SUV, which was parked on the street just up the road from the U-Haul lot.

Heather walked into the tiki bar and saw Alvaro flirting with a waitress at a table near the stage. He had his elbows on the table and a hand on his chin. He was giving her his puppy dog eyes and smiling. Heather had to admit that he was handsome, even in that tacky aloha shirt. Too well groomed for her tastes, but she could understand why the waitress was falling for his charm. She spotted his men at the bar. Both had a Budweiser in front of them, and she was sure that they'd seen her come in.

"Hi, honey." She put her hand on Alvaro's back and said, "Did you order me a cocktail, dear?"

Alvaro was relieved to see her. He played along: "No, cupcake, not yet. What would you like?"

The waitress' smile turned awkward. She noticed Heather's broken nose and two black eyes. "Can I, um, get you a drink?" she asked.

Heather wasn't surprised to see Alvaro with a big, tropical cocktail. It was in a large wooden cup with a traditional Hawaiian warrior carved on the side, complete with a bendy straw and paper umbrella sticking out of a giant pineapple wedge on the side. It looked like a lava flow and reminded Heather of the *Brady Bunch's Hawaiian Vacation*. Most customers were drinking out of the same type of cup.

"I'll have a Longboard," she said to the waitress.

"Oh, so boring," said Alvaro. "And predictable." He shook his head and held up his cup. "Doesn't my little wahine princess want to drink out of a traditional Hawaiian totem?"

Heather looked at the waitress. "Longboard."

"Be right back," said the waitress.

"A Longboard it is." Alvaro held his hands wide and looked around the bar. "Well, what do you think? Is this not the coolest place you've ever been?"

Heather looked around again. She felt like she'd taken a trip back in time. She'd never seen anything so stereotypically Hawaiian in her life. "I have to admit, this place ain't half bad. And not a bad crowd for one o'clock in the afternoon. Don't these people have jobs?"

Alvaro looked pleased with himself. "I told you. Johnny's is the best bar on the island. Just wait until the ukulele player starts up. You'll never want to leave."

The waitress brought Heather's beer, and they ordered some lunch. Alvaro got an ahi sandwich, and

Heather ordered chicken strips with taro chips. Midway through lunch, Heather leaned over and suddenly changed the expression on her face. It was a look of concern. Alvaro took the bait and turned to see what she was looking at, at which point Heather stabbed the two black olives that came with Alvaro's sandwich. When he looked back, she was chewing with a grin on her face.

Alvaro figured it out instantly: "Did you just steal my olives?" His smile was gone. "I was saving those. Did you really just steal food off of my plate? Black olives are my favorite."

"Snooze you lose." Heather laughed hard enough she had to cover her mouth.

"I can't believe you stole my olives." He genuinely looked upset.

Heather couldn't stop laughing. "I can't believe you fell for that. You should know better."

They finished their meals and ordered two more drinks. Alvaro's men hung out at the bar nursing their Buds.

Alvaro's other two men returned from dropping off the boxes and returning the U-Haul; they sat at the bar with the other two men. Before they could order, Alvaro gave Iceman a nod, which meant it was time to go. Iceman paid and the four men left.

Alvaro paid his bill, and they met the guys in the parking lot.

"How was your lunch, boss?" Iceman asked.

"Excellent, but some bitch stole my olives."

Heather tried to give him her "fuck you" eyes, but she couldn't help smiling.

"Maverick and Goose, Heather's going with you guys," Alvaro said.

"Are we really doing this?" Heather said, rubbing both temples with one hand. "Really?"

"What?" Alvaro smiled.

"First Iceman, now Maverick and Goose? The fucking Top Gun crew?"

Iceman turned to the fourth guy: "Hey, that makes you Slider." He laughed and gave the guy a slap on the back.

"Hey, fuck that, I don't want to be Slider."

"Sorry, Slider," Alvaro said. "Blame your partner for calling dibs on Iceman."

"It's like I'm dealing with idiots," Heather said.

"This is bullshit," Slider said.

She got into the back of Maverick's SUV. The guys were all smiling.

****

Detective Solosolo Fauatea and Matt Gold dropped off CSI Shauna Ikawa at the Honolulu Police Department's CSI lab a little after one o'clock. They went for lunch at Hooters at the Aloha Tower Marketplace. It was Solo's idea. None of them liked the food, and they weren't there for the waitresses, but of all the restaurants near downtown, Hooter's had the best view of Honolulu Harbor. Solo didn't consider how many people would be in the area, and he couldn't have guessed how many would be sneaking pictures of Matt. They didn't have nearly as much attention as they had earlier at Zippy's.

Lunch started with them mostly talking about the case and Matt's friendship with Danny, but it quickly turned into Matt explaining the Superhero Jesus story. He was modest in his description, but because Shauna didn't catch any of the stories on the news, she couldn't quite picture how amazing Matt looked on the video. Solo noticed how Matt downplayed it.

After satisfying Shauna's curiosity about Matt's recent fame, the rest of the lunch was Shauna talking about her life. She wasn't the type to go on about herself, but Matt continued to ask her questions, and she felt comfortable answering them. Solo didn't mind. He was much more interested in hearing about Shauna than about pretty-boy Matt. Girls liked to talk, and Solo liked to listen.

Shauna went back to her lab and found a colleague who she was close with. She asked her if she'd heard of Matt "Superhero Jesus" Gold. The friend said she had, and that she heard he was there this morning. She was upset she missed him, and now she was jealous that Shauna got to have lunch with him.

"Oh, my God!" she had said. "What's he like? He looked soooo handsome on TV."

Shauna confirmed his handsomeness. And charming, she added.

Shauna admitted that she felt like an idiot. She realized after lunch that she spent almost the whole time talking about herself. He was such a nice guy. He was so down to earth, and yes, very handsome.

Now all she could think about was Matt Gold. And she felt like an idiot.

****

Kim Carson was back in Kinu's hospital room. This time, she was with a police officer.

"Mr. Anapu'ui, how are you feeling? Can you answer some questions?"

"Call me Kinu," Kinu said. "And I been bettah."

"Ms. Carson here was telling me about what happened. She thinks maybe you were drugged. Is that what you think?"

"Yeah, must have been. I've never done that stuff in my life." Kinu was sitting up in his hospital bed. He was feeling better, and the handcuffs were off.

"Okay, so can you tell me what you think happened?"

"Don't know. Like I told Kim, I got coffee at the Aloha Mart. Must have been that, eh? What else?"

The police officer wanted to believe Kinu's story. Kinu didn't look like a junkie, and most junkies wouldn't be ingesting crystal meth, they'd be smoking it, but he'd heard every story in the book. "Anything you can add to that? Did it taste funny? Did you put anything in it?"

"Nah," Kinu said. "I don't really drink coffee, so it tasted fine to me. I put some sugar in it, but that was from my truck. Not from the mart."

"And nobody could have put something in it, maybe when you weren't looking?" the officer asked.

"Nah, not possible." Kinu shook his head. "Unless it was already in the coffee, of course."

"And can you think of anything else it might have been? Something you ate or drank?"

Kinu just shook his head.

"All right," said the officer. "I'll check it out, see if I can turn something up. That coffee's long gone by now, but if it was laced, there'll be some other reports. I'll let you know if I find something."

"Am I in any trouble?" Kinu asked.

"Nope. We didn't find any on drugs in your possession, so you can't be charged with anything."

The officer said goodbye to Kinu and Kim and checked the hospital for similar cases as Kinu. He didn't find any. He wasn't going to waste his time going to the Aloha Mart, but he did call to report the possibility to the manager, who assured the officer that he'd heard no other complaints and that he'd check the machine personally.

That was about all he could do for Kinu.

Kim Carson could do more. After Kinu had been discharged from the hospital, she helped him track down his truck and gave him a ride all the way over to Waimanalo to pick it up. She tried to get him to stop for some food, but he said he couldn't eat. The doctor recommended against Kinu driving, but Kinu was determined to get his truck. The doctor said he'd be fine tomorrow, and Kinu wanted things back to normal as soon as possible.

Kim waited for Kinu in Towing Express' front parking lot. The office was a one-room building with only a few people working inside. Behind the building, she could see Kinu's truck. It was inside a large parking lot surrounded by a high fence with barbwire on top. She knew from experience that towing companies were crooks. They were known to tow aggressively, and if they towed a car, the only way the owner was getting back was if they paid the outrageously overpriced fine. *Scum of the earth*, Kim thought.

She watched Kinu through the window as he handed the morbidly obese woman behind the counter his credit card. He walked out two hundred dollars poorer, but he held up his keys and forced a smile.

Kim insisted on following Kinu back to his home in the Palolo Valley. She told him to pull over if it became too difficult to drive, which Kinu had no intention of doing.

Kinu pulled out and headed towards Hawaii Kai. He decided to head east instead of taking the Pali Highway across to Honolulu. He wanted to avoid the city traffic and the congestion that occurs around the H1.

Kinu noticed the briefcase on the floorboard when he got in the truck, and as he drove, he figured Kim or one of his friends must have put it inside his truck at Magic Island. He thought about the police officer asking him if he put anything in his coffee and tried to remember if he could taste the sugar. He wondered ...

Kim pulled in behind Kinu when they reached his house. She asked how he was feeling and if there was anything she could do. He said no, but thanked her for asking. He also told her how much he appreciated her help. He meant it.

She gave him a big hug and told him that she was going to bring him some dinner later. She was going to go to the grocery store and then go home and cook him some soup and biscuits. She'd be back by dinner. Kinu said he doubted his appetite would be back by then, but he didn't protest to her coming by.

He was starting to see a silver lining to this situation.

After watching Kim pull away, Kinu took the briefcase out of the truck. He decided he'd have another look at that sugar, and he thought about what the police officer had said: *We didn't find any on drugs in your possession, so you can't be charged with anything.*

CHAPTER THIRTEEN

Friday 4:00 p.m.

Heather Brown rode with Maverick and Goose into Waikiki. They made three stops.

The first stop was at a five-story walk-up apartment on the Ala Wai Canal, away from the beaches and tourist hotels. Maverick parked in front of a liquor store with bars on its windows while Goose ran a box up to an apartment on the third floor. He came back with an envelope full of money.

The second stop was at Fort DeRussy Park, which was directly on the beach near the Hilton Hawaiian Village. This time Maverick circled the block while Goose looked for his connection in the park. Again, he came back with an envelope full of money.

The final stop was just outside of Waikiki. They pulled up to a three-story walk-up on Date Street. Goose got out of the SUV and walked up with the final box to an apartment on the third floor. When he approached the apartment, he noticed the door was wide open.

He put the box down and put his hand on his gun, which was holstered under his arm inside his linen jacket. He peeked in and saw Frances sitting on the couch reading a book. There was something under his shirt.

"What the fuck's going on, Frances," Goose said. He peeked around the door towards the kitchen, still fingering his weapon.

"Come on in, I'm all alone."

"Why's the door open?"

"Trade winds. The breeze really whips through when I open the front door, and since I have neither money nor anything illegal in the apartment, I see no reason to keep the door locked."

Goose picked up the box and came into the apartment. He put the box on the table. "Here, this takes care of not having anything illegal. Now, about not having money … Tell me about that, Frances. And what's going on under your shirt there?"

Frances took a bag of frozen peas out from under his shirt. "Well, I had a visitor today. He tossed me a can of guava juice that I failed to catch. I'd say it was going about a hundred miles per hour. This was right after he pushed his way inside and threw me to the floor, all while pointing his gun at me. And then he robbed me of everything I had." Frances smiled and said: "At least he left his number so that I can get in touch with him."

Goose let it sink in for a second. "Well … sounds like you're lucky he didn't put a bullet in your head. Do you know who he is?"

"Never seen him before in my life, but I could spot him from a mile away."

"What'd he look like?"

"Oh, probably a little bigger than you. White guy. Buzz cut. Maybe late thirty's or early forty's. Mean.

Looked kind of crazy." Frances left out the part the man leaving his gun on the coffee table. He thought this said something about the guy's level of sanity, but he knew he should've done better with the opportunity.

Goose knew the answer before he asked it, but he had to confirm: "Did he have any tattoos?"

"Yep," said Frances. "He had something coming up his neck. Not sure what it was."

Great, thought Goose. *Heather was going to go batshit crazy.* "Why'd he leave his number?" he asked Frances.

"Get this: He wants me to call him when I get more Sweet Maui Brown. He wants to buy it with the money he stole from me."

"Is he retarded? How can he possibly think that that's going to work?"

Frances shrugged his shoulders. "He's not dealing with a full deck?"

"Any idea how he knows where you live?"

"I've been thinking about that. The only thing I can think of is that he got it out of one of the sellers. If one of them doesn't show up tomorrow, I guess I'll know why."

Goose knew they were in the car waiting for him. Heather was much higher up on the pecking order than he was, so he knew she'd expect him to bring this news directly to her, but he was afraid of what she'd do.

"Okay, Frances. I've got to go, but I'm going to leave the box and take the phone number. I'm sure we'll be in touch soon. I guess if he comes back, just shoot the bastard."

"Sure thing." Frances smiled, not telling him that he didn't own a gun.

When he went back to the SUV, Goose didn't say a word. Heather didn't notice that he didn't have an envelope; she didn't concern herself with those things. However, Maverick did notice, but he didn't say anything. He knew better.

When they got back to the rented Kahala beach house, they saw Alvaro in a lounge chair next to the pool with an empty cocktail glass on the ground next to him. He was still wearing his aloha shirt and chinos, and his fedora was pulled down to cover his eyes. There was Hawaiian slack key coming from the speakers. Iceman and Slider were sitting at a table playing with their phones.

"Lord Jesus," Heather said. "Must be nice to have time for afternoon cocktails and naps."

Alvaro lifted his fedora and gave her a smile. He stretched and let out a big yawn. "Heyyyy, there's the team. Welcome home."

Heather shook her head and went back in the house.

Goose took the opportunity to fill him in. "Boss, we had a bit of a problem with a distributor."

Alvaro stretched again. "You don't say. What's up, Gooseman?"

****

Shauna was on her floor doing crunches. She usually didn't get home on weekdays until late, but on Fridays she tried to get out of the lab around four o'clock. That was the typical Hawaiian "pau hana" attitude. Friday's happy hour couldn't wait until the regular quitting time, so a lot of businesses finished early. If Shauna had to bet, she'd put money on no other state in the country being quite as unproductive as Hawaii on a Friday.

Shauna usually skipped the pau hana drinks with coworkers. Instead, she would swing by her apartment in Makiki, grab her surfboard, and head to Ala Moana

125

Bowls to surf for an hour or two, and then she'd stick around to watch the fireworks from the Hilton Hawaiian Village, which was just next to Ala Moana Beach Park. If the waves were good, sometimes she'd stay in the water past dark, catching waves until the fireworks started, and then paddling in to call it a day.

Today Shauna was doing crunches. She was using an app on her iPhone: *200 Crunches*. If she followed the program, she'd eventually be able to do two hundred crunches in one set, which she'd accomplished a few times already. Shauna would use the app until she hit her goal, and then she'd forget about it for a month or two, and then she'd go back to it to tone up.

After her lunch with Matt Gold, she was motivated to tone up again. Now she was on her back in front of her TV looking at Matt. She turned on the five o'clock news to watch during her workout, and there was an update of Superhero Jesus' trip to Hawaii. It was the first time she'd seen him on the news.

"It turns out Los Angeles Officer Matt "Superhero Jesus" Gold is in Hawaii for more than a little R&R. A graduate of the University of Hawaii, Matt was college buddies with recently murdered Officer Daniel Palakiko, and it looks like he might be here to assist the HPD in solving Officer Palakiko's murder."

The news was showing photos of Danny and Matt together at UH, and they had photos of Matt at some of Danny's family barbecues. There was a short interview with Danny's younger brother, Duke Palakiko.

"Yeah, Matt's like an uncle to me. He was always around. He and Danny, they were tight. Our family is happy knowing Matt is helping find Danny's killer. That's what we want. I think that's what the community of Waimanalo wants as well."

Next, Shauna was shocked to see a picture of Matt, Solo, and herself eating lunch together at Hooters.

"Matt, seen here with two HPD detectives, took a break from investigating to have lunch over at Aloha Tower Marketplace."

Thank God we didn't order beers like Solo had wanted, Shauna thought.

"Looks like there's a little time for R&R after all," the co-anchor laughed.

The app on Shauna's phone was beeping to warn her that her next set of crunches was about to start, but she just sat there shocked.

"If anyone has any information regarding the death of Officer Palakiko, please call the number on the screen or contact your local police station."

Before they even flashed the number on the screen, Shauna's phone started blowing up with text messages. She wouldn't have guessed she knew so many people who watched the news on a Friday night, but apparently this was the case. She'd later find out that the same photo made it to all the networks, and was picked up the next day nationally. Superhero Jesus' fifteen minutes of fame hadn't died down yet, and now she was riding its coattail.

She ignored the messages and finished her crunches. Now more than ever, she wanted to get out on the ocean. Therapy, Hawaiian style.

Coming from Makiki, even in Friday traffic, it only took Shauna ten minutes to get to Ala Moana Beach Park. She parked next to the beach at the west side of the park. From here, it was only a short distance to the water, and then a quick paddle out to the waves. Shauna stripped down to her bikini and was taking her board off the top of her car when she heard her name.

"Shauna? That's you, right?"

Shauna couldn't believe it. She turned around to see Matt Gold taking out his headphones. He was wearing a University of Hawaii ball cap and was dripping with sweat.

"Hey, Matt, wow! This is a surprise. What are you doing here?" She was suddenly self-conscious of standing in front of him in a bikini. She hoped her abs still had a little pump from the workout.

"Solo dropped me off early. Said he was going to make calls from the office, so I thought I'd get out for a jog. This is what I miss about Hawaii." Matt looked out at the ocean. From where they were standing, they could see Ala Moana Beach, Magic Island, and all the way down to Waikiki and Diamond Head.

"And this is why I live here," said Shauna. "Hey, have you seen the news?" She asked as she turned back to finish getting her board off her car.

"No, why?" He tried not to look, but there she was, standing in front of him in a bikini, looking like a model.

"Well, we made the news. You were the highlight, but there was a picture of all of us eating at Hooters. Embarrassing, but they did call me a detective, so, you know, that's kind of cool."

"Yeah, sorry about that. I've stopped watching the news since the whole Superhero Jesus video came out, but I hate to hear that I'm bringing people down with me."

"Not your fault. No big deal, really. Danny's brother was on there too. You know him?"

"Yeah. Duke. He's a good kid. A lot like Danny."

"Hey, sorry, I didn't mean to interrupt your jog," Shauna said suddenly. "You don't have to be polite. Get running. Work off those Hooters chicken wings."

"No, no, I'm just finishing up, but I'm sure you've got waves calling your name, right? I don't want to hold you up."

Shauna looked at her board like she had forgotten she was carrying it. "Um, yeah … I guess I should get out there," she said, not making a move.

Matt noticed she didn't put her board down."Okay. Well, it was nice running into you. Maybe we'll run into each other again before too long."

"Yeah, that'd be nice," she said.

There was enough of a smile there that Matt thought she meant it. "Okay, Great. Well, until then, I guess." As he jogged off, he watched her walk into the water and hop on the board to paddle out. Her surfboard sliced through the small shore breaks, and she paddled out through the calm waters of Ala Moana. She wore the small-cut bikini bottoms that left little to the imagination.

Matt had to force himself to stop staring.

****

Shauna wasn't the only one who saw Matt Gold on the five o'clock news.

Iceman was sitting in the rented Kahala beach house. He was near the back at the dining table, right next to the back doors. From the end of the table, he could see the pool and keep an eye on what was going on out there, and he could see the TV from the living room. With Alvaro, Slider, Goose, and Maverick all outside, he was mostly paying attention to the news.

He kept up on the Superhero Jesus story. He first saw the heroics when the video went viral on Facebook, but his interest was sparked further when he saw the story in the Honolulu Post. Now he was interested to see that Matt was connected to the Danny Palakiko murder, another story he kept up on.

"Argh, why are you watching this shit?" Heather asked as she came into the living room.

"They're talking about Superhero Jesus. He's in Hawaii," said Iceman.

"Superhero Jesus? Seriously? Can you hear yourself?"

"Wait ... you know who I'm talking about, right?" he asked.

"Yeah, I've seen the video, but who gives a shit? He's just some cop ... probably wouldn't even be famous if the guy who shot the video wasn't so stoned."

"He's here working on the case of that dead cop. You hear about that? He's been all over the news too. Superhero Jesus was his buddy."

"Again, who gives a shit?" Heather said as she went into the kitchen.

"Hey, you know what, why are you always such a downer? Seriously, do you ever lighten up?" Alvaro's other guys would've been impressed to hear Iceman have the balls to ask this to Heather, but he was starting to feel that her bark was worse than her bite. And besides, they were supposed to be on the same team.

"What the fuck is this?" Heather said, ignoring his question. "Who made coffee last?" She was holding the coffee container out at Iceman.

"Beats me. I think Alvi made an espresso earlier?"

"God damn it! You've got to put the lid back on or the oxygen gets to the coffee grinds. It's bad enough that we're buying ground coffee, but this is ridiculous. Speedy Gonzalez out there has to have his fancy espressos, but he doesn't give a shit about the quality. We've got a coffee maker, espresso maker, milk foamer, and a coffee grinder, which we don't even use because you ass-clowns buy ground beans."

"Yeah, so as I was saying, why so grumpy …?" Iceman trailed off and scratched his balls.

"Fuck this," Heather said as she grabbed a set of keys from the table. "I'm going to Starbucks."

"Whoa, hey, I think you'd better not … Hey, boss!" Iceman yelled out to Alvaro, but he was down near the back of the property near the beach. It looked like he was explaining something to Slider, Maverick, and Goose. They were looking at a small tree.

Iceman jogged back just in time to hear Alvaro say, "… and so while we call it a plumeria tree here in Hawaii, in many parts of the world it's called a frangipani."

By that time, Heather was already reversing out of the driveway.

****

Detective Solosolo Fauatea sat at his desk in the HPD's detective unit. He was following up on some of his leads for Heather Brown, the owner of the fingerprints found in the Montauk on Waikiki beach.

He had a file on his desk with information on Heather's time spent at Maston Shipping. She worked for their office in Los Angeles and spent a lot of time between her desk and the docks. Her last held position with the company was Lead Supervisor, Logistics Supply Chain. Maston Shippings HR department was kind enough to include a job description.

Solo considered the possibility that Heather Brown had come to Honolulu to find work. She'd been unemployed for a while, so maybe the savings ran out and she was looking for a fresh start. With so much cargo coming into the islands, Solo assumed she'd have good job prospects on the island.

He called her parents, but they didn't provide much. His hope was that they could provide something to point him in a direction, any direction. Heather's dad answered the phone, told Solo that neither he nor his wife had heard from Heather in a couple of years, and remained stoic when he heard that the Honolulu Police Department wanted her for questioning.

Before getting off the phone, Solo asked Drill Sargent Brown if he thought Heather might be mixed up in something illegal. His answer was short and to the point: "Yes," he said, "and if she is, she's probably the brains behind it."

Solo looked back over the information that he got from Maston Shipping. Out of the twenty-seven people in Heather's department at the time she quit, two of them were now living in Hawaii, and one, Mr. Chester Pile, was still working for the company. The other, Mr. Norman McClintock, was working for another shipping company.

Maston Shipping said that Heather worked closely with several other departments, but there was no telling how many employees she could possibly be close to. Solo was happy to start with two. If those turned up nothing, he might go back for more names.

Solo's hope was that one of these former co-workers was still in contact with Heather, and since they couldn't find a reservation for a Heather Brown at a hotel, it was possible that she was staying with one of them.

He also went over everything that was dug up on Joshua Allen, the junkie that Ms. Dotty Dubois discovered at the Lilikai Garden Apartments.

All the leads for Joshua led to the same conclusion: He'd fallen out of touch with most of his family, and they didn't know if he was living on the streets or dead in an alley somewhere. His mom and dad both broke down and cried when they got the phone call, but it was a call they were expecting. The dad said what so many parents say about their dead, addicted kids: "At least we know where he is now. We can stop worrying."

Solo considered Joshua a cold lead for now. He was much more interested in finding Heather Brown, if she were still alive. There were too many question marks about her, and if Solo could figure out why she was in Hawaii, and why she would have been in a boat in the middle of the night with a guy who lost a hand, he just might be able to get some traction on this case.

What he did know was that Ms. Dotty Dubois saw a man with a neck tattoo leave the apartment where Joshua Allen was found without a hand, and he knew that the bullets pulled from Joshua's body came from the same gun that killed Officer Danny Palakiko.

The man with the neck tattoo was Danny's murderer. Solo believed it. And Heather Brown probably knew how to find him.

Solo had to get out of there. He'd already worked later than usual for a Friday, and he knew his wife was going to complain, especially after finding out that he'd have to work tomorrow.

Solo printed out the names and addresses of Heather's Brown's two ex-coworkers: Chester Pile and Norman McClintock.

He hoped one of them had a neck tattoo.

****

Shauna paddled in after about forty-five minutes. It was a short session because the waves were a little flat. She'd thought about Matt the whole time. She wished she'd asked him more about how he planned to spend the weekend. Danny's funeral wasn't until Sunday, and she didn't know what he had planned. Possibly nothing.

She was replaying the day over and over in her head, wondering if she should have given him some kind of hint. He seemed like he might have been interested, but she wasn't the type to be too forward.

She was thinking about where she might see him next as she was pulling her board out of the water, and when she came onto the beach, there he was. He was sitting on the sand smiling at her.

"Hey, Shauna, what a surprise. I *totally* forgot you were out there surfing," Matt said.

"Really? Well ... I *totally* forgot that I saw you run by earlier." They both smiled at each other's bullshit. "It's a bit flat out there. Let me grab a couple of towels. Hang on." She couldn't hide her smile.

She put her board down next to Matt and stopped by the beach shower on the way to her car. Matt watched her ease under the cold water of the shower, her hands working the fresh water through her hair. He watched her rinse the salt off her arms, and then he stopped and looked out over the ocean. It took all his will not to turn back and stare.

****

Heather left the rented beach house and looked for the shitty Ford Taurus Iceman described after coming back with the malasadas. She assumed the man with the neck tattoo followed Iceman this morning when he went out, but she didn't think he'd be stupid enough to be sitting out front twice on the same day.

Heather headed for Kahala Shopping Mall. There she bought a couple of sundresses and some new sunglasses. She wanted something a little more Hawaiian-casual than she brought with her from LA. She thought the clothes would help her blend in a bit, and the sunglasses would help hide her black eyes.

Heather also stopped by a trendy yoga store and paid a ridiculous amount for a pair of new yoga pants. She knew the pants would drive the guys at Alvaro's crazy. They were terrible at not getting caught checking her out, and she'd look good in these. She also bought a pair of running shoes and some sports bras.

Heather's recent workout of choice was CrossFit, but she wasn't sure how much of that she wanted to do on the island. As a bit of a workout freak, she'd already considered her future workouts, and she thought it'd be a good time to move into yoga, marathons and maybe even triathlons.

Before leaving the mall, Heather stopped by Starbucks for a coffee and a new bag of whole coffee beans. She checked her phone and noticed six missed calls from Alvaro. Days ago he wouldn't have noticed her leave, and now he wanted everyone on lockdown.

Heather was in an unusually friendly mood, so she decided she'd stop by the grocery store and pick up some supplies, maybe even food to grill if they guys hadn't eaten yet. She found the SUV in the parking lot and put her coffee on the roof while she put her bags in the back. As soon as she closed the trunk, she felt someone behind her, and then she felt thousands of volts shoot into her body. She dropped to the pavement, looking up at the man with the neck tattoo, unable to do anything except mutter a few obscenities.

He zapped her again, smiling as she went stiff as a board.

Once he stopped, Heather felt like the voltage sucked all the energy out of her. She lay there, hoping the zapping was over.

He grabbed her by her hair and waistband, throwing her in the trunk of his car.

Heather hadn't noticed his car parked next to hers.

CHAPTER FOURTEEN

Friday 7:00 p.m.

Kim Carson made her grandma's famous chicken soup and corn bread. As a nurse, Kim was always trying to take care of people. By the age of eleven, she'd made her grandma's soup so many times that she'd already made improvements, but she'd always give her granny credit.

She put the soup in a portable crockpot, covered up the corn bread, and headed over to Kinu's house. She also stopped at a Redbox and rented a DVD. She didn't think Kinu was the romance-comedy type, so she talked herself out of renting *Love Actually* and instead went for a new release that had helicopters and fire on the cover. She hoped to spend the evening with Kinu, not only to take care of him, but also to see if any sparks flew.

When Kim arrived at Kinu's little house in the Palolo Valley, there was a black sports car parked behind Kinu's truck in the driveway. It was a little Japanese car, probably only an inch off the ground with tinted windows and a giant spoiler. Kim knew these were commonly referred to as rice rockets, and she was surprised to see one in Kinu's driveway.

Kim grabbed the crockpot and bread, and she threw the movie in her bag and went up to the door. It was just dark enough outside that she could see Kinu through the window, but she doubted he'd be able to see her. He was sitting on a chair and talking to a younger guy sitting on the couch. There was a shiny silver briefcase and a bottle of Longboard on the coffee table.

"Hello!" Kim shouted as she walked up to the door. "The soup lady has arrived."

She noticed the guy on the couch seemed to jump a little, but Kinu hopped up and raised a hand to let him know it was no problem.

"Hey, come on in," Kinu said as he opened the door for her.

She handed Kinu the crockpot: "Here you go, sir. Chicken soup as promised. How are you feeling?"

"Much bettah. Finally getting hungry," he said with a smile.

Kim turned to the other man, who was now getting up to greet her. He was quite a bit younger than Kinu. Probably mid-twenties. He was short, chubby, and he was covered in tattoos. "Aloha," he said as he gave her a kiss on the cheek.

"This is George," Kinu said. "My nephew."

"Aloha, George," Kim said. "Are you hungry? There's plenty of my granny's famous soup. And cornbread."

"No, but thanks. I need to be going. I just wanted to stop by and check on Uncle Kinu."

"Are you sure? Grandma's secret recipe. No better soup in Hawaii."

"Yeah, thanks anyway. Maybe Kinu will save me some," George said as he picked up the briefcase off the table.

"Yeah, don't count on it. I haven't eaten in twenty-four hours." Kinu went full pidgin. "This soup's gonna break da mouth, cuz."

George said his goodbyes and left with the briefcase. Kinu and Kim stood outside to watch him leave. When he started his rice rocket, Kim could feel the vibration coming from the car.

"Seems like a very polite young man," Kim said as George pulled away. "What's his story? I mean, you know, the car and tattoos ..."

"He's family. I called him, asked him to come over. That briefcase ... that's what messed me up yesterday. Had to get it outta here. That wasn't sugar in those packets." Kinu held the door open for Kim, but she didn't go inside.

"So what was it?" she asked.

"I found that case when I was surfing yesterday morning. It was just floating in the water near Diamond Head. Sure I'm gonna take it and see what's inside, but it was just sugar packets. So I threw it in my truck. Well ... I stopped to get coffee, and I put some sugar in. When I got home today, I kind of put two and two together, you know? And then I called George. I had to get that stuff out of here."

"Kinu, you should've called the police." Kinu went inside and put the crockpot on the coffee table. Kim followed. "Why did you call George?"

"Well, George is the first person I thought of who knows about that stuff."

"And what's George going to do with it?" Kim asked.

Kinu looked guilty. "Maybe sell it. Don't really know. I don't think he uses it."

Kim covered her mouth: "Kinu, no! You can't put that on the street. How could you do that?"

"Well … I wasn't thinking about it. When I came in and opened a packet, I was almost tempted to try a little. I didn't think about it much. I just called who I knew could help."

"But Kinu, that stuff is poison. Look what it did to you. You should've called the police. We should call the police right now."

"George asked if he could take it. I needed it gone. That's all I was thinking. We can't call the cops yet. I'll call George. We'll figure it out."

This was not going to be the romantic movie night that Kim was hoping for.

"So your nephew's a drug dealer?" she asked.

****

While Heather was shopping at the mall, Alvaro was having a bit of a panic attack. She wasn't answering her phone, which probably meant she was ignoring him, but it could've meant something worse. If she just went for coffee, she should've been back in less than an hour, but as it got later, Alvaro got more concerned. As soon as it was dark, Alvaro decided to go looking for her.

Alvaro, Iceman, and Slider got into their SUV and started driving by the coffee shops in the area. The closest one was a Starbuck's across from the Waikiki Zoo, but there was no sign of Heather inside, and because parking in the area was a challenge, they figured she wouldn't have gone there anyway. They headed to a Starbuck's on Kapahulu. There were three others on Kapahulu that they knew of, but there was no sign of

Heather or the SUV. They continued to Waialae Avenue and worked their way towards Hawaii Kai.

No luck.

When they got to the last Starbuck's in Hawaii Kai and still found no trace of Heather, Alvaro decided he'd get Frappuccino and have his guys drive him home. They'd continue the search without him.

It wouldn't be until a couple of hours later that Iceman and Slider would find the SUV Heather was driving. It was in the Kahala Shopping Mall parking lot. They immediately called Alvaro and let him know they found it. They told him that there was no sign of Heather, but they did find a cup of coffee on the roof of the car.

Alvaro hung up and let out a gigantic "Fuuuuccckkkkk!" Maverick made things even worse when he admitted that the spare keys were in the glove compartment. He failed to provide a logical reason as to why.

Alvaro reached down into his pocket and pulled out the phone number that Goose got from Frances. It was about time for him to call the man with the neck tattoo.

****

When the trunk opened, Heather Brown knew what she would see: It was the man with the neck tattoo. He kept his hands on the trunk as he opened it and look at her with a smile. He had her purse over his shoulder, and as soon as she could see that he wasn't pointing a gun at her, she swung her leg and kicked him hard, landing a solid shot in his side. He didn't even flinch. It was like kicking a tree.

She tried to cock her leg and thrust at him below the belt, hoping to get a lucky shot at his balls, but as soon as her knee went up, he caught her ankle and yanked her clear out of the trunk. He had her by the elbow and was dragging her inside in one motion, and she could tell by his grip that she had no chance of breaking free.

"What the fuck do you want?" she yelled. "Who the fuck are you?" She could feel her skin scraping on the pavement.

They were in an alley, and he dragged her through the back door of a Chinese restaurant. He yanked her to her feet and grabbed her around the waist, pulling her high off the floor. The kitchen staff gave them a look and then went right back to talking. There wasn't much cooking going on.

Heather tried throwing an elbow and struggled to get loose, but the man with the neck tattoo was too strong. As they went through the kitchen, she looked for a knife to grab, but there were none in sight, so she grabbed a pan from a counter and swung it as hard as she could. She caught him on the elbow as he raised his arm to block, but if it hurt him, he didn't show it. He yanked her toward him so hard that she thought her shoulder popped out of place. He grabbed the pan and threw it down with a mild annoyance.

The man with the neck tattoo took Heather Brown into a back room and threw her on a brown leather sofa. She popped right up. With one hand on her shoulder, he threw her back down.

"Sit down and be a good girl, or daddy will have to hold you on his lap." He smiled, and she didn't try to get up. "Now there's a good girl."

"Go. Fuck. Yourself," Heather said. She gave him a death stare.

He took her purse off his shoulder and tossed it at her. "Get your phone out." The man with the neck tattoo took his phone out and put it on the table. "Let's see which one of us your boss calls first."

****

Alvaro met the man with the neck tattoo at his Sand Island storage unit. He rode there with the Top Gun crew, making Maverick sit in the very back. Since they'd found the SUV Heather took, Maverick was constantly berated for keeping the spare keys in the glove compartment.

About a block before they arrived, Iceman pulled over and let Maverick and Goose out of the car. Alvaro wanted them to sneak around to the opposite side of the storage units to set up a position "in the rear," as he put it.

They parked at the end of the road leading to Alvaro's storage shed and waited. Maverick and Goose hopped a fence in the back and were hiding at the end of the units, roughly twenty yards from Alvaro and Iceman. Iceman spotted them in the headlights as they took their positions. When Iceman saw the other car pull in, he led them to Alvaro's storage unit nice and easy, never taking his eyes off of him in the rearview mirror. The man with the neck tattoo knew they had bulletproof glass, so Iceman knew he wouldn't shoot, but he wasn't going to let him out of his sight. He turned off his lights.

When Maverick and Goose saw Iceman coming their way, they circled behind the units and came up on their rear. They waited.

The man with the neck tattoo turned off his car, got out, and stood in the road. He held his cell phone out to the side to show it wasn't a weapon.

Alvaro wanted to roll down the window and talk to him from the safety of the SUV, or send out Iceman and Slider, but he knew he'd look weak, so he got out to face the man. Iceman and Slider fanned out to the sides of the SUV. They both had their guns in their hands.

The man lifted his shirt and turned around to show them that he had no gun. He slowly held out his cell phone and pushed a button.

Alvaro was surprised that the man would be standing here like this without a weapon. He hoped to avoid blood, but this problem might be solved easier than he thought possible. He looked around, wondering if he really came alone.

"Aloha," Alvaro said.

The man held up a finger: "Wait … just a sec." He gave them a smile and waved his phone in the air.

"Where's Heather?" Alvaro asked.

"Wait for it … one second …

"Where's Heather?" Alvaro repeated.

"Wait for it …"

From Alvaro's pocket, *Domo Arigato, Mr. Roboto* started playing.

The man with the neck tattoo pointed to Alvaro's pocket: "… and there it is!"

Alvaro knew instantly who was calling. He couldn't find a funny Korean song, so inspired by Heather's racist categorizing of Asians, he choose the 1982 Styx classic. It was the ringtone he set for Woo Lee.

The man with the neck tattoo lip-synced the chorus: *Secret, secret, I've got a secret.*

Alvaro felt his testicles shrink a little; he knew this was bad news.

"I think you should answer that, Ricardo Montelbon. It's important."

"Ricardo Montelbon? From *Fantasy Island*? What's that supposed to mean? Do I look like Ricardo Montelbon?" Alvaro lifted his fedora. "Do you see any gray hair? No, I didn't think so."

The man with the neck tattoo smiled: "Look, boss! Zee plane. Zee plane."

Alvaro wanted to tell Iceman to shoot the bastard. "Hey … Ricardo Montelbon was a handsome man."

"Boss!" said Iceman, trying to get Alvaro to focus.

"Anyway," Alvaro said.

"Anyway," the man with the neck tattoo said. The song continued to play.

Goose and Slider held their positions hiding in the rear, guns drawn.

"Hello," Alvaro said as he answered the phone.

"Alvi, how are you?" Woo Lee asked.

"Oh, I'm wonderful," said Alvaro. "I mean, you know, besides dealing with this asshole who I'm thinking about filling with bullets. You know who I'm talking about?" Alvaro was looking at the man with the neck tattoo.

"You talking about Sasha?" Woo Lee asked.

"Sasha?" Alvaro said. "Really?" He raised an eyebrow in disbelief.

"Dude, your name is Sasha?" Iceman asked. "Isn't that a girl's name?"

"It's Russian," Sasha said calmly.

"Sasha, huh? I never would've guessed," said Iceman.

Alvaro held up his hand at Iceman. "Look, Woo Lee, what's going on here? Can you fill me in here on what the fuck is going on?"

"Alvi, you give Sasha what you have in the storage unit. And then I want you to go home. Everything okay. No probrem."

"Are you robbing me here, Woo Lee? Is that really what's going on?"

"Alvi, no. Prease trust me."

"And what if I don't feel like doing that? What if I don't want to give this asshole my shit? What then?" Alvaro was stalling for time. He was trying to calculate the odds. They blindsided him, and he knew it.

"Well, Alvi ... Heather is a very rovery girl. So breautiful, but her mouth ... Many bad sayings coming from her mouth. She tell me fuck my mother. She tell me put my balls up my ass and eat a dick. What does this mean, Alvi? So bad mouth. Where you find this wahine, eh?"

The shock of the situation was starting to set in. He knew he was getting fucked over by the old Korean. "What about Sasha here? Say we fill him full of bullets and dump him in the Ala Wai. What then?" Alvaro asked.

"Oh, Alvi, I know you not a kirrer. You not going to hurt anybody when you know there's an easier way."

Alvaro looked at his men, and then he looked at Sasha. "And how do I know you'll let Heather go?"

"Alvi, you can trust me ... We partners."

"Partners, huh?" Alvaro kept his cool, but he was exploding on the inside. "And what happens to our partnership now? You just bent our partnership over and fucked it in the ass."

"Alvi, we'll talk later. You do what you want tonight. I'm going to spend time with this rovery girl. I hope to see Sasha soon. Aroha."

Alvaro looked at his phone in shock. "He hung up on me," he said to Iceman.

Iceman just shrugged. "What do you want us to do, boss? Should I put a bullet in him, or we could give him a beating ... He is a big motherfucker, so maybe we should put a bullet in him, and then give him a beating."

Alvaro looked at the ground and shook his head. "No ... not yet ..." He looked up at Sasha, who had a big smile on his face. "Get the boxes into his car."

Sasha gave Iceman a wink.

CHAPTER FIFTEEN

Friday 8:30 p.m.

After watching the sunset, Matt and Shauna decided to meet for dinner. It was actually Shauna who asked Matt, but it was Matt who made it clear he didn't have any dinner plans.

They met at a small Japanese place on King Street famous for sushi and sake. They were on their third bottle when Shauna got a text message from Solo: *Working tomorrow? Need a favor.*

She shared the text with Matt. "Say what you want about Solo, but he is one dedicated police officer."

"So you work with him often?" Matt asked.

"Yeah, all the time," Shauna answered. "You probably think he's a little grumpy, but once you get to know him, you realize it's mostly just an act. He just likes people to feel a little intimidated by him."

"I don't think he likes me much," Matt said.

"Nah, don't take it personally. He's always hard on the guys, especially handsome, younger guys. I wouldn't say he's jealous or anything, but he needs to have a reason to respect you."

"Well, he's been all right with me. Can't say I'd want to be showing me around if I were in his shoes." Matt filled up their cups with more sake. "So, what are you going to tell him? Working tomorrow?"

"Yeah, sure, but let's see what he wants." She replied to Solo's text: *Maybe. What do you need?*

She got Solo's reply within the minute: *Photos and background of Chester Pile and Norman McClintock. Going to question them tomorrow.* Then another text came in: *Both worked with Heather Brown at Maston.*

"The problem with older detectives is …" Shauna was saying to Matt as she was replying to Solo's text, "… the problem is … they don't like technology." She sent the text: *Can help, but did you ask Google? LinkedIn?*

Matt and Shauna debated the pros and cons of ordering another bottle of sake, which led them to the realization that they were getting a little tipsy. Shauna suggested they move on to beer, and they decided to walk over to Magoo's on University Avenue, which was only a block away. Magoo's was a favorite spot of both of theirs in their college days, but neither of them had been there in years.

Shauna felt her phone vibrate while Matt was paying the bill, but she waited until they got outside before reading it out loud: *Google doesn't like old men. Couldn't find shit.*

"I wonder if he'll ask me to join him," Matt said.

"Let's find out," Shauna said as she sent Solo a text. It said: *Going to take Matt with you?*

The text came back within seconds: *Prettyboy Jesus? I'll have to ask.*

Shauna turned to Matt: "Want to go with Solo tomorrow?"

"Yeah, of course," Matt answered.

Shauna sent a text to Solo: *Matt wants to go. I'm with him now.*

"Did you tell him we're together?" Matt asked.

"Yep."

"Ouch, not sure that was a good idea. I bet he gives me a hard time about it. For some reason, I don't think he'd approve."

"Approve of what?" Shauna said. "We're just two colleagues out for dinner and drinks, right?"

"Right," said Matt. "Wait, how often do you do this with 'colleagues' anyway?"

"For dinner and drinks on a Friday night? Hmm, I think this is the first."

Shauna and Matt were at Magoo's and well into their second pitcher of Longboard Lager when Solo finally texted back. His message was short and to the point: *I'll pick him up at 10:00.* Shauna didn't see the message. She was way too involved in her conversation with Matt. They were talking about the state of their current love lives. Shauna confessed to her disastrous attempts at online dating, and Matt confessed that he didn't date during his stint undercover.

"Not one date?" Shauna asked.

"Nope. Not one date for almost nine months."

"Bullshit. There must have been some girls. The whole operation started with you hanging around some gym, right? Weren't there any girls there?"

"Yeah, but I couldn't get involved. I wasn't going to date someone going to the same gym where I was trying to catch some bad guys. And then I guess I just got too involved to make time for anyone new outside of work. I just stopped meeting people."

"Dang, and I thought I was going through a rough patch," Shauna said.

"How about you? Tell me about your online lovers? Any of them get a second date?"

"Nope. One guy had a shot, but he blew it at the end by throwing a fit that I wouldn't give him a goodnight kiss."

"Yikes," Matt said. "Not even a peck? And you liked the guy?" Matt was both relieved and disappointed with this news. He'd been wondering what his chances were.

"Yeah, not even a peck. You think I'm going to make out with a guy I just met online? Seriously, do you know what kind of people are out there?"

"Enlighten me?" Matt said.

"Okay, but tell me honestly, have you ever tried online dating?"

"Nope."

She squinted at him: "Seriously?"

"Swear to God."

She let out a sigh. "Online dating … Let me tell you, when I created a profile, I had probably around thirty messages in the first hour. Not day, but hour! Thirty! And out of those thirty, I had at least six or seven dick pics."

Matt gave an impressed nod. "Not bad. And not to take their side or anything, but I'm sure you have quite the impressive profile." Matt poured the last of the second pitcher into their glasses.

"That's kind of you to say, but here's the kicker: I hadn't even uploaded a photo yet. Never did. I sifted through the crap to find a few guys who looked the most promising, and I wrote them back with a picture. These were the guys that had honest looking profiles, but ... didn't work out. None of them."

"That's hard to believe," said Matt.

"Really! And each date had two things in common. First, they couldn't believe I looked like my photo, and second, none of them looked like theirs. Meanwhile, the messages and dick pics kept rolling in. I've never seen so many penises in my life. Big, small, crooked, hairy ... I've seen them all." Shauna realized what she was saying and knew that she was a little more than tipsy. "I'm done with it. No more online dating for me."

Matt was interested. "Fascinating," he said as he shook his head.

"What?" Shauna said smiling. "It's the truth."

"Not even a goodnight kiss? And you liked the guy? I was wondering how you felt about those." Matt realized what he was saying and knew that he was a little more than tipsy.

Shauna leaned in over the table and said: "It's been a long time since I've met a nice guy." She was smiling.

Matt leaned in and replied: "I tend to consider myself a nice guy."

Then he leaned over the table and kissed her.

****

Alvaro sat next to the pool in the back of his rented Kahala beach house. He had the Top Gun crew with him. Iceman was behind the bar mixing a mai tai, Slider was sitting near the back door, and Maverick and Goose were sitting at the bar drinking Hinanos. Alvaro figured they could all use a drink.

"Hurry it up with that mai tai," Alvaro said to Iceman. "And don't forget the umbrella."

"Coming right up, boss."

Alvaro needed to call his boss, but aware that it was almost midnight in Mexico, he figured he could wait until morning. He needed time to think. He felt totally caught off guard with the way things unfolded.

"That crazy old bastard," Alvaro said to nobody in particular. "What the hell is he thinking?"

"We could go over to that restaurant where you met him. See if he's there. Shoot him in the head or something," Iceman said as he handed Alvaro the mai tai.

"I appreciate the enthusiasm, but I'd like to see this get done without anyone getting shot in the head, at least for now. Thanks, though."

"No problem, boss. You change your mind, just let me know ..."

Alvaro and his crew sat in near silence as they drank their drinks and listened to some Hawaiian slack key on the Bose outdoor sound system. Alvaro had the tiki torches lit and kicked back in a lounge chair. He watched the Pacific clouds roll under the moon. "Another day in paradise," he said. None of the crew replied. They couldn't tell if he was being ironic.

Shortly after midnight, Heather Brown rang the buzzer on the gate of the Kahala beach house. Maverick jumped to open the gate, and the rest of the Top Gun crew stiffened in anticipation. They all reached for their guns as a matter of habit. Alvaro didn't move. He just lounged next to the pool and sipped his fourth mai tai of the evening. He was thinking about the trade winds and how quickly they moved the clouds through the sky. He could see the top of Diamond Head, and he tried to think of whether he'd ever seen a more perfect view.

He knew a hurricane was blowing through the gate, but he wasn't worried. He knew what he was going to do.

****

Woo Lee was in a Korean karaoke room just off of Kapahulu Street. After letting Heather Brown go, he stopped by his bar on Apanui Street where he made the rounds and checked up on business. He wasn't too concerned with turning a profit, but he expected things to run a certain way, and he found that there was no better assurance than to drop in regularly to keep the staff on their toes.

Woo Lee's bar, the Dreamy Aloha, was locally referred to as a "buy-me-drinky" bar. Unlike a regular bar, the Dreamy Aloha mostly had booths, and most customers would sit in a booth and have one of the many Korean or Japanese hostesses join them to pour drinks and provide entertainment. All the customer had to do was buy the girl's drinks, which usually cost anywhere from ten to twenty dollars each, depending on the popularity, looks, and charm of the hostess.

Woo Lee bought the Dreamy Aloha when he first arrived in Hawaii. He had dreams of retiring and living a straight life as an honest businessman, but the drug deals kept falling into his lap and were always too profitable to pass up, and they also provided him with the income to not stress about how his investments were doing. Along with the bar, Woo Lee owned a car wash, a Hawaiian shave-ice stand, rental property, a Chinese restaurant, and a flower shop.

The Dreamy Aloha had karaoke rooms in the back, and Woo Lee was in the middle of a duet with one of his favorite hostesses when the man with the neck tattoo walked in. They were in the VIP room, and two other hostesses were sitting on the sofa. There was a large flat-screen TV on the wall with the lyrics at the bottom and a video of an Asian couple dancing through a flower garden. The man with the neck tattoo felt like he was watching a bad Korean comedy movie.

Woo Lee burst into the chorus: "Rove, rove me, do. You know I rove you … Sasha! Come!" Woo Lee held the microphone out to Sasha. "Sing together."

Sasha looked at Woo Lee like he'd gone mad. He sat down next to the two girls on a sofa large enough to hold at least ten people. Both of the girls looked happy to see him. One girl grabbed a glass and dropped in two cubes of ice, and the other began to pour from a bottle of whiskey. Sasha could tell that the whiskey was expensive, but he didn't know the Macallan 21-year-old scotch whiskey cost over three hundred a bottle. He noticed Woo Lee was drinking it with Coke.

Sasha was tired. He planned to report back to Woo Lee and then call it a night. After moving the drugs that he stole from Alvaro and the Top Gun crew, Sasha thought his night would be over. Getting caught with that much crystal meth would put him away for a long time, and if the cops could put two and two together, he'd probably get fingered for a couple of murders to go along with the drug rap. It was a stressful day, even by his standards, but then he had to deal once again with Heather Brown. He wrapped her wrists together with an excessive amount of duct tape and put a piece over her mouth before throwing her back in the trunk of his car. He didn't want to hear her yapping all the way back to Alvaro's. He threw her out down the block and headed to the Dreamy Aloha.

Now he was sitting next to two beautiful Korean girls and watching Woo Lee belt out a terrible rendition of a Beatles song. Sasha was surprised to find it enjoyable. He felt himself relax a bit as one of the girls poured him another drink. The girls were smiling and talking to each other in Korean.

Sasha let them talk for a while before saying to one of the girls, "You have a cute accent. That's called 'chat-do-ri,' right? Are you from Daegu?"

The two girls looked at each other in shock, and then they looked back at Sasha. The girl answered in Korean: "Yeah, I'm from Daegu. How do you know that?"

"I used to live in Korea," Sasha said in English. "I exported Korean cars to Russia. That's how I ended up working for him."

"Can you speak Korean?" the girl asked in Korean.

"Not much," Sasha answered in English. "I used to be better, but I don't use it much."

Both girls started laughing in embarrassment. They wondered if Sasha heard them talking about him.

"Can you girls speak English?" Sasha asked in English.

"A little," they both answered in Korean.

Sasha continued the chitchat, him speaking in English and the girls speaking in Korean, while Woo Lee moved on to a heavily accented rendition of Don Ho's *Tiny Bubbles*. Sasha had worked in Korea long enough to know how hostess girls operated, and he was trying to figure which girl he wanted to take home. He was also wondering if he'd have to pay for it.

Woo Lee finished his eighth song in a row, Israel Kamakawiwo'ole's *Somewhere Over the Rainbow*, and went to punch in another song on the karaoke machine.

"Girls," he said as he held out the microphone, and the two girls chatting with Sasha jumped up to join the third girl in front of the screen. A Korean pop song started playing, and the girls started singing and dancing like they'd been through rehearsals.

Woo Lee sat next to Sasha and added a little of the Macallan to his glass. Then he topped it off with some Coke. "Sasha," he said as he held up his glass. "Cheers!" Woo Lee then took a big swig, and Sasha finished his drink. One of the girls was right there ready to pour him another with the microphone still in her hand. She sang the only part of the song Sasha could understand: "Bay-yaa-yaa-yaa baby, baby. Bay-yaa-yaa-yaa, baby, baby." Then she joined the other girls as the song went back to rapid-fire Korean lyrics that Sasha made no effort to understand.

Sasha thought about the day. Everything went well, and now he was drinking expensive whiskey next to his kooky Korean boss and looking at three beautiful, young Korean girls in a karaoke room. Of everything that happened that day, this was the only thing Sasha hadn't planned.

"Today ... very good!" Woo Lee said as he slapped Sasha on the knee. "But tomorrow ... mo' bettah." Woo Lee gave Sasha a wink and a shaka. Sasha smiled and shook his head. He almost had a soft spot for the old wannabe-Hawaiian gangster.

After going over the next day's plans, Woo Lee said his goodbyes and made a quick exit, leaving Sasha with the three girls, two of whom left minutes later. Sasha sat on the sofa next to the cute girl from Daegu with the country accent. It was the one he was hoping for.

CHAPTER SIXTEEN

Saturday 8:00 a.m.

Timmy's mom woke him at eight o'clock.

"Wake up, Mr. Sleepy McGrumperson. Time for another day in paradise."

"Mom, Jesus Christ, what time is it? Close the curtains!"

"It's eight o'clock. Time for breakfast. French toast or pancakes?"

"Need sleep. Go away evil woman!" Tim pulled his pillow over his head.

His mom yanked the pillow off on her way out. "French toast it is. It'll be on the table in fifteen minutes. Don't be late. I'd hate to have to change the Wi-Fi password again." She tossed the pillow back at Timmy's head.

Tim knew it was a hollow threat, but he managed to pull himself up and make it to the table on time. Deep down, he didn't want to disappoint his mom.

Tim sat at the table, and his mom brought over a cup of coffee and poured him a glass of orange juice. As much as Tim liked to sleep, he enjoyed his breakfasts with mom even more. This was a new habit they developed when they moved to Hawaii, and Tim had to admit it was a nice way to start the day.

"Try the coffee. It's called Kopi Luwak. Very expensive."

Tim took a drink: "Not bad. Where'd you get it?" Tim asked as he took another drink.

"Just from a friend." Tim assumed this meant either a boyfriend or potential boyfriend, and he didn't care to hear more.

"It's good. Nice and dark," Tim said as he took another sip.

"It's from Indonesia. Apparently, there's a type of cat there that eats the coffee beans and then poops them out. I guess it does something to the flavor of the beans."

"Poops them out?" Timmy looked at his mom in horror. "You're giving me coffee that's been in cat shit? Mom, what the hell?"

"Oh, don't be so close-minded, Mr. Drama Queen. I'm sure they wash the beans. I heard it's the most expensive coffee in the world," his mom said, as if that'd make Timmy enjoy it more.

Tim pushed the cup away. "Yeah, maybe, but I'll stick with the non-fecal matter dark roast next time, thanks."

"Fine, I'll drink it myself," his mom said. She brought him a plate full of French toast and bacon.

"Is there anything I should know about this? Like, was the bacon soaked in dog pee or anything? Is the bread made from owl spit?"

"You're welcome," she replied. "Enjoy your breakfast."

Tim did enjoy his breakfast. He ate everything on his plate and then lingered around sharing the Saturday morning paper with his mom.

Around ten o'clock, Tim did his twenty-minute core workout, flexed his abs in the mirror, and then threw on a pair of board shorts. He grabbed his backpack as he flew out the door, yelling to his mom that he was heading for Waikiki beach.

He planned to go by Frances' apartment and pick up his daily supply, but he wasn't feeling too eager to be sitting in the park dealing to meth heads. He decided to stall and take the long way, swinging by the Starbuck's on Kuhio for a coffee that didn't pass through an animal's intestinal tract.

Like any teenager, Tim was starting to get bored of his job. It was fun when he was selling pot to his classmates, but selling meth to strangers in the park was a different ballgame. He'd never really considered the possibility of getting caught by the police, but what was starting to scare him were the customers. Tim barely weighed a buck-forty, and he knew he wouldn't stand a chance if someone decided to roll him.

He decided that his days of selling meth were coming to an end. He managed to save a few grand from his dealings, and considering that his mom bought him almost anything he asked for, he really couldn't think of any reason to continue.

Tim decided to head to Frances' and have a talk with him. Frances never pressured Tim, and considering how old the man was, he never came off as intimidating. He hoped Frances could hook him up with weed, which he planned to keep selling to his classmates. If not, he'd say his goodbyes and be on his way.

He knew Frances would want him to work today, and maybe even a few more days, but as soon as he could, Tim would stop spending his days dealing meth in Kapiolani Park.

****

Sasha was up early for a Saturday. He let his new Korean friend sleep while he showered and ate.

He lived in a one-bedroom apartment in Chinatown, directly above a flower shop. He chose the area when he first arrived on the island because it was cheap, but he stayed because he grew to like the neighborhood. Sasha spent ten years of his life in Asian countries, so he didn't feel out of place. The only downside was the criminal element. Chinatown was full of homeless drug users, transgender prostitutes, and street thugs. His size and skin color made him stand out, and it also helped keep people away.

Sasha finished his coffee and got his things: keys, wallet, sunglasses, and gun. He checked his bedroom, but there was still no movement from the girl from Daegu. She wanted to leave last night, but he made her stay. He put some money on the table, a little extra to make up for the bruises he gave her, and he left—he knew she wouldn't be stupid enough to rob him.

The entrance to the apartment was out back, and the stairs led down to his private parking spot—one of the main reasons he chose this place. He got in his shitty Ford Taurus and pulled out to work. It'd be a busy day.

Woo Lee's distribution chain wasn't as centralized as it was in the past. He mostly sold drugs in bulk, relying on his buyers to handle their own sales. Woo Lee himself rarely had any contact with the drugs. He placed himself as far away as possible, which was why he let Sasha handle this operation.

Sasha loaded up his car with the drugs he stole from Alvaro. He met with Woo Lee's three biggest buyers, and by nine-thirty, the operation was completely out of Woo Lee and Sasha's hands.

Sasha worked hard to set up the plan. Woo Lee's buyers didn't want to do what he was asking them to do, but in the end, Sasha convinced them. Woo Lee was a major lifeline, and if they were asked to help with one of his half-crazy schemes, they knew they had to play ball.

The first buyer was a long-time business associate of Woo Lee's named Jack Kim. Jack was a fellow Korean and known as one of the top suppliers of rims, spinners, and spoilers in the Honolulu area. He ran four custom design shops aimed predominately at local Asian kids trying to trick out their rice rockets. Jack's shop managers had no trouble finding people to get in on the action. They'd target the customers who looked like they could use a buck or two, and with very little effort, Jack Kim had an army of small-time drug pushers unknowingly working for him throughout the island. Within an hour of his man picking up the drugs from Sasha, Jack's small army was ready to go ahead with the plan.

The second buyer was Andrew McGabban, a haole from the mainland and one of the kookiest guys Sasha had ever worked with. Andrew was the only drug dealer he'd met who dressed like a homeless version of Magnum P.I. and resembled an ogre. He wore an aloha shirt, short khaki shorts, boat shoes, a large red beard, and about two hundred extra pounds around his waist. Sasha found it comical and assumed Andrew was trying to blend in with the local burnout fisherman crowd, which was true. Despite Andrew's sloppy appearance, he ran a tight ship, and his men had the drugs distributed and ready by ten-thirty.

The third buyer was Roland Cruz, a Hawaiian-born Filipino who owned a handful of shrimp trucks and shave-ice stands around the island. He sent trusted employee George Anapu'ui to meet Sasha and pick up the drugs.

When George met with his team, or "foot soldiers" as Roland called them, he opened the boxes and saw the same packages of Sweet Maui Brown that came in the briefcase from his uncle, Kinu Anapu'ui. He couldn't imagine how the briefcase came across Kinu's path in the water, or why it would've been out there, but he thought it best to keep his mouth shut. George planned to sell the contents of the briefcase on the side, but now he wasn't sure that would be a good idea. He considered opening the briefcase and adding it to what he passed out, but the contents were worth at least a couple grand. It wasn't easy for him to piss away that kind of cash.

After getting the drugs to the foot soldiers, George drove down an alley in the industrial area near Kaka'ako. He found a dumpster, and after thinking hard for a minute, George got out of the car and grabbed the briefcase from the trunk. He wiped it down as well as he could and put it next to the dumpster. He figured it was safer to let some bums take it than have a garbage man find it. He wondered how long it would take for the lucky bum to realize he found a month's supply of ice, not Sweet Maui Brown sugar.

Something didn't make sense to George. He hated to waste an opportunity, but when things didn't add up, the smart thing to do was to play it safe.

****

Detective Solosolo Fauatea started his Saturday morning by visiting Norman McClintock, a former co-worker of Heather Brown at Maston Shipping.

Norman McClintock was sitting on his front lanai when Solo pulled up to his house in the Manoa Valley. It was a one-story house with a large front yard and large banyan trees that covered most of the yard with shade. Considering the size of the land, the location, and the crazy Hawaiian real estate prices, he guessed it would go for a million or two.

"Mornin'," Norman McClintock said as Solo made his way up the concrete path to the house.

"Mr. Norman McClintock?" Solo asked.

"Yup. What can I do you for?" Norman looked younger than Solo by a few years, but he was equally as chubby. He didn't have a neck tattoo, and nothing about him looked like he was capable of killing. He wore an aloha shirt and sat drinking coffee with the morning paper.

"My name is Solo Fauatea, detective with the HPD. Sorry for the early Saturday morning visit. Mind if I ask you a few questions?" Solo flashed his badge and noticed Norman looked happy to see him.

"Sure thing, detective. Come on up." Norman met Solo on the steps with a big handshake and a smile. "Can't imagine how I can help you, but I'm always willing to help out law enforcement. How about a cup of coffee?"

Solo's instincts told him Norman McClintock wasn't involved in anything illegal, but he had an hour before he had to pick up pretty-boy Jesus at the Outrigger Hotel, so he figured he could sit outside with Norman and have some coffee. Hopefully, he could get some background on Heather Brown and Chester Pile.

"I never say no to a cup of joe," Solo answered.

"Have a seat in the rocker there. How do you take it?"

"Black," Solo said. He made his way up to the porch and took a seat, watching the screen door swing shut behind Norman. The rocking chair was big and black, and it reminded Solo of Georgia for some reason. Solo rocked back and forth while looking out over the lush neighborhood. Norman McClintock had quite the setup.

"Here you go, detective," Norman said. "One-hundred percent Kona coffee. That's from the Ka'u region over on the Big Island. Caramel notes with hints of citrus and nuts. That's some of the best coffee in the world. Hope you like it."

"Um, yeah." Solo looked at the coffee. "Yeah, caramel notes, huh? Sounds great." He gave Norman an approving nod as he took a sip. "Beats the tar that we have down at the station, that's for sure."

Norman started telling Solo about the different coffee plantations on the Big Island, Maui, and Oahu, which led him to the story of other crops on the islands, which somehow led him to the story of the first missionaries who settled on the islands. Norman was a talker, and Solo let him talk. He half listened as he sipped his coffee and rocked on the beautiful Manoa Valley porch. Finally, Norman wrapped up his short history lesson of the islands and Solo took back the conversation.

"Norman, do you know a Heather Brown?"

Without flinching, Norman laid down everything he knew. He started with a summary of their work history, and then he moved on to what he knew of her personal life, and finally he added his personal feelings towards her. It was so complete that Solo didn't even ask questions.

"How about Chester Pile? What do you know about him?"

Norman's account of Chester was much less complimentary than of Heather's. He described Heather as competent and hardworking while his description of Chester was less flattering. "Clusterfuck!" Norman started. "That man is a walking clusterfuck. Excuse my language, but how he ever managed to get a job with anyone anywhere is beyond me. If I remember correctly, he has more ex-wives than I can count on one hand, and I'm sure there are some sexual harassment claims against him, not to mention rumors of drug use. Total clusterfuck."

"Okay, he's a clusterfuck. Got it. So ... it sounds like you're not a fan. Any particulars you can share?"

"No ... no, I'm not a fan of Mr. Chester Pile. We did not see eye to eye, him and I. I had to file a complaint against him with HR. He wasn't doing his job. I'm telling you—clusterfuck. There is no better word. Did you say he's still working for Maston? That's nothing short of a miracle."

"Yeah, he's still there. He have anything to do with why you left?"

"Nah, I just got a better offer, but I can't say I wasn't happy to get out of there. Can I ask what happened? He in some trouble?"

"I'd like to tell you what we have, Norman, but the truth is, we don't have much. Just following some leads. Chester Pile and Heather Brown—we need to ask them a few questions." Solo set his coffee mug down and rocked up to his feet. "Thanks for the coffee, Norman. Those caramel notes really hit the spot."

"Anytime, detective. I hope the information was helpful. And I have to ask, you've been working with Matt Gold, right? I saw your picture in the paper." Norman dug through the read newspaper and showed Solo the article. "That must be exciting, huh? He's practically a celebrity."

"Oh, yes, terribly exciting," Solo said deadpan. He shook Norman's hand. "Mahalo for the help. And the coffee."

Solo gave Norman a wave goodbye as he pulled away. He headed directly to the Outrigger Hotel in Waikiki to pick up Matt, who was waiting near the valet when Solo pulled up, a full twenty minutes late. He was holding two cups of coffee.

Solo gave a non-apologetic shrug when Matt got in the car: "Hawaii time, eh? You know how it goes."

"No worries," Matt replied. "What's the plan?"

"I swung by Norman McClintock's house this morning. He gave a full dissertation on the agricultural history of Hawaii and how the missionaries laid down the framework for the islands to be taken over by the white colonizers. Then he gave some info on Heather Brown and Chester Pile."

"Sounds fascinating. Anything good?"

"He has no love for Mr. Pile, that's for sure. That's where we're heading. Based on what Norman said, I expect ol' Chester to come out of a trailer wearing a wife-beater with a ring of powder around his nose."

"Again, sounds fascinating."

"Speaking of fascinating, how was your evening?"

Matt noticed a shift in Solo's expression. His brow wrinkled, and he gave Matt a look out of the corner of his eyes.

"It was nice." Matt expected this, and for some reason, he hoped to get Solo's approval. "Had some dinner, a couple of drinks, and was in bed by eleven."

Solo gave Matt another look.

"Alone!" Matt added. "Back in my hotel room all alone by eleven."

"Had a good time, then?"

"Yeah, she's great."

Solo let it go.

They pulled into the parking lot of a three-story walk-up apartment in Kalihi. Matt closed the file of Chester Pile and took off his sunglasses.

"Is this what the other guy's place looked like?"

"Compared to Norman McClintock's house, this place is a shithole, and I'm sugar-coating it a bit," Solo said. "Hard to believe these guys have practically the same jobs. Norman's got a house in the valley, and this guy is living on Hawaiian Skid Row."

"Maybe he's just thrifty," Matt said.

Solo parked next to a shiny new truck. "Yeah, or maybe he's broke from child-support payments and an eight-ball-a-day coke habit."

Matt could see the apartment numbers from inside the car. "Looks like his apartment is that one in the corner. Second floor, with the door open."

"And this here looks like Mr. Pile's truck, if I remember correctly from the file. It looks like we're in business. You head up those stairs, and I'll go on the other side. Let me get there first. I don't want your celebrity face to be the first thing he sees."

"Whatever you say, boss."

Solo quietly walked up to the door before barking: "Chester Pile—Honolulu Police." With the door open, Solo could see a man bolt upright on the couch. Solo smiled as he took a step inside and made eye contact. "Mind if we come in?"

Chester Pile's hair stood straight up, and his eyes scanned his living room. Besides a few beer cans, an ashtray, and a few dirty dishes on the coffee table, it was clean. He knew Solo was scanning the place as well.

"Um ... sure, yeah ... come on in ... I guess, uh ... police, you say? Um, let me put a shirt on."

"I'm Detective Fauatea, and this is my associate. Hope we didn't wake you." Solo walked in and plopped down on an oversized chair between Chester and the kitchen. The back door to the lanai was open, and Solo could feel the trade winds blowing through.

"Yeah, have a seat, sure ..." Chester was mumbling. He ran his hand through his hair while looking on the floor for his shirt.

Solo whistled: "Boy, Chester, I like what you've done with the place. Nice TV. What is that, fifty-one inches?"

Chester squinted as he looked at Matt standing in the doorframe. Then he looked back at the television. "It's fifty-five."

"I'm sorry?" Solo said.

"Fifty-five inches," Chester said a little louder.

"Boy oh boy, that's a nice one. It's got that curved back." Solo looked at Matt. "You see that? Got a curved back. Boy, that's fancy."

"Um, thanks ..." Chester pulled his shirt over his head and took another look at Matt. He was leaning on the doorframe and looking out at the parking lot.

"Chester," Solo said louder than necessary. "Mind if we ask you a few questions?"

Chester fumbled for a cigarette. "No ... no problem. I mean ... what's this all about anyway?"

"Where you working these days, Chester?"

"Maston Shipping."

"Come again?" Solo asked.

"Maston Shipping," Chester said a little louder.

"Do you know a Heather Brown?"

Chester looked back at Matt again, who was still standing in the doorframe. "I did. We worked together before."

"Any contact with her lately?" Solo asked.

Chester shook his head and fumbled to light his cigarette.

"Was that a yes or no, Chester?" Solo sat upright and put his elbows on his knees.

Chester tried to think. He felt trapped, and he had no idea what these two detectives already knew. "We keep in touch."

"When's the last time you talked to her?" Solo could see Chester's brain thinking up his story.

"I'm, um ... I'm not sure. I ..." Chester looked back at Matt again and ran his fingers through his hair, which shot straight back up. "It's been a while."

"Was that a question?" Solo asked.

"What?"

"It sounded like you were asking me, like, 'It's been a while?' As if you weren't sure."

"No, um …" Chester took a long drag of his cigarette and exhaled before answering. "What's this about, huh? Heather in some trouble?"

"Focus, Chester. When's the last time you talked to Heather?"

Chester stood and picked up the ashtray. "I don't know … I um … Let me think." He started towards the kitchen. "Hey, you guys want some coffee?"

Before they could answer, Chester took off past Solo and through the kitchen. He jumped over the lanai's railing and dropped out of sight. Solo ran to look over the railing and saw him roll out of the bushes. By the time he turned back to the doorway, Matt was already halfway down the stairs and caught a flash of Chester as he scaled the back fence.

"He's heading mauka. Toward the mountain. Toward the mountain." Solo yelled to Matt, who was already bounding down the stairs.

Solo lumbered down the stairs and headed for the car, belly shaking and sweat already beading on his forehead.

By the time Matt got over the fence, Chester was out of sight. There was a high-rise apartment complex where Matt saw two possible routes. One was through the parking garage, and the other was around the side of the building, which is the one Matt followed. He knew he could catch Chester if he caught sight of him, but when Matt reached the front of the building, he was alone.

He ran up the street trying to look between parked cars and anywhere he thought Chester could hide. The street was quiet, and there was no sign of Chester.

Matt saw Solo's car coming around the corner and jogged back to meet him.

"I never saw him after I jumped the fence."

"You check the parking garage?" Solo stayed in the car. He was breathing hard.

"No, I thought he ran out here, but ..." Matt continued to scan the street.

"I don't think he ran too far," Solo said.

"Why's that?"

"Well, no shoes for starters. Second, he looks like he smokes like a chimney, so I don't think he's running marathons on the weekends. I'll bet you lunch that he's hiding in that garage."

"Why not? If he's hiding in the garage, Zippy's is on me."

The parking garage was small, only room for about twenty cars, but it was dark, and the back entrance was only a door. Solo backed the car into the entrance of the parking garage, but he stayed close to the curb, ready to pull out if Chester made a run for it. Matt entered the garage slowly. He knew Chester wasn't armed, and Matt outweighed him by at least a hundred pounds of muscle.

It only took Matt a few seconds to find a footprint of blood on the concrete. He followed it to the side of a truck, but there was no sign of Chester. He followed the blood, and when he figured out what happened, he shouted back to Solo: "I think he circled back."

Solo punched it and headed back to Chester's apartment.

The trail was obvious: Chester hid in the garage and then went back the way he came. From inside the garage, he would've been able to see Matt fly right on by.

Matt scaled the fence to Chester's apartment complex, and Solo parked in the same spot as before, but this time, Chester's truck was gone.

Matt was walking down the stairs before Solo had time to get out of the car. "Can you believe it? He even locked his door."

Solo shook his head: "Well, he probably had to grab his keys." Solo noticed some blood on the ground. "And maybe some shoes. Look at that blood. He probably scraped himself up pretty good jumping off the lanai."

"Should we talk to his neighbors?" Matt asked.

Solo looked over the apartment complex. Even with the commotion, not one neighbor came outside. "Nah, let's go. I have a feeling Mr. Chester Pile will turn up soon. It's hard for someone like him to hide for long on this island."

"Well, at least he wasn't in the garage." Matt looked at Solo. "That means you owe me lunch."

Solo let out a grunt. "No, he *was* hiding in the garage. You flew right on by, letting him get away. Nice one, Superhero Jesus. Too bad we don't have a clip of that for the five o'clock news."

"Alright, if you say so, that's fine. I think you got me on a technicality, but that's okay. No problem. I don't mind buying lunch."

"He just watched you going flying by, that hippie hair blowing in the wind."

"Zippy's sounds good. You get a senior-citizen discount right?"

"I can see the headline: Superhero Jesus Outsmarted by Chester Clusterfuck."

"Chester Clusterfuck—that does have a ring to it."

Solo wiped the sweat from his head. "At least we agree on something."

"So what's next?"

"Get in the car. We need to take a trip over to Waimanalo. Mrs. Palakiko left a message for me this morning. "

"Something important? I missed a call from Duke earlier. Didn't have time to call him back."

Solo shrugged. "Who knows? She said it was. I'll put an APB out on Chester's truck. That'll give us some time for him to turn up."

Matt looked at the clock. It was a little after ten o'clock.

"So," said Solo, "tell me more about your date last night, lover boy."

****

Alvaro had Heather and the Top Gun crew rallied around the outside pool bar. He sat next to Heather on a stool at the tiki bar. "Just got off the phone with the boss. We're going to move the rest of the Sweet Maui Brown, and then we'll go back to the old ways until Heather can arrange us another shipment." He looked at Heather: "Think you can speed that up a bit?"

"Shouldn't be a problem," Heather said, thinking about how it might be a problem. "What about Woo Lee and his gorilla?"

"We're not going to forget about this, but that said, we can't exactly kill the old bastard. This isn't LA, and it sure isn't Mexico. We've got to let that shit slide for now. So …"

The crew gave a collective sigh.

"Now, hold on," Alvaro continued. "Business first. We'll keep moving product through the airport, chunk by chunk. There's good money there, and it'll keep us up and running. That's how the game's been ran here for decades. We've got people for that, and we'll keep using them. We don't give up our bread and butter."

"That's weak," Heather said.

Alvaro gave her a sharp look. He took off his fedora, slicked back his hair, and addressed her in a calm voice: "When the time is right, we'll find a way to get back at Woo Lee and his gorilla. First, however, we need to work on our foothold on the island. Business first. Is that clear?"

"Foothold on the island? I'm not sure 'foothold' is the right word there, Montezuma," Heather said.

"Hey," Alvaro snapped. He pointed a finger at her and paused. Then he blinked and shook his head. "What does that even mean? Montezuma?"

"Why don't we just kill the old bastard?" Iceman asked.

"Not yet. Things are different out here. You know that. We kill someone like Woo Lee, we burn a lot of bridges. Nothing goes under the radar on this rock."

Iceman nodded his head in understanding. "Okay then, let's just kill the gorilla with the neck tattoo."

"Hell yeah!" Heather said, pointing at Iceman. "For once I agree with one of your goons."

Alvaro let out another deep breath. "All right, Iceman, I love the enthusiasm, you know I do, but for now, let's focus more on making money and less on killing the competition. Business first. Comprende? Now, that said, if that big bastard keeps sticking his neck around our product, well, I guess we'll have to do something. But for now, we focus on making money."

"Okay, so what's the plan, boss?" Maverick asked. "What do you want us to do?"

"Yeah, what's the plan, boss?" Slider added.

"Shut up, Slider," Goose said.

"Yeah, shut up, Slider. You stink." Iceman added.

"Hey, that's my line," Maverick said.

Heather was ready for this meeting to be over. "For fuck's sake. All of you idiots shut the fuck up. Keep talking Alvi. Let's get the show on the road."

"You don't stink, Slider. Don't listen to these guys," Alvaro said.

Heather took off her sunglasses and shot laser beams at him.

Alvaro continued: "Okay, let's get on with it then. Get a delivery of the Sweet Maui Brown out today. We'll bleed that until it's gone, and then we'll go back to the regular stuff. Let the distributors know what's up. Business as usual, folks."

"Done, boss." Iceman took the lead as usual. "Let's hit it, boys. Slider, you're with me."

Alvaro waited until the crew was gone before talking to Heather: "So, what should I know?"

"What do you mean?" Heather put her sunglasses back on.

"You know what I mean." Alvaro took his sunglasses off—his smile was gone. Now it was time to be tough. "Last night. With Woo Lee."

"I told you everything. I went from the trunk to the office and back to the trunk. Neck tattoo guy threw me around a bit, and that goofy old Korean smiled at me a lot. I'm telling you, he's not right in the head."

Alvaro still wasn't smiling. "What did he ask you?"

"Nothing."

He stared at her and waited. Despite Alvaro's vanity and near-constant smile, Heather knew he could turn violent, and without the guys around, she felt herself become uncomfortable. "Nothing ... much," she said. "He smiled, like ... a lot. He was really nice, actually. Just strange. I'm seriously not sure he's all there."

"And what, you just smiled back?" Alvaro hopped off his stool and walked behind the tiki bar.

"I might have yelled a thing or two, can't be too sure." Heather turned on her stool to face him.

"That's all? Nothing you're forgetting to tell me?" He had both hands on the bar. Heather could see the muscles in his arm tighten.

"No, Alvi, nothing! What the fuck?"

Alvaro shook his head: "This shit isn't supposed to happen. That's one of the reasons we came out here. Hawaii has one of the lowest rates of violent crime in the country, even among drug dealers. Low supply and high demand. There's a piece for everyone."

"Yeah, you've mentioned that. Jesus, I remember your PowerPoint."

"What's the old bastard thinking, huh? We offer him a deal on a silver platter, and he pulls this bullshit."

"Fuck it, Alvi. We don't need Woo Lee. It'll take longer to get going, but we've got the product. There have to be other players who'll want in on our shit. What'd the boss say? Any other connections?"

"Pretty much the same thing. He wants us to do what we can for now. Loosely translated he said, 'Fuck it. Keep selling.' He knows the connections will come."

"And can you do that? The 'fuck it' part? Can you let this shit go for now?"

"I can do that ... for now. But I've got a plan or two. That Korean bastard won't be getting off clean, that's for sure."

"Neither will Mr. Neck Tattoo," she added.

"You know what's really fucked up? I actually like the old guy. Thought he liked me. Never saw this coming." Alvaro shook his head and relaxed his grip on the bar. He looked up. The trade winds blew the clouds across the sky, briefly blocking out the sun. "Fuck it. He made his choice. We'll be fine." Alvaro opened the refrigerator behind the bar and took out a Hinano.

"Jesus, Alvi, do you know what time it is? Can't you even wait until noon?"

"Hair of the dog. You want one?" Heather didn't answer. "Oh, and you want to know what's funny? Woo Lee's man, the one with the neck tattoo, his name is Sasha."

"Really? Sasha, huh?" This brought a smile to Heather's face. "That's kinda gay."

Alvaro took a swig of his beer. "Yeah, I know."

****

Timmy arrived at the three-story walk-up apartment on Date Street just before eleven o'clock. He was just in time to see a large man get into a black SUV. Timmy had seen the man before. He was large, had a crew cut, and was wearing aviator sunglasses. Timmy guessed the man was dropping off the product for Frances, but he wasn't sure.

Today was the day Timmy planned to tell Frances he needed to quit. He figured if he gave notice, Frances wouldn't have a problem with it. He even knew a guy he could recommend taking his place, but he wasn't sure he wanted to get someone else involved. Frances was a nice old man; he'd understand.

When Timmy entered the apartment, Frances seemed like he was in a good mood.

"Aloha, Timothy. And how are you doing today?"

"Good." Timmy handed Frances his backpack. He sniffed a little and looked at the ashtray on the table. He could see a joint still burning.

"Medicinal," Frances said with a wink. "Hold on a sec. You're going to like what we've got today." Frances took Timmy's backpack into the back bedroom. Timmy stole a quick puff while Frances was away.

"What's all that coughing I hear?" Frances yelled from the bedroom. "Young Timothy ... are you smoking my weed?"

"I think I feel a cold coming on. You said it's medicinal, right?" Frances came back in and handed him the backpack. Timmy looked inside. "Sweet Maui Brown," he said with a smile.

"We should have it for a few days. Might want to let your customers know."

"Awesome."

Timmy knew this would sell fast. Because of his excitement, or maybe because of the weed, he forgot to tell Frances of his plan to quit. He could tell there was more product than usual, and knowing the interest in it, Timmy knew this would be a good payday for him. The money was just too easy.

Timmy left the apartment and headed for his normal picnic bench at Kapiolani Park where Rachel was already waiting for him.

"What's up?" Timmy asked.

"Hey."

Timmy checked her out. His Oakley's hid his eyes as they moved up and down her body. She was easily his most attractive customer, and today she was sitting on the picnic table wearing short little board shorts and a bikini top. She had a beach bag with her.

"Gonna hit the beach?" he asked.

"Nope. Got a business meeting. Ted from accounting found some discrepancies in the annual report. We need to crunch some numbers. See if we can hit the fourth quarter …"

"Okay, smart ass." He sat up next to her and scanned the area. He could see a police car near Kaimana Beach, but it didn't worry him.

"What have you got, Timothy? Tell me it's what I'm looking for."

He was happy she knew his name. "Well, what is it you're looking for? Maybe a little Sweet Maui Brown?"

"Fuck yes! How much?"

"Same as before."

She took her wallet out of the beach bag and counted her money. "I'll take six."

Timmy couldn't hide his surprise. "Six?"

"Yeah, six. I'd buy more if I had more cash."

"Jesus, you trying to kill yourself? Why so much? What's so special about this shit?"

"It's cheap. And it's good."

"Really?"

She could tell he had no clue. "Jesus, you don't even know? The other shit is like half this much for the same price. When you sold it to me last time, I thought you fucked up."

Timmy replied without thinking: "I just sell it for what I'm told. I don't set the price." He regretted saying it immediately. "I mean, you know, I make sure I get my cut."

"What'd you think, monkey boy, junkies are impressed with some clever packaging? I think it's cool that it's ripping off the Sweet Maui Brown company. I mean, it's better than putting it in Sweet'n Low or Equal packets, but the only reason you're getting away with selling something people can't see is because the price is so good. Anyone buying from you can tell that just by looking at it."

"Wait, is Sweet Maui Brown a real company?"

"Jesus, Timmy, do you know anything? Yeah, it's a real company. Remember me telling you I put it in my Starbucks? Those look just like the shit they have."

"Oh, hey, speaking of my other customers ... Do you know some local-looking asshole who you might have told I was up here selling this shit?" Timmy opened his bag and took out six packets of Sweet Maui Brown. Rachel took a peak.

"Yeah, maybe. Kind of ugly. Dark hair. Maybe your height. Lots of tribal tattoos?"

"Yeah, that sounds like him," Timmy nodded.

"His name is Marco. I work with him. Bartender. He deals sometimes, uses all the time. If you see him again, don't let him see that stash."

"Seriously? I should worry about him?" Timmy tossed the packets in her beach bag and took the money.

"Uh, yeah, he's a junkie. Of course you should worry about him. Or just don't keep that much stuff on you. Don't you guys have runners or something? You know, like a kid hiding somewhere who brings you more stuff when you're out?"

"Runners? Um ... no. I think you watch too many movies."

"Well," Rachel said as she hopped off the picnic table, "I think you need to watch some more movies. I saw what you have in your bag. Forget about Marco, you know what would happen if the cops caught you with that much shit?"

"There are never cops around here." Timmy looked back at the police car parked near Kaimana Beach. "I mean, yeah, they're always around the area, but they never come into *this* area."

"Right ... until they do. I'm just saying, you might want to think about this shit a little more."

"Thanks, mom."

"Hey, I'm just concerned for my favorite little drug dealer."

Timmy smiled at the compliment, even though he didn't like the "little" comment.

"Anyway, I'm late. Supposed to meet the girls at the beach."

"I'm going to have this stuff for a few days at least." He wished she'd stay a little longer. "You know where to find me."

"Good to know. Be safe, young Timothy."

CHAPTER SEVENTEEN

Saturday 11:00 a.m.

At eleven o'clock drug dealers entered coffee shops across the island. Waikiki was the biggest target, but the effort did not stop there.

Dealers entered coffee shops at Ala Moana Shopping Center, Windward Shopping Center, and Ward Center. They entered coffee shops in Hawaii Kai and Kailua. They found Starbucks in Mililani and up on the North Shore. They even visited the campus coffee shops at UH and the community colleges.

Twenty-three dealers hit forty-seven coffee shops across the island. They were in and out in less than thirty minutes.

They entered the coffee shops with their Sweet Maui Brown, and they left with the real sugar.

Before the last packet was placed, the first emergency call came from a Starbucks in Waikiki. A fifty-six-year-old woman from Des Moines added a packet of Sweet Maui Brown to her already sweetened vanilla latte. She thought she was having a heart attack.

Within thirty minutes of the first call, the island's emergency response units were already at maximum capacity.

Emergency rooms were overflowing with people. Some came alone; friends and family brought in others. Some patients were holding it together; others had vomit on their clothes and were unresponsive.

The authorities were quick to trace the cause back to the coffee shops, and with the cooperation of the island's news stations, island-wide warnings went out within minutes of the discovery.

News teams flocked to coffee shops and emergency rooms to cover the story. The HPD tried to tape off as many coffee shops as they could. The DEA were on the scene once they heard of the symptoms. Homeland Security reacted on the possibility of a terrorist attack. The mayor declared a state of emergency.

It didn't take long for Sweet Maui Brown to become the center of attention nationwide.

The company's logo was all over the news before noon, and the CEO was in full panic-response mode. News teams made it to his house in Maui before he could make it out of the driveway. He gave assurances that his company produced nothing but the finest sugar, and that the Sweet Maui Brown company was in no way connected to the Sweet Maui Brown making headlines across the islands. He said it was obvious that someone copied their packaging, but they had no link whatsoever to any wrongdoing. He was also trying not to shit his pants.

The DEA knew what was in the packets almost immediately, but they withheld this information from the public. If word got out that meth was in packets of Sweet

Maui Brown, they knew junkies would be dumpster-diving behind coffee shops and shoplifting the sugar from island grocery stores.

Unfortunately, not all of the authorities working the case were this forward thinking, and several officers shared their theory with reporters. It wasn't long before all the Sweet Maui Brown was either pulled from the shelves or shoplifted down the pants of some junkie. Those packets all turned up clean, much to the disappointment of the shoplifters.

Nearly every HPD officer on the island was called to work, and Shauna Ikawa was front and center when her lab confirmed that the packets contained crystal methamphetamines. She was also part of the team to discover the differences in the packaging of the Sweet Maui Brown containing meth and the ones containing sugar. It took the team a matter of minutes to determine that the packets were made in a different processing plant. The print was slightly off, and the glue was different, both chemically and in quality.

It didn't take long for the authorities to figure out what happened. Unfortunately, they would never figure out why.

****

Woo Lee watched the news from his barstool in Waikiki. He chose Lulu's for its location directly over the busiest Starbuck's in the area, and because it was directly across from Waikiki Beach. He sat in his ten-dollar aloha shirt and flip-flops, looking like any other Asian tourist.

Woo Lee thought the odds of anyone dying was slim, but when he saw the ambulance take away the woman from Des Moines, he felt some guilt in his stomach. Watching the show unfold was artful, and he enjoyed it immensely, but he didn't want to see any innocent deaths. He was long past that part of his criminal career.

He kept looking at his phone. He kept it on the bar in front of him and hoped Alvaro would call. He liked Alvaro, but business was business, and Woo Lee didn't like the idea of hiding drugs in everyday food products, especially drugs coming from Mexico. He could deal with Alvaro, but not on the scale Alvaro was looking for. He couldn't let Mexican drugs flood the island, and he couldn't make it easy for Mexican drug gangs to take over the territory. Woo Lee felt he had no choice except to scare Alvaro and his men away.

Now Woo Lee had a pang of remorse. Aside from worrying about someone accidentally overdosing, the trust he built with Alvaro was dead, yet he wanted to hear his voice, maybe to explain a little. He wanted to call, but he resisted. He knew they'd speak soon enough.

****

Timmy sat on the picnic table in Kapiolani Park wondering why business slowed down. Things started off on fire. Shortly after Rachel left, a few other regulars came by and bought more than their usual amount. He finally took her advice and raised the price. No one complained. He was proud of his entrepreneurial skills.

Things slowed down a little after eleven, and Timmy was trying to calculate how much he had left. Not much longer and it'd be quitting time. He had a fat wad of money in his pocket and second thoughts about quitting.

He realized he needed a new pair of sunglasses and maybe a new hat. Maybe a Jamba Juice first, and then he could check out some of the surf shops in Waikiki. Maybe a new skateboard. New shoes. A belt. Wallet. Timmy decided he have a little shopping spree.

But first business needed to pick back up. Just a little longer, and he was sure to sell out.

****

Alvaro and Heather watched the news at the Kahala beach house.

"You have to be fucking kidding me." Alvaro slouched in the oversized chair in the living room. His fedora was lower than usual, and he held an empty Hinano in his hand. "You have to be fucking kidding me."

"Alvi, I told you he's not all there. The old gook has lost his mind."

"How the fuck does this even happen? I mean … how? And why?"

"He's fucking crazy."

"Crazy?" Alvaro shook his head, "I don't know about all that, but … what the fuck? Did he really just give all that shit away? I mean … what the fuck? He just pissed it all away? And for what?"

"He's craaaaazy. Are you listening to me?"

Alvaro flipped back and forth from different news channels. He noticed CNN picked up the story. "He's gotta be trying to run us out, that much for sure, but why give the shit away?"

Heather didn't answer. She sat on the edge of the sofa watching the news. She looked at Alvaro. "For him to do this—to mess with you like this—you know he thinks we won't retaliate, right?"

Alvaro tossed the remote on the sofa. He put his empty bottle on the table and headed out to the bar for another. "All right, fuck it. Let's kill him."

Heather couldn't tell if he was serious. The walls to the house were open, connecting the outdoor area to the living room, but Alvaro still used the door in the kitchen. She watched him walk to the tiki bar.

"You want one," he shouted back to Heather.

Heather pointed to her non-existent watch and shouted out to him: "Not even noon, Alvi."

He sat back down with his fresh beer: "Let's do it."

"Kill him?"

"Yeah."

"And his gorilla with the neck tattoo?"

Alvaro took a swig of his beer: "Sure. You want to kill him, or you want me to have one of the boys do it?"

"Just like that, huh? We're going to kill both of them?" Now that she heard it out loud, Heather wasn't so sure. "What about the big boss? What's he going to say?"

"He'll be fine with it, I think." Alvaro nodded back at the television. The reporter held up a packet of Sweet Maui Brown and gave the same warning they'd heard for the last half hour. He leaned back and pulled his fedora over his eyes.

"Alvi, you know we have people selling that shit as we speak, right?"

Alvaro didn't answer.

"Alvi, you hear me? We have people selling this shit all over the island. Think we should get them off the streets?"

Alvaro took a drink of his beer. He still didn't answer.

****

It didn't take long before news of the overflowing emergency room reached the maternity ward at Queen's Medical Center. When Kim Carson first heard Sweet Maui Brown was responsible for the panic, she couldn't have been more furious at Kinu. Her first thought was the briefcase that Kinu gave to his cousin George. How or why George would poison innocent people at coffee shops was beyond her, but if Kinu had done the right thing in the first place, none of this would have happened.

Kim realized her hypocrisy: *If she'd done the right thing, none of this would've happened.*

Kim reminded herself that Kinu was a victim. She knew what happened to him wasn't his fault, but she couldn't help but to place some blame on him for what was happening. She couldn't understand why he hadn't called the police. *Or why she hadn't.*

She went to the emergency room to do what she could to help, and as soon as she found a break, she called the police to report what she knew.

Then she called Kinu.

CHAPTER EIGHTEEN

Saturday 11:30 a.m.

Solo and Matt were heading across the Pali Highway when news of the emergency came across the radio. Dispatch requested all available detectives report to the nearest coffee shop or police station. Solo decided to head to the Starbuck's in Kailua. They were only five minutes away.

"You might want to stay in the car. No need for a sideshow." Two squad cars were already at the scene. Solo pulled in the parking lot and parked in the middle, effectively blocking the entrance. There was a large crowd of foot traffic that stopped to watch. "Keep that hat pulled down."

"Of course."

"We're not staying long. If these guys have it under control, we're moving on."

Solo clipped his badge on his belt and headed over the officers. They had a perimeter set around the store, and he saw two more officers inside.

"Hello, detective," said the officer standing out front.

Solo recognized the man, but couldn't remember his name or see it on his badge. "Aloha, officer. What've you got here?"

"Well, had a few reports of people freaking out, but nothing too serious. It seems most just walked over to the clinic there."

Solo turned back to see the sign for Kailua Medical Clinic. "Ah, well, that's handy. They're open on a Saturday, huh?"

"Yeah, till noon. Good thing this didn't happen after lunch."

"Fortunate, I guess. So, you guys know what it is yet?"

"Some type of drug. Not sure yet. We're only boxing stuff up. Haven't actually opened any packets or seen any of it. We've secured the scene. We were told to box up the sugar and tape everything else off. Guess you guys'll take over, right?"

"Christ, this is going on all over the island, eh? You know how long it'd take to investigate every damn Starbuck's? We don't have the manpower for that." Solo looked inside at the officers collecting all the sugar. "We need to figure out a motive, and then we'll get the jump on it."

The officer and Solo watched the two officers inside the Starbuck's, both trying to process the scope of the situation. Neither had any idea how many coffee shops were on the island, or how many had been hit with the bad sugar, but they both knew this was a shit-storm.

Solo's phone rang. "All right, looks like you guys have this under control. I'm going to take this call and head out."

"Mahalo, detective."

Solo gave a wave to the other officers and answered his phone: "What's up, Jimmy."

"It's Lieutenant Nishi, Solo. Where are you?"

"Kailua. The Starbuck's on Hahani. What's up, boss?"

"We've got a lead on the Sweet Maui Brown. How are you on Danny's case? You get anything this morning?"

"Saw Norman McClintock and Chester Pile this morning. Mr. Pile jumped off a second-floor lanai in order to get out of the conversation. Norman makes good coffee." Solo sat on the hood of his car; Matt sat inside with the window down.

"So Chester Pile, huh? He's the one that still works for Maston Shipping, right?"

"Called in an APB. Figured it'd be easy to get a hit on his truck. But with this shit going on …"

"Well, I need you to follow up on a lead. Head over to Palolo. 342 Paalea Street. His name is Kinu Anapu'ui. We had a call that he was in possession of some of the Sweet Maui Brown. The story is that he found it in the ocean and gave it to a cousin. He checks out clean, but his cousin doesn't."

Solo repeated the number while looking at Matt: "342 Paalea. Kinu Anapu'ui. Got it."

"Are you writing this down?"

"No need. Got a mind like a steel trap."

"I'll text it to you. Solo … this is important. I'm pulling you from whatever this shit is with the coffee shops. Tell me you're not going to stop at Zippy's. Lunch can wait."

Solo pushed off the hood and walked around to the driver's side. "I'm offended, Jimmy. Truly offended."

"Just that we're stretched here. This is a big lead. I'm trusting you with it."

"Now that you mention it, some Spam and eggs sound awfully good."

"Solo."

"Yeah, yeah. Heading directly to 324 Paalea. Nothing to worry about."

"342 Paalea, Solo. I'll text you."

"Yeah, 342. Got it."

"Mahalo, detective Fauatea. Get back to me as soon as you have something."

"Sure thing, boss." Solo hung up and got back into the car. "We're heading back across the Pali," he informed Matt.

"I heard. 342 Paalea. Kinu Anapu'ui. In the Palolo Valley."

"Are you sure it wasn't 324?"

"I'm sure," Matt said. "I guess this is about Danny's murder?"

"You guess right. Sounds like a solid lead. We've got a call that a surfer found some Sweet Maui Brown in the water. He passed it off to his cousin. We need to figure out who that cousin is."

"You know what's in the Sweet Maui Brown?"

"Didn't ask. Sounds like crystal meth or something similar." Solo pulled on the Pali Highway. "That shit is poison. You know what they say about meth?"

"Yeah: 'Not even once.'"

"Bingo. We've got a real problem with that shit on the islands."

"So you think some of these people will turn into addicts?"

"Possibly."

"I don't know," said Matt, "it seems like once isn't enough. You know, if you're not in the type of environment where meth is easily accessible ... like a soccer mom isn't going to drink it once in her latte and then start scoring it in Chinatown."

"You never know. It happens."

Matt wasn't convinced, but he didn't argue. "Yeah, I guess it happens. Any theories on who'd want to do this?"

"Well," Solo said. "That's the million-dollar question."

****

It didn't take long for anonymous tips to come flying in. Many were dead ends. Others were calls from people reporting their neighbors. They wanted the police to follow up, hoping to get some of the scum out of their neighborhood.

Operators politely explained that officers were a little tied up at the moment, but they thanked the callers nonetheless, saying an officer would look into it as soon as one became available.

Police focused on reports of sellers, and after two calls had came in about a young white kid selling Sweet Maui Brown on a picnic table in Kapiolani Park, a patrol car was sent from a Waikiki Starbucks, a short three blocks away.

Officer Mike Hernandez drove down the backside of the park, scanning the large open fields for a match amongst its diverse population. The park had banyan trees scattered about, and there were several areas with picnic tables, all well spaced out from each other.

Officer Hernandez spotted a young man sitting across the park on a picnic table. It was hard to see from the distance, but the kid fit the description. It looked like he had a backpack next to him. Officer Hernandez slowed to take a better look. *Are you really this stupid?*

As he made his way around the park, Officer Hernandez kept one eye on the kid. He also tried to scan the park looking for other people who fit the description. Kapiolani Park was always full of foot-traffic. There were plenty of strolling tourists on the sidewalk, runners jogging on the path, and, of course, homeless people. However, there was only one person who fit the description—only one white kid sitting on a picnic table who looked like he was selling drugs.

Officer Hernandez pulled off to the side of the road for one final scan. He planned to park closer to Kaimana Beach and approach the kid from behind. The park was wide open, and Officer Hernandez had yet to be outrun by any suspect, but this kid was young, so he wanted to get as close as possible before being spotted.

Just as Officer Hernandez began to pull away, he noticed another man coming up on the picnic table from behind. The man was moving fast, and the kid on the table hadn't noticed him yet. The man grabbed the kid by the back of his shirt and pulled him down hard, effectively causing the kid to flip off the back of the picnic table. The man followed up with a hard right fist across the kids face. The kid dropped.

Officer Hernandez punched the gas and hit the lights, but he held off on the sirens. He didn't want to scare them off before he could get in range.

He had to drive around the end of the park and head back in their direction. Due to the banyan trees and the picnic table's location, he lost sight of the two suspects several times. But when he was able to see, all he saw was the kid taking a beating. The man was on top of the kid throwing punches, and then he was standing up, stomping the kid into the ground.

When Officer Hernandez finally arrived, the man stopped beating the kid, grabbed the backpack, and ran. The kid was on the ground, barely moving.

Officer Hernandez was in a full sprint from the moment he was out of his car. He managed to radio dispatch before jumping out, but he couldn't wait for their reply. The man had about a fifty-yard lead, but he'd just spent a great deal of energy beating the shit out the kid, so Officer Hernandez was confident he'd catch him. The kid on the ground didn't look like he was going anywhere. He had blood covering his face and was barely moving.

Officer Hernandez didn't say a word; he broke into a sprint and knew he was going to catch the guy. He felt his knees get high and his back straight. His arms were pumping, and despite his equipment belt flopping around, he felt like a professional sprinter. He knew it was only a matter of time until he closed the distance.

The man running put the stolen backpack on and headed towards Waikiki. He wasn't in the shape he used to be in, but he was still young and felt confident he could outrun a Honolulu cop. If he could just get past the zoo, he would have no trouble blending in with all the tourists in Waikiki. He turned to see how close the cop was.

"HPD! Stop running!" Officer Hernandez was less than twenty yards away. "Give it up, Marco."

"Awe, fuck ..." Marco muttered. He didn't expect the cop to recognize him, and he expected to be gaining ground. He was badly losing this race. He could see the parking lot of the zoo up ahead. If he could make it there, he might have a chance, but in open space, there was no way he'd outrun the cop.

"Marco, stop running."

He looked back again to see if he recognized the cop. As he did, he stumbled just enough for Officer Hernandez to close the distance.

Officer Hernandez was on him seconds later, grabbing him by the backpack. "Face down, hands behind your back." He helped Marco down by yanking his arm while pushing down with a stiff palm to the back. The cuffs were out, and in two swift motions, Marco was cuffed and yanked back to his feet.

"Fuck, man. Do I know you?" Marco asked.

"We went to high school together." Officer Hernandez swung Marco back in the direction of the picnic table. "Let's go."

Marco looked again but couldn't place the big cop. "Hey, um, this bag is the kids. I ... I don't even know what's inside ..."

"Go." Officer Hernandez gave Marco a shove. "Keep walking."

When they got back into sight of the picnic table, they were both surprised to see that Timmy was gone.

"Now whose bag did you say that is?"

"Oh, come on, man. You saw that kid. You had to run right by him."

"I saw you assaulting someone, yes."

"Yeah, we fought, but, hey, this is his bag. Really. I stole it, yes, but I don't know what's inside. That's his shit, not mine."

"You're going to have to tell it to the judge."

"Tell it to the judge? Man, I'm telling you—this ain't my shit."

Officer Hernandez looked around for the kid. He was nowhere in sight. He undid the straps of the backpack and put it on the hood of his squad car before putting Marco in the back. When he looked in the bag, he estimated there were forty or fifty bags of the Sweet Maui Brown. "Marco," he said, putting Marco in the back of the squad car, "you know this puts you in deep shit, right?"

"You saw me steal it, man. How the fuck you going to put that on me? It's the fucking kid's shit. Find that kid. I'll wait—I don't mind."

"What kid? Officer Hernandez asked. "I don't see any kid."

****

Timmy cried behind the trunk of a big banyan tree. He looked at the blood on his hands and felt his face to see where it was coming from. Marco got a good shot directly on his nose, which Timmy thought was broken, and he felt a cut over his left eye. He could also taste blood in his mouth and knew he had a busted lip. There was blood on his shirt and board shorts, and he had a big lump on his head. The pain wasn't bad yet, but the tears wouldn't stop. Timmy was scared.

Although the attack was a blur, Timmy knew his attacker was Marco. He hadn't seen him coming and had no chance to escape, but he had seen Marco's rage as he threw fist after fist at Timmy. It wasn't something he thought would happen, but now the memory of Marco's face and barrage of attacks would be burned into his memory.

Timmy looked out from around the tree and saw the big officer putting Marco in the back of the squad car. He tried to think of what he had in the bag. He knew there was a lot of Sweet Maui Brown in there, but he wondered if there was anything with his name on it. He felt his pocket and was relieved to feel the wad of cash.

As soon as Timmy saw the squad car pull away, he made his way to the public bathroom. There was no mirror inside, and thankfully no homeless people either. Timmy used the sink to rinse off as much blood as he could. He'd have to walk home, and the last thing he wanted was to be stopped by the police for being covered in blood.

After coming out of the bathroom, he took out his cell phone and looked at himself in the camera. His left eye was swollen, his lip was busted, and he had a knot on his temple. He could also feel several small knots on his head and one big one. He was going to be ugly for a while, but he was at least thankful to still have all his teeth. Hopefully, his mom would be out; she wasn't going to take this well.

Timmy had to make it home, grab some money he had stashed, and then head to Frances' to explain what happened. He planned to give Frances the full amount for the day's supply, and then tell him he was out— Timmy no longer wanted to be a drug dealer.

CHAPTER NINETEEN

Saturday 12:30 p.m.

George Anapu'ui stopped by his uncle Kinu's house in the Palolo Valley. After dropping off the briefcase in the alley, he wanted to talk to Kinu about what happened. He knew Kinu would hear about the Sweet Maui Brown on the news, and he wanted to assure him that it wasn't from the briefcase. He didn't want Kinu to feel responsible.

George pulled into Kinu's driveway and parked next to Kinu's little white truck. Before he even got out, a car pulled in behind him. George's heart sank—he could spot an unmarked police car a mile away.

His first thought was that they were there for him; being chased by cops came with the job, but his second thought was that his cousin called them after seeing the Sweet Maui Brown all over the news.

He noticed both men get out of the car behind him. They were slow and casual, and the fat one from the driver's side seemed to take more interest with the house than with George's car. He got out of the car at the same time that Kinu came out of the house. Kinu didn't look happy to see George.

"Hey, cuz," George said. He looked at Matt and Solo. "Who these guys?"

"I'm Detective Fauatea. One of you fellas Kinu Anapu'ui?" Solo didn't introduce Matt.

"I'm Kinu." Kinu hopped down to the lawn and shook Solo's hand. "I talk to you on the phone?"

"No, not me. Did you call the HPD?"

"I did. I saw the news."

George felt a sickness in his stomach. He figured there was no way to outrun Matt, who George recognized from the news. While Matt looked like a jock superstar, George would be lucky to make it two blocks without running out of breath.

Kinu began to explain: "I saw the Sweet Maui Brown a couple of days ago. I found a briefcase full of it. Put some in my coffee and ended up at Queen's. Gave a police officer a statement there, but he thought maybe it was the coffee from Aloha Mart. Or maybe he thought I was just a junkie."

George moved near the stairs.

"Didn't think it might've been the sugar."

"Where'd you find it?" Solo asked.

"Off Diamond Head. Was paddling out. It was just floating there."

"Hey, gonna use your toilet, uncle," George said. He moved towards the door and heard Solo's next question just before it closed behind him.

"So where's the briefcase now, Mr. Anapu'ui?"

Kinu looked at the ground and scratched the back of his head. "I don't have it anymore."

"Yeah?" Solo said.

"Yeah." Kinu looked back at his door.

It took Matt a second to register what Kinu meant, but he caught it a split second faster than Solo, who understood at the same time that Matt began a sprint around the side of the house. Kinu's backyard was separated from his neighbor's by a waist-high chain-link fence, which Matt hurdled with ease. He expected another chase like this morning when Chester Pile gave him the slip, and the last thing he wanted was to lose another suspect.

As Matt expected, George tried to sneak out the back. He caught sight of George rounding the corner just over the far side of the fence. With another hurdle over the back fence, Matt knew he wasn't going to lose him. George saw him coming and turned back just in time to run face-first into a clothesline, effectively stopping him in his tracks and putting him on his back.

"I think we've got a few questions for you," Matt said.

George was breathing heavily on the ground. He held his face where the clothesline hit him, mumbling a few obscenities. He made it to his feet and didn't put up any resistance. He knew there was no way to outrun Matt.

Matt knew it too. He walked George around the fence, leading him back to Solo, who had a bead of sweat across his forehead despite making no effort to help in the chase.

Matt waved off Solo. "I got him. No, really, you just wait there. No problem."

Solo ignored him. He looked at George. "Why'd you run?"

George was still rubbing the spot where the clothesline hit him. "Because I know why you're here."

Solo laid out their options: "I'll be honest with you guys. This Sweet Maui Brown is the biggest story to hit the islands since the tsunami hit Hilo in 1960. People have died. And what leads do the Honolulu Police Department have? I'm looking at 'em. You two are all we've got."

George glanced at Kinu.

"I take you both to the station right now, or you give me a reason not to."

"If you've got something, tell 'em," Kinu said. George had a police record for selling weed, and Kinu was worried there were other things that the police would be better off not knowing.

George looked at the ground, trying to buy time.

"You know what's going on across the island?" Solo asked. "Right now you and your uncle here are the main suspects. You don't look the mastermind to me, but if you two are all I've got ..."

"Kinu had nothing to do with it." Under normal circumstances, George would have kept his mouth shut, but he couldn't let his uncle take the fall. "I got rid of the briefcase he gave me. I ditched it in an alley over in Kaka'ako."

"And?" Solo asked. "You know ... you ran from us. That tells me something. You don't run if all you did was ditch a briefcase your uncle found in the ocean. Nope, that doesn't make much sense, does it?"

George shrugged. "I ... a ... I don't know ..."

"Suppose we find that briefcase with both of your prints all over it? Or maybe a CCTV feed of you dumping it? Or here's an idea: I could get both of your photos on the news. Maybe we'd get a witness. Maybe those photos make the national news ..."

"And if I talk now? I'm not saying I do know something, but if I do?" George asked. "What then?"

"Depends on what you've got for me. Seems worth a shot. Save us all some time."

George didn't like his chances either way. "Okay, what the hell. Better here than in some police station. What I told you was true—I really did ditch the briefcase in an alley."

Solo shook his head. "And?"

"The reason I ditched it was because I heard about what was going to happen today at the coffee shops."

"All right. Now we're talking," said Solo. "Keep going."

"Now, I just heard about this," George lied. "I hear rumors, so …"

"Just rumors. Got it."

"So, what, if I give you a name, you'll let me get in my car and go?"

Solo wiped the sweat from his head with the back of his hand. "That probably depends on the name."

"It's a big name. The guy running the show." George said. "At least, that's what I heard."

"Fine. If I like the name, we've got a deal."

George didn't hesitate: "His name is Woo Lee. Korean guy. He …"

Solo cut him off: "And how do you know this?"

"Hey, like I said, I hear things. And that's the name I heard. That was the deal. I know this because I know this, and if you tell him I told you this … I'm in deep shit."

Solo looked at Matt, and then he said to Kinu: "Mr. Anapu'ui, thank you for your cooperation today. George, you got a driver's license on you?" Solo took a picture of both George's driver's license and license plate. "You know if I don't get anywhere with your information, I'm coming back for you, right?"

"Yeah, I figured already. Just keep my name out of it and I'm good."

"Take care, fellas." Solo nodded for Matt to get in the car. He needed to tell him a little about Woo Lee.

****

Chester Pile tried desperately to contact Heather Brown. He called her phone and sent text messages repeatedly.

Chester cut his left foot and scratched up his legs when he jumped off of his lanai. It wasn't the first time Chester jumped into the bushes, but it was the first time he did it without looking first. He had slowly dropped himself off the lanai a couple of times last year when an ex-wife showed up at his door yelling for child support. He hurt himself worse than he expected, but he considered the cuts and bruises better than jail. At least at the moment.

He needed to talk to Heather.

When she finally called him back, Chester was sitting in his truck outside a liquor store in Waikiki. He had a half-empty pint of Jack Daniel's in one hand and a cigarette in the other.

"What's the problem, Chet?"

"Cops." Chester took a swig from the bottle. "Cops. They came to my apartment. Two of them. They asked about you."

Heather wasn't expecting this. "Cops?"

"Yeah, detectives."

"Well, what happened? What'd you tell them?"

"Why are cops coming to my apartment?"

"Fuck if I know." There was urgency in Heather's voice. "What'd you tell them?"

"This is really freaking me out. Why would they show up at my place? Something happen?" Chester took another hit from the bottle.

"Chester! What the fuck did you tell them?"

"I didn't tell them shit. The fat one came in and sat down in my living room. He asked me a couple of question. Asked if I knew you."

"And what did you say?"

"I think I told him we worked together. I don't know exactly. I panicked."

"Jesus. What else? What else did you tell him?"

"Nothing. I got nervous, so I ran. Jumped off of my balcony."

"For fuck's sake, Chet." Heather saw her plan crumbling. Her value to Alvaro was her ability to move product. She was good at it on the mainland, and now, almost immediately after the first major shipment to Hawaii, she was running into a major fuck-up.

"What should I do?" Chester asked.

"We need to meet. Can you be at Kahala Shopping Mall in thirty minutes?"

"Yeah, no problem."

"Second-floor parking garage. Park near the south end. Find a spot without many cars around."

"I'll be there in fifteen minutes."

"I know your truck. I'll find you."

Heather hung up and thought about how she'd get out of the house. She couldn't tell Alvaro about the detectives showing up at Chester's apartment, so there was no way she could tell him where she was going. She looked out the window and saw him drinking a Hinano with his shirt off and feet in the pool.

She went outside.

"Ho, howz it, sistah?" he said in an over-exaggerated local accent. "Put on your bikini and join me, you one sexy wahine." He pulled his sunglasses down as he said this, showing her his big brown eyes.

"You're going to get fat drinking all those beers."

Alvaro looked down at his stomach. He flexed. "I did three-hundred push-ups and four-hundred crunches today. I earned these beers."

"Proud of that, huh? You want a cookie?"

"Come on. Join us."

Heather looked at Maverick and Goose, who were sitting at the table under the umbrella. Both were looking at their phones. "I'm going to take a nap. Maybe you and your yahoos can keep it down?"

Alvaro pushed his sunglasses back up: "Suit yourself. You're the one wasting away this beautiful Hawaiian day."

She went back to the room she was sleeping in and left a note. She said she decided to go for a drive instead. He'd be pissed, but at least he wouldn't worry as much. She hoped she could meet Chester and be back before Alvaro even noticed she was gone.

She snuck out the front door and out the gate with no trouble.

Chester was already there. She pulled in next to him and got in the truck. She carried her purse with her. A quick scan of the parking lot revealed no surveillance cameras and very few people. Even on a Saturday, this part of the parking lot rarely got used.

"Jesus, are you drinking?"

Chester just shrugged.

She noticed the scrapes on his legs and bloody towel on the floorboard. She also noticed Chester was wearing cut-off jean shorts and a t-shirt that said "Bush-Cheney." She shook her head: "It's like you fell right out of the trailer park."

Chester shrugged again and took a drink. Heather could tell the bottle was almost empty.

She kicked the towel and trash away on the floorboard and set her purse between her legs. "Okay, tell me exactly what happened."

Chester repeated what he told her on the phone.

"What did these cops look like?"

"The one that came into my apartment was kinda fat and balding on top. He looked Polynesian—Hawaiian or Samoan or something. The other one didn't come inside. He stood at the door. Had a hat on and sunglasses. Big guy. He's the one that I watched go flying by when I was hiding in the garage. That motherfucker could move, I tell you."

"So to recap: the fat one asked you if you'd talked to me lately, you jumped off of your lanai to get away, and now you're here? That's all of it?"

"That's right."

"That ... doesn't sound so bad." Heather looked down at her purse. There was an empty Busch Light can that must have rolled out from under the seat. "Christ, do you ever clean this thing?"

Chester finished his pint of Jack and shoved it under his seat. "Uh, yeah, sometimes." He lit a cigarette. "So what happens now? What do I do?"

"Who did you get to help you with the shipment? You know, the person who actually got the drugs in the shipping container."

Chester shook his head. "Hey, I don't know … I don't think I should be giving you that info, you know? I mean, that's not something I think I should be sharing."

"Listen, Chet, I gave you a lot of money up front to make this shit happen, and now I want to know if any other assholes are going to be getting questioned by the cops. The last thing I need is to be blindsided by some ass-clown shitting his pants in LA and leaking my name."

Chester's cigarette hung on his lip, looking like it was going to fall out of his mouth, only to swing vertically with a large inhale. "I never used your name. Really, I didn't."

"Who'd you use, Chet? Who'd you get to help?"

"Awe, come on, man."

"Remember those guys I was with the other day? Big guys, right?"

Chester took his cigarette out of his mouth and ran his fingers through his hair. "Yeah, I remember."

"Well, you tell me, or you tell them. Your choice."

"Come on, man—Heather. I mean, you said it wouldn't come to this. You said I do my thing with my people, and you do your thing with your people, right? This … I don't know, man."

"Cops are involved, Chet. Now we all need to work together, right? You're going to need our protection, right? We're a team, right?"

"Yeah, shit, man, I guess so."

"So let's have it. Who you working with? Who's on the other end?"

Chester told her the name: Scott Combs. It was a guy Heather knew from her days at Maston Shipping, and she wasn't surprised.

"Thanks, Chet."

"So what do I do? If I go home, they're going to find me, right? They'll just come back, and what the hell would I tell them? Should I just—"

She cut him off: "Don't worry, Chet. Just let me think for a second."

Heather leaned down and looked hard out Chester's side of the truck. It was a trick she'd been pulling since she was a kid. She still used it to steal food all the time. Her secret was in not telling the person to look. If she looked hard enough and interested enough, the other person would always turn to see what she was looking at. She sold it every time.

When Chester turned to look, Heather grabbed the knife from her purse. She brought it up as fast as she could and got Chester right in the neck. Blood started spraying all over the truck. Chester reached for the wound, but Heather kept pressure on the knife, twisting it up towards his jaw. The blood sprayed on her, covering her hand and leaving spray patterns on her shirt. Chester slumped into his seat, his blood drained along with his life.

Heather never thought about the blood. She pictured the knife going in and blood running down his neck, never considering that it might spray. She cursed herself for the lack of foresight, pulling the knife from Chester's neck.

She looked at the bloody towel on the floor and hesitated to use it. Her thought was of the possible diseases Chester might have, but then she realized she was already covered in his blood. She took the towel and wiped off her hands and arms the best she could.

Heather scanned the parking lot to make sure nobody was near, and then she used the towel to open the door. She grabbed her purse, closed the door, and wiped down the truck handle the best she could. She quickly got back into her SUV.

She worked more blood off of her hands with the towel in order to keep the blood off the steering wheel and upholstery. When she looked in the rearview mirror to back out, she noticed blood on her face, which she tried to wipe away as she drove out of the parking lot. She kept the bloody towel on her lap.

After ditching the towel and knife in a trash can at the edge of a beach access point, Heather headed back to the Kahala beach house. The trashcan wasn't too far from the house, but it was a popular access point, and Heather figured there would be lots of empty beer bottles and trash thrown on top before it was picked up and taken to the city dump, or wherever trash ended up. She wiped the knife and didn't think there would be any trace of evidence linking her to the murder.

Heather snuck back into the beach house undetected. The guys were still out by the pool, so she tore up the note she left, rinsed off in the shower, and got into bed. She figured she could still take that nap.

****

Timmy's mom wasn't home when he got back to their apartment. He took off his clothes, stuffed his bloody shirt in the trash, and then he washed his face. His eye had gotten worse than it looked at the park. It was almost completely swollen shut, but after clearing away the dried blood, he didn't think he looked too bad. The cut above his eye that bled so much didn't look nearly as bad as he expected.

He looked at his phone. There were several missed calls from his mom, but he didn't want to deal with her now. He still hadn't worked out the lie he'd tell her— probably something about a couple of homeless guys jumping him for his backpack. He'd keep it simple.

He couldn't erase the image of Marco throwing punches. The more the image flashed in his head, the clearer it became. It even slowed down, each punch clearly making its way at his head. Marco's face was right between the fists. His hollowed eyes, wrinkled forehead, and look of pure rage burned in Timmy's memory.

It wasn't Timmy's first fight, but it was Timmy's first ass-beating. If it were a classmate or some kid Timmy's age, that would've been different, but it was a guy years older, much scarier, and from a world Timmy no longer wanted any part of.

And then there was the police officer.

Timmy saw the officer running from his patrol car. If Marco wouldn't have grabbed Timmy's backpack, and if the chase didn't last as long, Timmy could've been caught with all those drugs. He barely made it to a hiding place as it was, and if the officer had spent any time looking, Timmy's whole world would be quite different.

The realization of how lucky he'd been was sinking in as Timmy heard the front door open. He heard a man's voice, which was strange because although Timmy knew his mom was dating, she'd never brought a man back to their apartment since they'd moved to Hawaii.

Timmy felt a wave of panic. He looked around the bathroom, considering if there was somewhere he could hide. The shower was glass, so that was out. He looked under the sink, but there was no way he'd fit. He was trapped.

Somehow the police must have figured out his identity. There must have been something in the backpack with his name on it, or maybe someone saw him leaving the park and reported him. He froze and listened as carefully as he could.

The man's voice was soft, and Timmy couldn't make out the words. He realized that police couldn't just let themselves into an apartment, so maybe it was his mom's new boyfriend. He cracked the door as slowly and quietly as possible and listened.

"I'll get you some water," the man said.

"Thank you," said Timmy's mom.

When Timmy heard his mom's voice, the relief felt like a warm blanket wrapped around him, taking away all the bumps and bruises from Marco's fists. It must be her boyfriend.

"You just sit there and try to take it easy. Watch a movie or something. I'll try to come back later tonight. You'll be fine. You just need to take it easy."

Timmy heard his mom say something but couldn't make out the words.

The man said, "If I didn't have to go, you know I'd stay here and take care of you. I hate to leave you like this."

Timmy heard the door close and the television come on. The man must have left.

Timmy's shirt was buried in the trash and his shorts were on the floor in his room. He stood in the bathroom with a towel around his waist and thought about what to do.

As quietly as he could, Timmy slowly opened the door and began to sneak out of the bathroom. If his mom was watching television, there was a good chance she wouldn't see him come into the hallway and walk down to his room. Unfortunately, Timmy wasn't that lucky.

"Timmy, where have you been? I've been trying to call you." Her voice was different. "Come in here."

Timmy headed for his room. "Sorry, mom. Have to get dressed," he shouted.

Timmy got dressed and looked at his face once more in the mirror. Since cleaning himself up, his face really didn't look too bad. The swollen eye was ugly, and Timmy guessed it would turn nice and purple soon, but besides that, it wasn't as bad as it felt.

"Mom," Timmy said, "sorry I didn't call you back, but …"

She cut him off. "Good Lord, what happened? Your eye? What happened?" Her voice was much sharper than Timmy expected, as was her demeanor. She stood up in one motion, like a spring popped in her spine.

"Mom, are you okay?" Timmy could tell she wasn't.

"What happened to that eye? Did you get into a fight?" She grabbed him by the shoulders and moved her head in for a closer view.

"Yeah, it's no big deal. What's wrong with you? You're acting weird."

"I had some of that Sweet Maui Brown," she said flatly.

Timmy's heart sank.

"Did you get in a fight?" she asked.

"What? You had what?" He couldn't understand her.

Her sentences came in rapid bursts. "Did you see it on the news? Dave said it's an upper. I'll be fine. What happened to your eye?"

Timmy looked at the television and noticed what she was watching.

Yes, the officer was saying, *we have all coffee shops on the island closed, and we've requested all the Sweet Maui Brown be pulled from grocery stores and markets on the island, as well as any restaurants using the sugar. It's important to note that although there have been no reports of incidents anywhere other than coffee shops, we're not taking any chances.*

Timmy looked back at his mom. "What happened?"

"I was with Dave. After we had hiked Koko Crater, we stopped at Starbucks. I put a sugar in my coffee, and then I started to feel ... different." She smiled. "Thank God Dave was there, or I don't know what I would've done."

Timmy didn't fully comprehend what happened. He sat at the end of the sofa and watched the news.

"Dave said it's a type of upper. I need to relax. I'm just going to stay here. I'm not going to move. I'm just going to stay right here on this sofa. I need to relax. I'm not going to move. Just stay right here."

Timmy tried to listen to the news through her ramblings. He knew his mom was on meth. He prayed he wasn't somehow responsible.

She sat next to him on the sofa and reached for his swollen eye. "Timmy? Timmy, your face? What happened to your face?"

CHAPTER TWENTY

Saturday 2:00 p.m.

Solo drove down Kapiolani Boulevard. He was taking Matt to Chinatown for a little stake-out.

"So who's this Woo Lee guy?" Matt asked.

"This Woo Lee guy ... he's a legend. He's a Korean gangster from the old days. He has a few legitimate businesses, but he's been on our radar several times over the past decade. Nothing has ever stuck to the guy, but he's all kinds of dirty."

"On the radar for what?"

"Running brothels. Selling drugs. Murder. There's probably more that I don't know about." Solo took a left onto Piikoi Street. "And I say he's a bit of a legend because nothing sticks. That's how everyone knows him." He turned right onto Ala Moana Boulevard, passing a taped-off Starbucks with two patrol cars in front.

Matt noticed a news van in the parking lot near the Starbucks. "You think he'd pull something like this? Seems a little ... I don't know."

216

"Well, Woo Lee also has a reputation for being a little more than eccentric. I know first hand. About—I don't know—five, seven years ago, there was a double homicide in Waikiki. Two guys from the Ukraine. They were both shot in the head. Woo Lee was a suspect."

"And you worked it?"

"Yeah. Questioned him a couple of times. He never asked for a lawyer, and he never gave up anything. He just smiled, and he talked in a very broken local accent, or at least he tried." Solo entered the downtown business district, driving past the Aloha Tower Marketplace. "Never could put the pieces together. That's one case we couldn't close. I'm sure there are other stories just like it. Rumor has it the DEA has staked him out several times, but he always comes up clean."

"The murdered Ukrainian guys, were they dealing drugs?"

"Nah. They were pimps. They smuggled in Eastern European girls who would walk the streets or work in massage parlors. If you walk the right streets of Waikiki late at night, you can still see it going on. That's been going on since ... I don't know ... as long as I can remember. The Eastern Europeans arrived maybe fifteen years ago. Tourists seem to like that look better than the Asian girls. The Asians are in this area and over behind the Walmart on Keeaumoku. Actually, Woo Lee owns a place over there. The Dreamy Aloha, if I remember correctly." Solo turned onto Maunakea Street, right into the heart of Chinatown.

"When I was going to UH, rumor was the prostitutes down here were all transvestites."

"Yeah, that's kind of true. The girls downtown, over in the business district, they're usually trannies. That's a few blocks over. Here, there's a mixed bag. Lots of homeless and addicts around. Also a lot of massage parlors and back-room brothels. As soon as the sun goes down, this is not a good place to be. There're all kinds." Solo circled the block looking for street parking.

"But this is a nice place during the day, right? Good dim sum and the cheapest leis in Honolulu. Do tourists still come down here?"

"Yeah, sure. In the daytime it's great." Solo pulled into a parking spot in front of a closed Chinese herb shop. About half the businesses in Chinatown closed on the weekends, but most of the restaurants and flower shops were open. "You see that Chinese restaurant up past Lucy's Flowers? That's Woo Lee's."

Matt looked at the neon sign hanging out over the sidewalk: Woo Tan Fan. The first letters of each word were out, so it lit up: oo an an. There were only a few people on the street: two homeless and one old lady carrying some grocery bags.

"It's a shithole," said Solo, nodding at the restaurant. "I think the only people who go there are lost tourists." He took his phone out and went through his photos, finally finding one of Woo Lee. He handed the phone to Matt.

Matt saw an older Korean guy with a big grin throwing up a shaka with both hands. "Looks kind of local."

Solo shook his head. "He posed for that. Knew we were taking pictures of him. I'm going to take—" He stopped mid-sentence. "You see what I see?"

Matt saw a large white guy exit the restaurant and walk their way. It was obvious: "The man with the neck tattoo," Matt said.

"The man with the neck tattoo," Solo repeated. "Give me that phone back."

****

Woo Lee sat in the back office in his Chinese restaurant. He watched the news.

Deb Johnson put three Sweet Maui Browns in her coffee, two of which were filled with what we believe were crystal methamphetamines. By the time she finished, she was lying in her own vomit. Sixty-four years old and on prescription medicine for her heart, she went into cardiac arrest. She was pronounced dead at 11:58 A.M. Her husband watched in horror as Mrs. Johnson died on the sidewalk outside of this coffee shop. Rescue teams were simply too overwhelmed to reach her in time.

The reporter stood in front of a Starbucks. Woo Lee recognized it as the one at Ward Center, just behind Ala Moana Beach Park. He was there the other day with the woman from his lawn bowling club. They cut to a clip of Deb's husband, who mumbled something about celebrating their fortieth wedding anniversary.

Deb Johnson was just one of the many tragic stories from today. More stories, sadly, continue to come in from across the island.

Woo Lee didn't want to hear more, but he couldn't pull his eyes away from the screen.

Esteban Rivera was on vacation with his wife and three children. He put two Sweet Maui Browns in his coffee, and two packets in his ten-year-old son's iced tea. According to Mrs. Rivera, Esteban, a former drug user, had been clean for seven years, but he knew the rush when it started to come on. Mrs. Rivera said her husband smacked the drink out of her son's hand, instinctively knowing something wasn't right, but it was too late. Now Esteban and his young son are recovering at Queen's Hospital. There's no way to know the effects this will have on Esteban's life, nor that of his son's.

A photo of the Rivera family was on the television. They were at the Polynesian Cultural Center. Their son was behind one of the cardboard cutouts of a Hawaiian warrior, his head sticking through the cutout for the face, with his mom and dad on both sides. Mr. Rivera was smiling on top of the body of a hula dancer. Mrs. Rivera must have provided the photo.

For the Rivera family, what was a dream vacation has now turned into a nightmare.

Woo Lee knew he made a mistake. He underestimated the amount of sugar parents gave their children, and he underestimated the emotional pull of seeing a ten-year-old boy's picture on the news. A boy Woo Lee knew he was responsible for poisoning.

And then there's the story of young Isabelle Cooper. A photo of a smiling toddler was on the screen. *Isabelle is the youngest victim we know of so far. At only four years old, Isabelle's mother bought her a small iced coffee at the Honolulu Café, located in the lobby of the Halekulani Hotel. It's unknown how many packets of the Sweet Maui Brown Isabelle added to her coffee, but what we do know is that young Isabelle is lucky to be alive.*

Woo Lee didn't know four-year-olds drank coffee. He changed to CNN.

That's right, Wolf. They were going to the movies for little Jessica's seventh birthday party. The mom took the kids to Starbucks for a quick treat before the—"

Woo Lee turned off the television. He didn't want to hear any more.

"I think that kills the Sweet Maui Brown game," Sasha said. He sat on the small sofa in Woo Lee's office. Woo Lee sat behind his desk, reclining in his leather chair.

Woo Lee turned the television back on. There was a different reporter on the screen with the words "Breaking News" at both the top and bottom of the screen.

We have reports that Homeland Security is considering this a terrorist act, but we cannot get confirmation, and so far, they have not released any theories on a possible motive. What we do know is that security is tight here in Honolulu.

"Terrorist act? Psst." Woo Lee turned off the television again. "CNN, huh? You watch this?"

"I don't watch much news," Sasha admitted. "It's depressing."

"We had a few ... what's the word? I studied. You know, people dead."

"Deaths? Victims? Casualties?"

"Casuarties! That's it. Cas-u-ar-ties." Woo Lee tried to sound it out. "Children cas-u-ar-ties too. Why do mother and father give children sugar? And children drink coffee? Did you know this?"

"We talked about this, remember? I told you it was possible. Parents suck. They give their little shits anything they want. That's why this country is full of fat-asses."

Woo Lee leaned back in his chair and put his hands on his belly. "Yeah, well, you did say to me, yes, but ... anyway ... I guess it's done." Woo Lee pulled an envelope out of his desk drawer and tossed it at Sasha.

Sasha opened the envelope and thumbed the money. "You are very welcome. You think it's enough to run off your little Mexican buddy?"

Woo Lee turned the television back on. "I think so."

"What's next?"

"You bought the plane ticket?"

"Yeah. I fly out in the morning."

"Well, that's what next. When you get to Mexico, don't call me. I'll call you."

****

"There he is. Don't make a move," Solo said to Matt. They watched Sasha come out of Woo Lee's restaurant. He was walking their way. Solo snapped as many pictures as he could.

"We going?" asked Matt. "I don't think he spotted us."

"Wait." Solo let the man gain a little distance. "Slowly. And follow me. Nothing stupid. We just want to see where he goes."

Solo got out of the car and crossed the street. Matt followed.

The man with the neck tattoo glanced over his shoulder and then crossed the street back to the side where Solo parked, about forty yards ahead. He turned left at the next street, heading for downtown.

Solo and Matt crossed the street, and when they turned the corner, they saw the man running.

"I said nothing stupid," Solo shouted at Matt, but Matt was already in a full sprint.

****

Sasha ran. The cop car was easy to spot, and when he saw two men sitting inside, he knew better than to walk to his apartment.

He crossed the street and saw them get out of the car heading his way, so as soon as he was around the corner, he took off.

He wasn't sure they'd follow, but just before darting up the next street, he looked back. He saw the fat one turning to wobble back to the car, and the other one, the tall younger guy, was sprinting his way.

As soon as he turned, he knew he went the wrong way. The fat cop might be able to get in the car fast enough to head him off, but if he turned back, he'd run right into the other cop. He had the envelope full of money squished into his pants pocket and secured with one hand as he ran, and his gun concealed under his oversized aloha shirt. He'd use the gun if he had to, but shooting a cop was the last thing he wanted to do.

Sasha's body wasn't built for running. He was big and thick, and he knew he wouldn't last long lumbering through the streets. The streets were too quiet, and too many businesses were closed for him to try to blend in and hide somewhere, not that he'd have much luck, considering his size.

He stopped, turned back and lined up an angle about five yards from the corner. He dropped into a football stance, bending at the hips and knees and putting one hand on the ground.

Matt was running fast. He had to slow down a bit for the corner, but he rounded it without losing much momentum.

As soon as he was in Sasha's sight, the big man exploded from his three-point stance and drove at Matt, driving his shoulder into Matt's chest. The impact lifted Matt clear off of his feet, causing him to go vertical and crash down hard on the concrete sidewalk, jarring his hat and sunglasses clear off his head. Sasha landed on top.

An old lady across the street dropped her bag at the sound of the impact.

Sasha caught Matt totally by surprise. He quickly straddled Matt, throwing punches at his face. Matt, who had the wind knocked out of him and was dazed by the impact, struggled to block. One of Sasha's blows hit Matt with enough force that Matt's head bounced against the sidewalk. Sasha hopped off. He pulled his gun and pointed it at Matt. Matt rolled over and kept his hands over his head, dazed and expecting another blow; he never saw the gun.

Sasha looked up the street and saw no sign of the cop car coming his way. He looked back at Matt, the gun still pointed at Matt's head. Matt had one hand on the pavement and the other on his chest. He was trying to get up.

Sasha lowered the gun and ran back the way he'd came.

****

Matt tried to follow. He struggled to get to his feet and immediately stumbled, catching himself on a car parked near the corner. He took a few more steps before falling to the ground.

Solo circled the block in the direction they were heading, but because of the change of course and combination of one-way streets and traffic, it took him too long to get back to Matt. By the time he found him, Matt was sitting on the hood of a sedan with his head back and pinching his nose together. Solo could see the blood.

Solo double-parked next to the sedan. "Looks like you caught up to him."

"Other way around." Matt's eye was already swollen and his lip was busted. "He laid me out as I came around the corner. It was like running into a train."

"I thought I told you nothing stupid." Solo handed Matt a handkerchief. "That eye looks bad. You still got all your teeth?"

Matt ran his tongue around his mouth to check. "Feels like it." He spat out some blood.

"Well, I'm glad he didn't shoot you." Solo bent down and picked up Matt's broken sunglasses, which were beyond repair. "Think of the paperwork."

"Thanks."

Solo's phone rang. "Detective Fauatea, at your service … Yeah … Yeah … Got it." He hung up.

Matt shoved two pieces of tissue up his nose to stop the bleeding.

"Good news. We've found Chester Pile."

"Great."

"Well, not so great really. The bad news is he's dead. Found him in is truck over at Kahala Shopping Mall. Stabbed in the neck."

"Holy shit!"

"We'll go check it out. I can give these photos of your friend with the neck tattoo to one of the CSIs there. Save me a trip to the station."

Matt wanted to ask if Shauna was the CSI. "What about this Woo Lee guy? Are we going to talk to him first?"

"Nah. Chester first. I have a feeling Woo Lee wouldn't be available." Solo looked at his watch. "Maybe Chester, dinner, and then Woo Lee."

CHAPTER TWENTY-ONE

Saturday 4:00 p.m.

Four o'clock in the afternoon and stories of Sweet Maui Brown still dominated the news. Reports continued to come in of people who put the sugar in their drink. There were tourists, locals, family members of politicians, kids, adults, law enforcement officers, and even an actor with a minor role on *Hawaii Five-0*. The most dramatic reports always started with a crying family member and a photo of the victim. Reporters on all channels were starting with a back-story and milking the drama before finally revealing the victim's condition, keeping viewers in suspense of whether or not the story would end in death, which it rarely did.

Speculation varied. Most news channels were focused on the likelihood of a terrorist attack, but they gave some consideration to other possibilities. Fox News questioned the possibility of the company being a front for the organized production of drugs.

News agencies were desperate for the story. Reporters flew out on the first flights to the island as soon as the story broke, but at over five hours from the west coast, most stations were unable to get their people to the Hawaii fast enough, which made them turn to local reporters.

Cub reporter Amy Ito and intern cameraman Justin Bush received the assignment to "find a story." Amy, a recent graduate of UH-Manoa, started working with KHNT News Channel 4 less than a month ago. It was the least desirable news channel on her wish list, but she knew she was lucky to get the offer. So far, her main contribution to the News Channel 4 team was her ability to fix the copy machine.

Justin had been working for the news channel since the beginning of the year. His internship period was just about over, and he knew he had no chance of getting a full-time job with the station.

"Waikiki," Amy ordered as soon as they got the assignment. "That's where the story's at." She knew tragedy meant opportunity, and she had high hopes to hit the jackpot. She needed it. She knew it took a crisis for her boss to send her into the field. This opportunity didn't happen very often.

Justin was more realistic. "There won't be any parking," he told her.

Justin drove. They went up and down the streets of Waikiki looking for signs of drama. "We need ambulances and police cars. That's where the story'll be," Amy said.

"There's too much traffic. And you'll have to pay for parking. I don't get paid for this, you know?" Justin replied.

They passed several coffee shops with police cars in front, and they saw some ambulances, but by the time they got out of Justin's truck and got to the scene, they either couldn't find much of a story or there was already another news team there.

Amy Ito's dream to find the big story faded, and she was just hoping for something good enough to get her on air. Everyone she talked to had the same boring story, and without something big, she knew she'd never get airtime over the veteran reporters. Justin was sweating, and she knew he was tired of lugging the camera from block to block.

"Let's get out of Waikiki," she suggested.

"Thank the Lord," said Justin. "How about we go somewhere with good parking, and air conditioning." And with this suggestion, Amy Ito and Justin Bush decided to go to Kahala Shopping Mall.

After cruising around the mall and seeing little action, Amy spotted a lone police cruiser on the second floor of the parking garage. Justin wanted to give up and just turn in the shitty footage they got in Waikiki. He suggested they go to Cold Stone for some ice cream. It took some arm-twisting by Amy, but she convinced Justin it'd be worth checking out. "Then we'll get you some ice cream," said Amy.

When they pulled onto the second floor, they could see the patrol car parked as far away from the mall as possible. It was angled behind a red truck, both about forty yards from other cars. The police officer they saw from the road was sitting on the hood, and when they approached, he casually waved them away. Through the window of Justin's car, the officer thought they looked like a young couple looking for a parking spot.

Amy hopped out. "What happened?"

The police officer wasn't ready for this. In his most official voice, he said, "Nothing to see here, young lady.

Find another place to park." Since arriving on the scene, the officer hadn't seen another person in the area except mall security.

"My name is Amy Ito, reporter for KHNT News Channel 4." Amy had her interview-voice going before Justin had the truck in park. "Does this have something to do with the Sweet Maui Brown?"

"Shit," the officer said, hopping off the hood of his patrol car. "Um, no ... not exactly." He positioned himself in the best way to stop Amy from seeing inside the truck. The windows were tinted, but from the side of the truck, it wasn't hard to see the man slouched against the driver's side window. A few steps closer, and she'd probably be able to figure out there was blood splatter on the windows as well.

Justin got out of his car. "Should I get the camera?" he asked Amy.

****

When Solo and Matt drove up the ramp to the second floor of the Kahala Shopping Mall's parking garage, they saw a police officer standing with his arms crossed staring straight ahead. Next to the officer they saw a woman with a microphone. She seemed to be pleading with the officer. About ten yards away there was a camera set up on a tripod.

"Are those kids?" asked Solo. "That girl looks about twelve."

"Campus news team, perhaps?" Matt answered.

The officer noticed Solo's car first, and a look of relief came across his face. Amy and Justin noticed. Amy saw the car approaching and nodded for Justin. He turned the camera in the direction of where Solo was pulling in.

Solo let out a grunt. He looked at Matt, who held a bag of ice on his swollen eye and had fresh blood on his busted lip. "Well, Superhero Jesus, how are we going to hide you this time?"

"I'll keep my hat pulled down. If you do the talking, maybe they won't notice me."

"Right," said Solo.

Amy stood next to Solo's door, waiting to question him as soon as he got out of the car. She stood erect and looked into the camera. She started before Solo was all the way out: "This is Amy Ito for KHNT4, here at Kahala Shopping Mall where there appears to have been a murder or possible suicide." She turned to Solo, "Officer, what can you tell us about what happened here?"

Solo looked at Amy Ito and then at the officer on the scene.

The officer held his hands out: "Sorry, Detective. I tried to keep them back."

Solo looked at Amy. He shut his door a little harder than necessary. "Amy Ito, for KHNT4, I haven't got a fucking clue. Didn't you see me just get out of my car?"

Amy flinched, but she powered through: "There appears to be a lot of blood in the cab of the truck. Do you suspect foul play?"

"Foul play?" Solo looked at the truck. "Nah, I suspect it was a tickling match that got out of hand." Solo shook his head. "Didn't you see me just get out of my car? Just now. I literally just got out of my car. How the fuck do I know what happened?"

Matt was out of the car and walking behind the camera, making his way around to the side of the truck. He had his hat pulled down and tried to avoid eye contact, yet he watched Amy Ito. She lowered the microphone to her side and looked uncertain of what to do. Matt wanted Solo to lighten up on her, but he wasn't about to get involved.

"Amy Ito," Solo continued, "let us do our job. Do not interfere with our investigation. That means you need to turn the camera off and back up. Go stand on the other side of your car. If you interfere in any way, I will confiscate your video tape and have you wait in the back of the officer's patrol car." He motioned her out of his way and started toward the truck.

Amy dropped her shoulders and gave her foot a little stomp. "You can't do that. There are laws for the freedom of press. I have every right to—"

Solo turned back, and in a small, condescending voice said, "I know all about freedom of press, Miss Ito. But if you interfere, I have every right to take action. Now, turn that camera off, wait over by your car, and sit tight. If you're good, I'll give you a proper interview once we have a clue what's going on here." Solo turned to approach the officer.

Amy looked at Justin, unsure what to do. Justin was nodding and pointing towards Matt. He had a smile on his face.

Amy looked at Matt, whose face she couldn't quite make out. He had his hat pulled low and his head down. He was trying to look into the window of the truck, working his way around to the front. She looked back at Justin.

"Superhero Jesus," Justin said as quietly as possible. "That's the detective he's working with on the murder of that dead cop. Didn't you see the story?"

Amy looked back at Matt. She noticed the swollen eye and busted lip. Here it was—her jackpot. She couldn't believe her luck. She just needed to get him on camera without the fat cop bullying her.

****

Heather Brown got out of bed and changed into her bikini. She put on a cover-up and grabbed her iPad. She swung by the kitchen on her way outside and shoved a plastic bag deep into the trashcan with the bloody shirt and pants she was wearing earlier.

She took a bottle of water from the refrigerator and her sunglasses from the counter, and she went out to join the guys near the pool.

"Well, aloha. Nice of you to finally join us," Alvaro said from his position on the edge of the pool. He had his feet in the water, and his head was propped up on a rolled-up beach towel. There was an empty cocktail glass next to him with a paper umbrella in it.

"It's not like I have a choice. You've got me locked up like this place is Fort Knox." She was smiling.

"Tell me again what happened last time you went out."

"What happened last time I went out?" Heather thought about it, erasing the smile for a second. *I drove to Kahala Mall and stabbed Chester Pile in the neck. I murdered our inside man. I killed him and killed our chance to smuggle shipping containers full of drugs to the island. I just cost this operation millions of dollars and am unsure whether I can find someone to pick up where Chester left off. The contact I worked so hard to get, the only reason I'm here, and the centerpiece of our plan to make money in Hawaii … I just stabbed it all in the neck.*

"I don't imagine it'd happen again," Alvaro continued, "but now we know to be more prepared. You don't want to end up in the back of a car again, or in Woo Lee's office, right?"

"That's right, Ricky Martin. We don't want any of that happening again." She looked at the Top Gun crew. Maverick, Goose, and Slider were sitting at the table in the shade looking at their phones. Iceman was floating in the pool on six noodles, three under his arms and three under his legs. The noodles barely kept him above the water. "How many of those have you had?" Heather asked Alvaro, nodding to his empty cocktail glass.

"I think this is the same one I had when you went in for your nap."

"Wasn't that a beer?"

"Might have been. Not sure. Anyways, since you're up …?"

Heather put her bottle of water and iPad on the lounge chair near Alvaro, and then she grabbed two Hinanos out of the refrigerator behind the bar. She put one down next to her chair and handed the other to Alvaro along with the bottle opener. "Anyone else want something?"

The Top Gun crew looked at each other. Iceman perked his head up from the water and lifted up his sunglasses. "Are you serious?" he asked.

"Sure. What do you want? Beer?"

Maverick, Goose, and Slider all mumbled their no thanks, but Iceman wasn't so timid. "Is this some kind of trick?" he asked.

"How about a Hinano?" Heather was walking back to the bar. "Are you guys sure you don't want something? There are quite a few beers in here."

"Hell yeah. I'll take a Hinano," said Iceman. He began to paddle himself to the side of the pool.

Heather grabbed three bottles by the neck and set them on the table in front of the guys. "Don't be pussies. Let's have a few beers." Then she went back and grabbed one more. She put it down for Alvaro to open and then took it to Iceman before sitting in her lounge chair. "Oh, sorry." She hopped back up and grabbed the bottle opener from where Alvaro sat it down. She tossed it to Maverick. "Forgot you needed that."

Maverick caught the bottle opener and looked at Goose and Slider. Then they all looked at her, and then back at each other.

"Who are you and where is the real Heather?" Iceman asked as he paddled back to the middle of the pool with his beer.

"Like I said, it's been a crazy day. I think we'll all be better off with a little stress relief." Heather grabbed her beer, flipped her sunglasses down, and sat back on the lounge chair. "Isn't there some meat inside? Maybe we should barbecue."

Heather knew there were four more beers in the pool bar's refrigerator and a twelve-pack in the house. Once those were gone, someone would need to do a beer run.

****

Matt felt sorry for Amy Ito. She was standing a good distance away with her arms crossed and a pouty lip sticking out. After ignoring Solo's initial warning and trying to film them and Chester's truck, Solo unleashed a scolding like nobody's business. Matt thought there was a real possibility she would break down in tears.

"Stop feeling sorry for her," Solo said. "She's young. If I give into her now, I'll have to battle her for the rest of my career. She needs to remember me. She needs to know to play by my rules."

"I didn't say a word," Matt said. They both stood on the passenger's side of the truck with the door open. They could see Chester Pile's dead body, the blood all over the truck, and no sign of a murder weapon.

"I see you looking at her. Do you want her plastering your jacked-up face all over the news?"

"No, not at all, but you were a little harsh. And that line about arresting her for impeding a police investigation ..."

"Hey, if she doesn't know that's bullshit, that's her own fault. As far as I'm concerned, I'm teaching her a lesson." Solo leaned inside the truck and carefully looked around for a knife. He put on one latex glove and lifted some trash on the floorboard and tried to look between the seats.

Matt looked over Solo's shoulder from the outside. "Anything?"

"No sign of a weapon." Solo put one hand on the seat and leaned as close as he could to Chester.

Matt wondered if Solo should be waiting for a CSI, but he didn't want to say anything.

Solo poked at Chester's pockets and then began to reach between his legs.

"When do you think a CSI will be here? Maybe we should ..."

"Bingo," Solo said, pulling an iPhone out from between Chester's leg. He held the phone up with his thumb and index finger, examining it closely. There was a drop of blood on the front of the screen, but the rest of the phone looked clean. Solo adjusted it into his palm and looked at Matt. "Cross your fingers that there's not a passcode.'

"Should you be touching that with your finger?"

Solo looked at Matt as he pushed the Home button. The phone came to life. "It's our lucky day," Solo said, seeing that there was no passcode. He swiped the phone open with his thumb.

"Whoa, I didn't think it'd work with the latex glove."

"That's the problem with your generation. Once you hear a rumor, you give up. If you were running the show, we'd have to wait to hear this dazzling piece of evidence." Solo showed Matt the phone.

"A recording app." Matt's eyes lit up. "He recorded his own murder?"

"Let's hear what we've got."

Solo and Matt both took a quick glance at Amy Ito, who was still standing behind Justin's truck, just like Solo ordered her to do. She had her arms crossed, but the expression on her face had softened. Between Chester and Justin's trucks, the patrol officer stood just outside his cruiser's door. He kept an eye on everyone.

Solo pushed play on the phone. Both of them cocked an eyebrow when they heard a woman's voice.

Tell me what they looked like, the woman said.

Chester's voice was obvious: *The one that came into my apartment was kinda fat and balding on top. He looked local— Hawaiian or Samoan or something.*

"Kinda fat?" Solo looked at Chester's dead body. "Asshole."

They continued to listen. The woman probed Chester for information, and Chester gave it.

"Did you get those names?" Solo asked.

"The first one sounded like Heather, and the second one, maybe Scott Combs, from Maston Shipping? That's what it sounded like."

"Yeah, that's what I heard."

They finally heard the sound of a commotion, followed by a brief moment of silence, and then a door opened and slammed shut.

"That must be our Heather Brown," Solo said.

"How in the world does a woman stab Chester here so easily?" Matt looked back at Chester, whose eyes were still open.

"I guess we'll have to ask her when we find her." Solo looked back at Amy Ito. "So, mister nice guy, what do you think we should do about her? Should I give her that interview I promised, or can we just get out of here and let the CSI clean up?"

Matt had been working on an idea. He put his hand on Solo's shoulder. "Why don't you let me take care of it?"

****

Justin Bush drove as fast as he could without exceeding the speed limit. Amy Ito sat in the passenger's seat, barely able to contain her excitement.

"Drive, man, drive," Amy said.

Justin focused on the road. "I. Don't. Get. Paid! Do you understand that? You gonna pay my ticket?"

"Yes! Yes, I'll pay. Just go, go, go!"

Justin couldn't have sped if he wanted to. He drove down McCully, catching a stoplight every fifty yards or so. "I can't drive through cars, you know? Just relax. We'll get there."

"Oh my God! I'm so excited. Soooo freaking excited! Get me to that station!" Amy had her hands on the dash, gripping it as tightly as she could and bouncing up and down in her seat. "I've never hated Hawaiian traffic more in my life!"

"For the love of God, relax woman."

Justin pulled into the KHNT4's parking lot, and Amy jumped out before he had the truck in park. She ran to the door with the tape in her hand and went directly to the producer's office. She knew she had to hurry to make the six o'clock news.

****

Duke Palakiko sat with his mom in their backyard. The barbecue was in honor of Danny, and the yard was full of uncles, aunties, cousins, and friends. The funeral was tomorrow, but Mrs. Palakiko felt she needed a day for them—a day without the media involved. A picture of Danny in his police uniform sat on the small table just outside of the backdoor, and there were so many leis stacked over it only the top of the frame was visible.

Behind Duke and Mrs. Palakiko, there was a crowd of people looking at Duke's laptop and listening to him explain what he found. For most of the barbecue, talk focused on the Sweet Maui Brown and whether or not anyone they knew was a victim. It was a momentary distraction from Danny's death, but now they focused on Duke.

"So ma said when Matt and that detective stopped by, the detective said they had a lead. He said there was another man killed with the same gun that Danny was shot with."

"That's right," Mrs. Palakiko confirmed. "He did say that."

Duke continued: "He said the man had a neck tattoo."

"Shit, that's hardly a lead," Duke's cousin said, tilting his head to the side, which revealed a tribal tattoo leading up the side of his neck. "Neck tattoos all ova' da place."

"Right, but look at this." Duke clicked a folder on his laptop. "Check these out. This looks like files for everyone Danny ever arrested. I went through all of them. Look at these." Duke enlarged three photos for the crowd. All three men had neck tattoos. "All haoles, just like the detective said. All have short hair, also like he said." Duke gave the crowd a confident look.

Duke's uncle asked: "Have you told the detective about this? I mean, it seems like they'd already know about it, right?"

"Don't know if he knows," Mrs. Palakiko answered. "I called and left a message for Detective Fauatea after Duke discovered this. Called Matt, too, but they haven't called back. Detective Fauatea was supposed to stop by this morning, but with all this Sweet Maui Brown business going on, I think that might have sidetracked them."

The photos rallied the family, and by now nearly everyone at the barbecue was trying to get a look at the computer, hoping they recognized one of the men. Nobody did.

"You got to call them back," Duke's uncle said, expressing the sentiment of the crowd. "That business with the sugar must've died down by now."

"Go through those guys one more time," Duke's cousin said.

The crowd packed even closer around Duke and the laptop. He took his time cycling through the three men, stopping between to read the file. The file was the original arrest report, and there was no information on the whereabouts of the three men today, nor was there information on whether or not they served time.

"You look these guys up online?" Duke's uncle asked.

"Yeah, I tried. Couldn't find much on Google, but I didn't search long. Just found this. Also searched Facebook—no luck."

"What about that other site: LinkedIn?"

"I ... I don't think criminals have LinkedIn accounts, uncle. That's, like, a resume website."

"Never know, right?"

"I'll search more, but you're right—we need to get this to Detective Fauatea."

After a day dominated by talk of the Sweet Maui Brown, everyone's attention was now fully back to the murder of Danny Palakiko. Most of the people at the barbecue credited Duke with discovering a big lead, and they were excited that Danny's killer seemed one step— one huge step—closer to being caught.

It wouldn't stop the hurting they felt from losing Danny, but it eased the fear of the murder never being solved. The idea that the killer could get off, could escape, was in the subconscious of everyone with ties to Danny.

Now they had hope.

CHAPTER TWENTY-TWO

Saturday 8:00 p.m.

Woo Lee sat in his office at the Dreamy Aloha. After watching the news in his Chinese restaurant, he needed a change of scenery.

And a drink.

The bar and karaoke rooms were just opening, but things were still quiet. Business didn't pick up until around ten o'clock, but with all the workers showing up and getting the place ready for the night, the atmosphere was much livelier than the restaurant, which rarely had anyone coming in.

Although he had a change of scenery, Woo Lee couldn't stop himself from turning on the news. He sat behind his desk in his small office and watched News Channel 4's coverage of the day. He mixed himself a whiskey and Coke and tried to talk himself out of any guilt that popped into his mind.

When the six o'clock news came on, the first thing that flashed on the television screen was a photo of Sasha. Woo Lee was mid-drink and nearly sprayed it all over the television.

It was a grainy photo, but it was obviously Sasha, and it was taken just a couple hours ago. Woo Lee knew this because he could see his Chinese restaurant in the background, which meant somehow the police were on to him, and somehow they knew to look for Sasha.

After flashing the photo of Sasha for a few seconds, a young female reporter came on the screen standing next to Matt Gold. Matt towered over the reporter. He had his hair slicked back behind his ears. One eye was swollen, and his face had cuts on it. It was obvious he'd recently been in a fight.

The young reporter introduced herself as Amy Ito, and then she introduced Matt as the undercover police officer who recently gained much attention for work done in Los Angeles, and who was known around the world as Superhero Jesus. She maintained a professional demeanor but looked as if she were struggling not to bust out in a full giggle.

Woo Lee's mind worked as he listened to the interview. His first thought was Alvaro. It was possible that Alvaro would point the police in his direction as payback, but that seemed unlikely. His second thought was Sasha. He had a long history with Sasha that went all the way back to Korea, and although there was trust there, he wondered if Sasha would turn on him to save himself. Woo Lee was careful. He never came into contact with the drugs, never used a traceable phone or said too much when talking on one, and never committed any crimes directly himself, or so he tried not to. That's what people like Sasha were for.

And people like Sasha were expendable, if that's what was necessary.

Matt explained the reason they were looking for the man in the photo. He said the man was wanted in connection with the Sweet Maui Brown. When Amy Ito asked how the man was connected, Matt said they received an anonymous tip, and when they caught up to him to ask him some questions, well ... Matt shrugged and motioned to his face. "He didn't exactly want to talk." The viewers knew there was a fight.

One fact hit Woo Lee: Sasha wouldn't be able to catch his flight tonight. It wouldn't take long for his face to be all over the news, which would make it very hard not to be recognized on the island, especially with Sasha's size and features. And he doubted Sasha was sitting around watching the news, which meant he'd be unaware that he'd be the most wanted man in Hawaii in a matter of minutes.

If there was any hope of the Sweet Maui Brown story dying down, it was now gone. The interview with a bruised Matt Gold just guaranteed the story would go into super drive, and Woo Lee knew it.

Woo Lee had a big decision. He could let Sasha fend for himself, try to hide him, or have him taken care of.

Letting Sasha fend for himself wouldn't work. Sasha would have no chance on his own. It'd be a matter of minutes before he was spotted at the airport, if it even took that long.

Trying to hide Sasha might work. Woo Lee had the means to hide him, but there were a lot of risks. It'd just take one slip-up, and Sasha would be in the hands of the police.

Killing him would definitely work. Having Sasha killed would guarantee he couldn't point the cops in his direction. Woo Lee had taken such measures in the past, but he liked Sasha, and he wanted to believe he was no longer a killer, despite the overdoses of the day.

And maybe because of the overdoses of the day, Woo Lee was leaning towards option two. He could help Sasha. No more killing, especially someone who'd been loyal.

****

Hyejin Lee sat in the back room at the Dreamy Aloha. She got ready in front of the mirror, putting on her makeup trying to cover up the faint bruise marks she got from going home with the wrong kind of guy. He seemed nice enough when they met, and they had a few things in common. He'd been to Korea, could speak a little Korean, and he worked for her boss. She thought it'd be fun.

In Hyejin's line of work, there were all types of guys, but most of them were older Koreans and Japanese, mostly married men who come to the Dreamy Aloha to drink. Hyejin liked to think of herself as a modern-day geisha, pouring drinks and entertaining the men. Most men just wanted a pretty girl at their table, and they were willing to pay good money for it.

But there were other customers who wanted more than someone to pour drinks and laugh at their jokes. She'd often get called to a booth to entertain a group of guys. She'd pour their drinks, they'd laugh, and Hyejin would think she had the best job in the world. But after a bottle or two of whiskey, even the nicest guys might get handsy. Their jokes would start to cross a line, but all she could do was laugh and keep pouring their drinks. They were paying for her services, after all.

Most nights she would get propositioned a few times for sex. A Viagra-popping old-timer would ask how much, and Hyejin would have to decide how badly she needed the money. She knew this was part of the job; the part that paid her rent.

On a good night, she'd get a group of men who'd take a few girls back to one of the singing rooms. They could lounge around taking turns singing karaoke and share the drink-pouring duties. This too would often result in offers for sex, but it was often with a higher caliber client. These were the clients she hoped for.

But not tonight. Tonight she was too sore.

Hyejin finished getting ready and headed to the bar. She walked down the long hallway past the singing rooms and remembered the night before. They were singing and drinking expensive whiskey with the boss. Hyejin was fond of Woo Lee. He gave her a job and was known to treat his girls well. He never pushed any of them for sex, and when his business associate came in, she thought she felt a connection. It was nice to see a handsome, well-built guy. She never could tell the good ones from the bad.

The hallway was quiet. In an hour or two most of the singing rooms would be full. Hyejin entered the bar, which was also quiet. Most of the other girls were already working, doing their duty as servers until an invitation came to join a table, not that there was much business yet. Most were standing around the bar.

Hyejin stopped dead in her tracks. There he was. It was the man whose name she never learned. She must have heard it, maybe he even told her, but she couldn't remember. Now he was just the man with the neck tattoo. He was in the corner, a full photograph of him on the television screen. The television was on mute, but she could tell he was in some kind of trouble.

She felt a wave of anger wash over her. She'd experienced several uncomfortable sexual encounters, but none as emotionally and physically painful as with him. She went along with what he wanted at first, but he crossed the line, and he didn't stop. Now he was on television, wanted by the police. She felt some satisfaction in that.

Other girls were standing by the bar watching. They had seen him around, and the two girls who were with Hyejin in the singing room were also staring at the television. Someone turned up the volume, but the reporter spoke too fast for most of them to understand the English.

One thing was clear: he was wanted by the police. There was a number on the screen, and Hyejin was able to understand the words "considered dangerous."

She wanted to call the number. She wanted him caught, in jail, and unable to show up again in her life. She thought of the last thing he said to her before he fell asleep: *We'll have to do this again sometime.*

She felt a shudder and turned from the television. She hadn't cried from the experience, but she felt tears coming on. She hurried back down the hall, past the singing rooms, and into the dressing room.

She didn't think about the consequences. She didn't think about what Woo Lee would do if he knew, or what it might mean to him. She just opened her phone and looked for the Honolulu Police Department's phone number. She'd make the call. She'd explain in her broken English everything she could about the man with the neck tattoo.

****

Solo and Matt decided to give Chinatown one more try. It wasn't exactly on the way to Matt's hotel, but they both hoped the news broadcast would bring in a lead tonight, and they wanted to be available when it came in.

Solo had to call his wife. He talked to her as they drove down the H1, promising her he'd be home by ten-thirty. Matt couldn't understand what she was saying, but he could hear her barking through the phone. Solo mostly listened and apologized.

While Solo was on the phone, Matt checked his. He had a couple of messages from Shauna and several missed phone calls from Duke Palakiko. Duke also sent a few messages, one of which was a photo of the man with the neck tattoo. It was a mugshot.

Matt held the phone up for Solo to see.

"Honey, gotta go. Love you." And he hung up on his wife. "Who's that from, HPD?"

"Duke Palakiko, Danny's little brother."

Solo's phone rang. "So he's in the system. Got anything else? How'd he get that?" He looked at his phone, expecting it to be his wife, but the caller ID said *Lt. Nishi.*

"Says it was on Danny's laptop."

"Detective Fauatea," Solo answered.

Matt looked at the mugshot of Sasha Novikov. He remembered the last time he saw his face. It was just a flash before impact and then glimpses as giant fists rained down on him. Sasha's face was big, and Matt noticed his jaw muscles were clenched.

Solo hung up. "That was my lieutenant. We've got a lead at the Dreamy Aloha, Woo Lee's bar. Anonymous caller said our guy meets Woo Lee there." Solo darted over to catch the exit ramp for Punahou. "We'll swing by there. The tip said Woo Lee's there right now."

"Sasha. Sasha Novikov. Nothing here on why he was arrested."

"Listen, Woo Lee's going to like you. He'll know you from the news, and he'll probably act like a thirteen-year-old schoolgirl. That's how he is. I told you he was a kook. So I'm thinking, maybe you should …"

"Hold on. Don't even tell me to wait in the car."

Solo made a right onto Beretania, moving with the flow of traffic. "No, I'm not saying that, but his place, the Dreamy Aloha, is … well, it's a buy-me-drinky bar. You know, where you pay the girls to drink with you. Singing rooms in the back. You can imagine what goes on there, right?"

"You've been."

"Once, back when we were looking at him for those murders. He's got an office in the back, behind the singing rooms. Lots of staff. He's got lots of girls working, and those girls need some protection. You can imagine, yeah? They'll be more than a couple bouncers, and he's got cameras, I'm sure." Solo headed down Keeaumoku.

"Sounds like more of a reason I should go in."

"It's early. I doubt there's much going on. And Woo Lee isn't the type that'd let something bad happen to a cop on his property. Like I told you, nothing ever sticks to him. He's too smart for that."

"So what do you want me to do, stand outside and talk to the valet?"

"I'm going to park on a side street. They have valet parking, but we ain't going to do that." Solo turned right on Makaloa and then slowed to look for parking. "Here we go. Look, you can see the back entrance of Woo Lee's place from here."

"Oh, nice, I'll stand out back next to the dumpsters."

"See that Mercedes sitting all by itself? That's Woo Lee's," Solo guessed. "If he sees me coming in the front, he might decide to go out the back, right?"

"You sure that's his car?"

"Yeah, of course. I told you I know this guy. If he comes out, just stall him."

"Stall him? Sure, I'll ask him directions or something."

"Just say hi. He'll recognize you. He'll probably want to take some selfies or get an autograph."

Matt reluctantly agreed. He made his way to the back, finding a hidden little spot next to dumpsters where he could lean against a fence, avoiding the path of the security camera he saw over the door.

He watched Solo rub the sweat from his bald head as he made his way around to the front.

****

Heather Brown gave the guys the slip. Once the beer ran low, she suggested she run to the store to pick up some more. Alvaro quickly shot down that idea. Not that he thought she'd be in any real danger, but he was still borderline paranoid over his recent bad luck. He'd been blindsided too many times, and he wasn't in the mood for more trouble.

He said Iceman and Slider could go, or they could just switch over to cocktails. There was plenty of booze stocked in the tiki bar. "Let's get the paper umbrellas out," Alvaro said.

The sun was almost completely down, and they had the tiki torches lit. Alvaro had Hawaiian music playing on the speakers, and Goose was getting ready to fire up the grill.

Iceman poked his head up. He was now sprawled next to the pool with his feet in the water, using the pool noodles as a pillow. "Slider, we're going to the liquor store." He held his beer in the air. "Right after this one."

All the guys had a few beers in them. Heather thought about pointing out that she was probably the closest to the legal limit to drive, but she backed off. She agreed, asked Alvaro to make her a mai tai, and then she went inside. She grabbed the keys off the counter, changed clothes as fast as she could, and headed out the front door.

She also grabbed a gun from Alvaro's bedroom.

For the second time that day, Heather had an easy getaway. This time, however, she knew she wouldn't be able to sneak back in.

If they'd seen the latest breaking news, her plan might have been different. If Alvaro wouldn't have insisted they turn off the TV, they might know Sasha's face was all over the news, and she might really be going for beers. But she killed once already, and she knew she wouldn't be able to put her mind at rest until she killed again. If Alvaro wasn't going to help her get revenge, she'd have to take matters into her own hands.

CHAPTER TWENTY-THREE

Saturday 8:20 p.m.

Woo Lee wasn't surprised when he saw Sasha enter his office. But he was concerned with the look on his face—it was expressionless. He closed the door and sat down across from Woo Lee, not saying a word.

"Sasha, have you seen the news? You ... all over the news. Your picture. You fight Superhero Jesus? I saw."

Sasha let out a deep breath and looked at the picture on the wall behind Woo Lee's desk. He didn't answer.

"Prease, Sasha, talk to me. This big trouble. We need hide you. You can't come through front door like everything ok. Are customers here yet? Anyone see you come in?"

Sasha stared at the painting. It was a print. One of Diamond Head painted in the old Hawaiian style, similar to the vintage postcards and Hawaiian Airlines advertisements.

"Sasha? Who saw you come in?"

"You going to hide me?"

Woo Lee didn't like the way Sasha said it. His voice was flat, almost like it wasn't a question. "Yes, good plan to do. Hide you. No problem."

Sasha looked back up at the painting. He paused long enough for Woo Lee to begin to understand what he was getting at. "What's behind that painting? Seems like I remember a safe back there, right?"

Woo Lee turned to look at the painting and then back at Sasha. He didn't answer.

"I think I can hide just fine. But I'm going to need some money." He looked Woo Lee in the eye. It might have been the first time Sasha hadn't seen a smile on his face.

Woo Lee squinted his eyebrows and bit one side of his lip. He could understand the desperation Sasha must be feeling, but he wasn't about to let Sasha shake him down. "Yes, I have money here. How much you need?"

"Why don't we play it safe and give me all of it?"

"Sasha, you risten to me. You risten to me good." Woo Lee's voice was calm, softer than usual. "You know I take care of you. You hide. I get you what you need, find you how to go mainland. Everything going to normal in short time."

Sasha remained expressionless. "So ... let's open it up and see what you've got."

"Listen, singing rooms probably all open. Too early for customers. Go back and lock the door. Take whiskey. I can make phone calls, get money. Trust me."

This was the moment of truth. Woo Lee laid out what he had to offer, and Sasha could make his choice. Ten minutes ago Woo Lee thought Sasha would've jumped at the chance, even beg for it. Woo Lee took care of his employees, and they were loyal because of it. Now, as

Sasha sat across from him, not moving and staring at Woo Lee with no trace of emotion or willingness to move, Woo Lee knew Sasha wasn't here for his help.

"Ok, you want money, yes? Don't need any hiding?" Woo Lee brought his smile back. "No problem." Woo Lee gave a sincere laugh and pushed the whiskey across his desk. "Sasha, here, have a drink. I open safe." Woo Lee turned as Sasha made a move for the bottle. He slid the painting out of the way and could hear Sasha moving behind him.

Woo Lee hoped Sasha was pouring himself a drink. He didn't want to get caught pulling the gun out of the safe.

****

Solo's plan was to walk back to Woo Lee's office like he knew right where he was going, but he didn't make it two steps in the door before one of the hostesses greeted him.

"Table for one?" She smiled as if Solo were about to tell the funniest joke in the world. She wore a tight miniskirt and a half-shirt revealing her midriff. Although not a uniform, most the girls wore almost identical outfits.

"Sorry, honey, I'm not here for a good time." He lifted the left side of his oversized aloha shirt to reveal his HPD badge. Her smile was gone. He held the shirt and turned slightly as if the badge were scanning the room. Some of the girls at the bar noticed; they stiffened, a few taking a couple of steps backward. Solo knew what they were worried about—immigration. He was sure most of the girls didn't have a working visa. Most of the buy-me-drinky bars were the same. Immigration could raid one on any given night and probably find ten illegals to deport. They don't, of course, but they could.

"Relax," Solo said. "I'm only here to talk story to your boss. Just a friendly visit." He flashed them a smile and started to walk towards Woo Lee's office.

That's when he heard the gunshot.

****

Heather didn't have a plan. She heard Alvaro talk about Woo Lee hanging out at his girly bar behind Walmart, the Dreamy Aloha. She knew the area. There were a few shady places back there, and she knew she wouldn't blend in well with the other customers, but it wasn't like she could get Sasha to meet her at a park.

She took her cell phone, and this time she planned to answer it if Alvaro called. She'd tell him she was out getting beer, that he should relax, and that she'd be back in no time. It'd buy her time, but she knew even if she were lucky, she wouldn't be back for a while.

She had the phone on the passenger's seat, and the gun in her purse on the floor. She drove the black SUV past the Dreamy Aloha, around back, and then passed by one more time. She finally parked on the street behind, nearly a block away.

Heather grabbed her purse and took off down the street, leaving the cell phone. She reached in to make sure the gun was positioned with the handle up, ready for an easy draw. If she were lucky … If the opportunity came up … If she saw the bastard with the neck tattoo … She planned to shoot. Growing up on military bases, Heather was exposed early and often to shooting ranges. If her chance came up, she wouldn't miss.

She headed in the opposite direction of the back entrance, circling the block. The front of the bar was well lit, but with a small parking lot and valet stand in front, she was able to walk across the street inconspicuously. There wasn't much going on yet, and Heather started to realize she was probably too early.

She continued around the block. When she approached the back, she saw two men walking across the street towards the back. One continued walking towards the front, and the other stopped and leaned against the fence, taking out his cell phone. Heather recognized the second one from the news. It was Matt Gold, which meant the other guy, the rounder one, was likely a cop as well.

She crossed the street and went back to her car, thinking she should pick up some beer and head directly back to the beach house. This would not be the night for revenge. If the cops were hanging around Woo Lee's, she wasn't.

As soon as she turned the ignition, the phone rang—it was Alvaro.

****

Matt was leaning against the fence replying to Shauna's text message when he heard the gunshot. Or what he thought was a gunshot.

He froze, unsure what to do. He knew the door was locked from the outside, and it'd be reckless to go charging through the front. It sounded like a gunshot, but it was faint, and there was just one. He couldn't be sure. Solo said there wouldn't be trouble inside. He said Woo Lee was too smart for that.

He called Shauna. She answered on the first ring: "Hey, Mr. Detective. How's it going?"

"Hey, I think I just heard a gunshot. I may need you to call backup."

"Wha—"

"I'm in back of the Dreamy Aloha, watching the back door. Solo went in the front to talk to Woo Lee. We had an anonymous tip. Solo said it was safe, but …" Matt heard two more gunshots, and then a third. "Holy shit. Those are definitely gunshots." He tried the back door once more, hoping it'd open. "Call backup. I gotta …"

Matt stopped when the back door flew open. It came open with such force that it knocked him back, causing him to drop the phone. He saw Sasha stumble out carrying a bag and gun in the same hand. His other arm looked limp.

Sasha raised his gun and fired twice as he started to run towards the street. He fired once more once over his shoulder as he hit the sidewalk running.

Shauna was still on the line. She heard the shots and her heart was nearly beating out of her chest. She shouted for Matt, but she knew what she had to do. She hung up and called 911. Then she tried to call Matt back. There was no answer.

****

Heather put the SUV in drive and answered Alvaro's call. Before she took her foot off the break, and before Alvaro had time to ask her where she was, she saw the man with the neck tattoo coming directly at her.

He was running in the middle of the road. She could see the bag and gun in one hand, and it looked like something was wrong with his other arm, but he was moving well. He kept looking back over his shoulder.

Heather dropped the phone. She didn't have time to get her gun; he was coming fast, zagging down the middle of the street as if he couldn't decide which side of the road he wanted to take.

She was on the side of the road, foot on the brake and engine on, waiting. When he was in range, Heather put her foot on the gas and tried to run him over. He had a split second to react, but not enough time to fully get out of the way. She clipped him. Hit him square on the hip as he spun to try to miss her.

She thought she got him good enough to put him down. The impact of the collision rattled the SUV, but when she stopped to back up, to hit reverse and back over him to finish the job, he wasn't on the ground as she expected. He was up and stumbling away. One arm was hanging and he had a major limp, but he was still moving. He fired a shot over his shoulder, not even trying to aim. He crossed the sidewalk and entered the Walmart parking garage.

Heather banged the steering wheel. She missed her chance. Had him lined up in her sights, and she missed. She started to pull away, only to slam on the brakes when another man raced in front of her. She could see him clearly in her headlights—it was Matt Gold. He paid her no attention; he was chasing the man with the neck tattoo.

Heather hit the gas. She missed her chance, and she felt lucky for it. She was happy to pick up some beers and head back to the house. Back to the guys. Back to the tiki torches in the backyard of the rented Kahala beach house. She figured game over for the man with the neck tattoo.

CHAPTER TWENTY-FOUR

Saturday 8:40 p.m.

When the back door smashed into Matt, he was fortunate it knocked him near the space between the two dumpsters. He didn't have to see Sasha's face to know whatever was coming out that door spelled trouble. He did a panicked crab-walk into a reverse somersault, taking what cover he could between the dumpsters.

Sasha fired one shot, not even sure what he was aiming at, and to Matt's surprise, he missed.

Matt hid behind the dumpster, unsure of where Sasha was.

Matt's heart raced. He waited, hoping Solo would come through the back door. He couldn't hear Sasha, so he dropped to the ground, trying to look under the dumpster for Sasha's feet, but it was too dark and low, and he couldn't see a thing. The sun was now fully down, and the only light came from a street lamp and the back door.

He tried to think. Three gunshots inside. He knew what that meant for Solo. He knew there was a chance he was down. Then Matt heard another gunshot coming from down the street.

Without hesitation, Matt took off. The back door was still open, and Matt thought he caught a glimpse of a man on the floor at the end of the long hallway.

****

Sasha ran. He had a bullet in his left shoulder, and his left hip was throbbing, but he still ran. He cleared the bushes and entered Walmart's parking garage. With one way in and one way out, the garage always had a line of cars. Sasha moved between them, gun in hand.

He thought about going to the second floor, heading up the stairs and finding a place to lay low, but he kept moving.

He looked over his shoulder, but he didn't see anyone. After getting past the first row of cars and closer to the entrance, he slowed down a bit, trying his best to walk normal, hiding the limp and pain as well as he could. He dropped the gun in the bag that held the contents of Woo Lee's safe. Sasha didn't know how much he got from Woo Lee, but he felt satisfied. There were several stacks of cash, as well as some jewelry. He liked the weight of the bag—made it all feel worth it.

He passed the entrance, continuing on to a very busy Keeamoku Street. The sidewalk was thick with people, and they were getting out of his way, moving to the side, as if the sea was parting. They were pointing, whispering to their friends, and he saw jaws drop.

His shoulder was bleeding, but he thought the aloha-print was doing a good job of hiding it. He put his head down, just wanting to get out of there.

And then he remembered the news. Remembered what pushed him to Woo Lee's in the first place. He should've hidden in the parking garage. Or ran the other way. Anything except trying to blend into a crowd.

He started to run, scanning the street for a police officer or anyone crazy enough to stand in his way. He had to get back to his car. With his hip hurting, left arm dragging, and his right arm gripped tightly around his bag of money, he tried to run.

****

Matt spotted Sasha move past the entrance of Walmart. He took off in a sprint just as Sasha rounded the corner.

Matt knew the area well. He knew that the sidewalk would split, one path leading down to the street, while the other elevated up slightly along the side Walmart. The path would bend out there to pass a few businesses. He knew the first was a Starbucks, complete with tables outside that were always full.

Matt tried to think. He rounded the corner and saw Sasha take the high path, moving through the tables and beginning to run again. Matt noticed a wave of onlookers in Sasha's path, and he saw one guy pointing his phone at him.

Here we go again, Matt thought.

He made his decision as soon as he saw that Sasha wasn't holding his gun. He remembered Sasha laying him out in Chinatown, and now it was Matt's turn.

He sped up, sprinting as fast as he could, bending at the hips, driving his shoulder into Sasha's back, and pushing him over the sidewalk's railing. They fell into the landscaping—a small flower area that separated the upper and lower sidewalks—and they landed hard. Matt was behind him. He put one arm around Sasha's neck and squeezed hard with the other hand, wrapping his legs around Sasha's hips. He pulled back, trying to get all the pressure he could muster on Sasha's neck.

Sasha struggled to get up. He tried to roll and managed to get to one knee, but his injured hip wouldn't let him stand. He tried to pry Matt's arm from his neck, but with a bullet in one arm and a bag wrapped around the other, he couldn't manage to break the grip. He felt himself beginning to lose balance.

With all the power he had left in his legs, Sasha pushed backward, slamming Matt hard onto a Chinese hibiscus.

Matt had the wind knocked out of him, but he held his grip.

Sasha tried once again to pry Matt's arm away, but Matt had too much leverage. Sasha felt Matt's arm on his windpipe and started to feel desperate. He reached back with his right hand, the bag still looped around his wrist. He felt for Matt's head, trying to find an eye socket to jam his giant thumb into, but he couldn't reach.

The gun. Sasha needed the gun. He dropped his arm to the ground and easily found the opening of the bag. He reached in and pulled the gun out, Matt still squeezing with his arms and legs, knowing if he let go he wouldn't have much of a chance.

Sasha mumbled something Matt interpreted as "die motherfucker."

It was just enough of a warning for Matt to notice Sasha's arm coming back up. He saw the gun. He saw Sasha's finger on the trigger. The barrel was turning, making its way towards Matt's head. He didn't have time to react. There was a blur and a sharp pain on Matt's head. There was a crash. And then another. Matt felt the weight of Sasha's body increase, and then he realized there were more people on top. The pain to his head was someone's knee. More weight was added to the pile. Matt could see at least two guys on Sasha's right arm, likely struggling to the get gun. He could tell there were more, but he didn't stop squeezing Sasha's neck. The pile of bodies trying to hold Sasha down was beginning to suffocate Matt, but he squeezed, and eventually he felt Sasha beginning to stop his fight.

Someone came away with the gun, and slowly the pile was able to pull Sasha off of Matt.

Matt saw two police cars pulling up from different directions, about five guys wrestling Sasha down, and a huge crowd watching, many of whom were recording the ordeal.

Matt didn't wait for the officers to arrive. Still breathing hard, he turned and ran back to the Dreamy Aloha.

****

Matt heard the cheers from the crowd as he ran. He moved back through the parking lot, crossed the street where he saw a black SUV clip Sasha earlier, long gone now, and he came to the back of the Dreamy Aloha.

There were police cars on the scene, and an ambulance was pulling up to the front. Matt heard more sirens in the distance.

He went through the back door, which was still open. He could see Solo, still on the ground at the other end of the hallway. Two police officers were with him. As Matt got closer, he could see one officer was holding pressure on Solo's left shoulder area, and the other was talking to him. Solo was conscious.

"Here he is," one of the officers said. He looked at Matt. "Solo said he heard more gunshots out back, where you were. We were just getting ready to look."

"What happened? You're shot?" Matt asked. He could see a look of relief on Solo's face.

"Just a flesh wound. I should've never left you back there without a gun," Solo said. "That was stupid."

"Hey, I wanted to come in the front door with you. Look how that turned out."

The paramedics came in, and Matt and the two officers backed off.

"What happened?" Solo asked, ignoring the paramedics. "He get away?"

"I seriously doubt it. Last I saw he was being held down by a gang of good samaritans. Two patrol cars were on their way."

Solo let out a sigh. "Fucker shot me."

Matt noticed the bar was nearly empty. No customers and no waitresses. The paramedics and two officers lifted Solo onto a stretcher.

"I heard a shot when I walked in," Solo said. "In the back. Take a look before they get me out of here."

Matt walked down the hallway. The two officers followed. When he peaked in Woo Lee's office, he saw the blood on the wall next to an open safe. The blood splatter next to the safe looked like a headshot, and Matt looked over the desk to see a small Korean man on the floor with his head in a pool of blood. Matt could see enough of his face to recognize Woo Lee from the picture Solo showed him.

When Matt left the office, he ran into Shauna in the hallway.

"Hey, you okay?" She asked.

Matt could see the look of relief on her face. "Barely a scratch," Matt said.

She gave a slight hesitation, and then she hugged him. "I heard the gunshots on the phone. I thought …"

"I was lucky. Lucky he missed, and lucky he didn't know I wasn't carrying a gun."

They heard Solo yell: "Uh-hum, hello, over here. Wounded detective with a bullet in his arm. You going to tell me what happened? Is it Woo Lee?"

Matt looked up and saw Solo on the stretcher. The paramedics were looking too, waiting for the answer before pushing Solo out to the ambulance. Matt shook his head, not letting go of Shauna. "Yeah, it's Woo Lee," he called down the hallway. "Headshot."

Solo's head fell back, and the paramedics pushed him out. Matt didn't know for certain, but he didn't think Solo liked the news.

****

Heather made it back to the rented Kahala beach house with a case of Hinano and a case of Longboard Lager. Alvaro gave her some shit about leaving and wanted to know what took her so long. She said she got carded at Safeway, so she had to go to another store. He bought it.

The Top Gun crew cheered when they saw the beer.

Heather could smell the barbecue. The party would go on. She put some of the beer in the kitchen refrigerator and watched the guys take the rest out to the tiki bar. Then she turned on the small kitchen television to News Channel 4 where Amy Ito was on location. She stood on Keeamoku Street with Walmart and Starbucks visible behind her, looking very serious into the camera.

… and after Officer Matt "Superhero Jesus" Gold tackled the suspect, they wrestled in the flowers before the man pulled a gun.

That's when multiple bystanders jumped the man and were able to subdue him.

They cut to an amateur video showing how everything unfolded. Several videos had already been uploaded on Facebook, YouTube, and other social media sites. CNN was interrupting normal broadcasting with breaking news of the event, and people in Asia were waking up to the story on their morning news channels.

Amy continued:

It appears from the video that this is the same man that Officer Matt Gold asked for the public's help in finding earlier today. Officer Gold indicated that the man was wanted for questioning for his role in the laced Sweet Maui Brown found throughout coffee shops on the island. An inside tip also tells us that the man is wanted in connection for the recent death of Honolulu Police officer Daniel Palakiko, but this has not been confirmed by the Honolulu Police Department. Stay tuned to News Channel 4 for more updates.

Heather turned off the television. She wondered whether anyone saw her hit Sasha. She thought about the knife she used to kill Chester Pile, and how she dumped it in a nearby trashcan. She thought about the name Chet gave her—the guy he used to smuggle the drugs. She looked outside at Alvaro. He was standing behind the tiki bar mixing a cocktail. He had that big smile on his face. Slider was taking food off the grill. Iceman still had his feet in the pool. He had an unbuttoned aloha shirt on and a beer in his hand. Goose and Maverick were sitting at the table. Iceman said something and they all laughed.

Heather grabbed a beer and went out to join them.

****

Shauna and Matt were both at the Honolulu Police Department. Shauna had helped process the scene, and she was finishing filing the evidence when Matt came into her lab.

"So, they let you down here without an escort, huh?" She tucked her hair behind her ear.

Matt fell into a small chair in the corner. "After the amount of paperwork I just did, I should be able to do whatever I want around here."

"Right. If only it worked that way." She took off her lab coat and gloves. "Have you heard from Solo?"

"Yeah, they already let him go home. Can you believe taking care of a bullet wound takes less time than paperwork?"

"Yes. Yes, I can." Shauna signed a file and tossed the pen on the table. "That does it for me. I guess I'm giving you a ride?"

"Yeah, so, I was thinking about that." Matt leaned forward, putting his elbows on his knees. "So … I'm thinking I might have a little trouble at my hotel. I'm worried there might be a crowd."

Shauna smiled. "Yeah, I can see that."

"Well … I'm wondering, and you can say no, but I'm wondering how you feel about me crashing at your place?"

"Hmm," she shook her head, but her smile didn't disappear. "I don't know if that's a good idea … and what about your clothes and things?"

"I already called the hotel. They're willing to have my suitcases taken to your place. They were very nice about it."

"Wow, you've already called the hotel, huh? And they agreed to pack up your things and deliver them to wherever you desire? Must be nice being a celebrity."

"Oh, I'm better than just a celebrity." Matt leaned back in the chair and put his hands behind his head. "I'm a celebrity with a badge."

Shauna burst out in a laugh. "Okay, cheeseball. Let's not be ridiculous. Let me get my things and we'll get out of here. But hey, it's sofa city for you. Don't be getting any ideas in your head. I'm not that kind of girl."

Matt held his hands in the air. "I wouldn't want it any other way."

****

Timmy woke up in the middle of the night. He was on the sofa with his feet in his mom's lap. She was sitting straight up with the remote control in her hand.

"Mom, what time is it?"

"I don't know. Maybe around four."

"Why aren't you in bed?"

"Not tired. Wide awake. And the New York Sunday morning news should be starting up soon. I want to see what they have." She turned from CNN to Fox News, and Timmy saw that Hawaii was still dominating airtime on both channels.

He sat up next to his mom and stretched. "How are you feeling?"

"I'm okay. Just not tired at all. How are you? Let me see that eye."

Timmy pulled away as she reached out to touch his swollen, purple eye. "It's sore."

"I can't believe you got into a fight. You know what'll make you feel better?"

"Shooting the asshole in his kneecap?"

"Watch the language, mister." She hopped off the sofa. "Bacon and eggs? Pancakes? French toast? You name it, I'll cook it."

Timmy watched her pull the eggs and milk out of the refrigerator. She buzzed around the kitchen prepping for his feast, and all he could think about was that his mother was on crystal meth. Crystal meth that he was dealing in the park. Meth that somehow found its way into coffee shops and poisoned more people than Timmy could imagine.

And here she was, cooking him breakfast because she felt sorry for him. Because he got beat up by a junkie who wanted to rob him. Because he was dealing drugs on a picnic table in Kapiolani Park.

Timmy loved his mom, and he hoped she never found out the truth.

CHAPTER TWENTY-FIVE

Sunday 9:50 a.m.

Heather Brown sat on the sofa in the rented Kahala beach house. She had her feet up and a cup of coffee in her hand. The Top Gun crew was busy with their morning runs, and Alvaro was tanning on a lounge chair next to the pool. She had been flipping through channels all morning watching the coverage from last night. She was hoping for new developments when she came across an update on News Channel 4.

This is Amy Ito reporting from outside the Dreamy Aloha. It was here that last night a local businessman and suspected gangster was shot and killed in his office. Police say a Mr. Woo Lee was shot in the back of his head while being robbed. Mr. Lee is the owner of several local businesses and has been investigated by the Honolulu Police Department several times in the past.

The prime suspect is a Mr. Sasha Novikov, who we see here being chased down and tackled by Officer Matthew Gold, better known around the world as Superhero Jesus.

Heather had already seen the video numerous times, but she still enjoyed it. News Channel 4's footage was better than the video they showed last night. Her favorite part wasn't when Sasha was tackled over the sidewalk railing, and it wasn't when the crowd rushed him, pinning him down and waiting for the police officers to put the cuffs on. Her favorite part was before all that. It was when she saw him limping past the cameraman. Limping in pain. A pain she caused, and a pain she could see on his face.

Mr. Novikov is wanted in a number of crimes, and our sources inside the police department tell us he is now the prime suspect in the death of Officer Daniel Palakiko. Mr. Novikov was arrested by Officer Palakiko early last year for assault and resisting arrest, for which Mr. Novikov served two months at the Halawa Correctional Facility in Aiea. Sources tell us it was Officer Palakiko's testimony that helped convict him.

Heather smiled. She knew Sasha's next sentencing would be much longer than two months. Game over for Mr. Neck Tattoo.

Besides being the prime suspect in the murders of Mr. Woo Lee and Officer Daniel Palakiko, police sources tell us Mr. Novikov is a suspect in at least one other murder, a Mr. Joshua Allen of Kalihi. Mr. Allen was found shot to death in his apartment earlier this week.

"Adios, muthafucker," Heather said as she turned off the TV.

"Adios?" Alvaro stretched in the doorway and let out a big yawn. "Don't you mean hola?"

Heather stood up and tossed Alvaro the remote. "I'll be out by the pool. You, on the other hand, might want to catch up on the news."

"Oh, come on. I don't want to hear about the Sweet Maui Brown. What's done is done. It's time to move on."

"Yeah, you got that right." Heather nodded to the TV. "Turn on the news, Speedy Gonzales. There have been some developments."

****

Matt rode with Shauna in the long funeral procession for Officer Daniel Palakiko. They were both dressed in their full police uniforms, driving up to the Punchbowl National Cemetery where Danny would be buried next to other fallen servicemen.

"I don't know," Matt said. "This might be a bad idea."

"You have to get out of the car. You can't miss Danny's funeral," Shauna said.

They came to a stop. The procession was approaching the cemetery, and Shauna could see police cars slowly filling up the parking lot.

"I don't want to create a media circus. I'm so over the attention."

Shauna laughed. "Maybe you should embrace it. Have you seen the videos? They're pretty awesome. You should search your name on YouTube. There are tons of videos of you."

"You searched for me on YouTube?"

"Yeah. A couple of times." Shauna pulled into a parking spot.

Matt put his hand on her neck, running his hand behind her hair. "Great, so here I am with a girl who's stalking me online."

"I'm not the only one. You should see how many views those videos have."

The car next to them came to a jerky stop. Solo's wife got out and scuttled around to the passenger's side to help him out. He had his arm in a sling and his officer's jacket on over his shoulders.

"Solo looks good," Shauna said. "That uniform makes him look slimmer."

Matt laughed. He didn't know if Shauna was serious, but there was nothing slim about Solo. "His wife's cute. Look at her take care of him."

"Well," Shauna said. "How about it? Are you ready for this Mr. Superhero Jesus?"

"Come on now, don't be calling me that."

"You could get a haircut you know? Maybe shave that five-o'clock shadow. Try to look a little less Jesus-ish."

Matt tucked his hair behind his ears and put on his officer's cap. "Cut the hair? Go clean-shaven? No way. I'd look twelve."

"Good. I like the hair." Shauna opened her door. "Come on. Let's say goodbye to Danny."

Solo and his wife were waiting for them. "Don't walk too close to me," Solo said to Matt. "I don't want to be all over the papers."

"I do," his wife said. "You can walk as close to me as you want." She took Solo's good arm and they led the way.

"She is cute," Shauna said.

"We could walk like that." Matt held out his arm.

Shauna took it.

"Great," Solo said. He shook his head. "Don't tell me you're going to do something stupid like transfer out here."

Matt looked at Shauna, and then back at Solo. "Nah, I'd never do anything like that."

Thanks for Reading

If you liked what you read, nothing makes an author feel as good as a positive review on Amazon. It's quick and easy, and I'll love you forever.

Keep an eye for more Matt Gold stories and other works coming soon.

Mahalo!

About the Author

Thomas Bishop was born on the mainland, but his heart belongs to the tropical paradise of the Hawaiian Islands. An English professor and nonfiction author by day, he spends his evenings and weekends creating stories from the land of aloha. Find more by this author by visiting Amazon.com.